# BREAK ME LIKE A PROMISE

REBECCA STONE

All rights reserved. No part of this book may be reproduced in any form or by any electronic means, including information storage and retrieval systems, without permission in writing from the author, except by a reviewer who may quote brief passages in review.

This is a work of fiction. Any resemblance to actual persons, living or dead, events, or locales is entirely coincidental. Any trademarks, service marks, product names, or named features are assumed to be the property of their respective owners, and are used only for reference. There is
no implied endorsement if any of these terms are used.

Copyright © 2022 by Rebecca Stone
All rights reserved.
Cover design by Rebecca Stone
ISBN

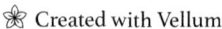

*For A.G.*
*Thank you for being my first, but not my last or only.*

# 1

With one slam of the moving truck door, Ruby saw her life in New York City disappear. The cold December air cut into her skin, burning her lungs. Crossing her arms over her chest, she willed the tears not to fall. She'd fought so hard to get to this point... and now she was going right back where she started.

Rachel's hand rested on her shoulder. Her boss at Maven Media had quickly become a friend, and her presence was reassuring.

"I hate this."

"I know, babe."

"And you're sure you don't mind me working from home?" Ruby turned to her friend, squaring her shoulders. Rachel had taken a chance when she hired Ruby. Her state college degree didn't compare to those of private schools, and Ruby had bounced around the city trying to find stable housing while she tried to prove she was a hard worker, a smart hire, while sending money to support her mom.

Rachel smiled, rubbing Ruby's arms. "Positive. You know Ella and I don't really care about attendance, so long as the work gets done. Your mom needs you, and we're all here for you. As friends, coworkers, whatever you need."

Ruby nodded, not fully believing it. But Ella and Rachel — Maven Media's co-founders — were always generous. In this case, they were not only allowing her to work from home, two hours north in the small town of Oak Valley, they were giving her three paid weeks off. She knew it was partly because of Christmas, but she also knew they wanted her to settle in and not have to worry about working while she dealt with doctor's appointments and moving.

"'Scuse me? Could you please sign?" One of the movers thrust a sheet of paper at her.

"Here you go," Ruby said, handing him the signed receipt. "And if you could just take a picture of the storage unit when you're done and text it to me, that'd be great."

He nodded before climbing back into the truck, turning the engine.

She watched the truck leave with her non-essential belongings, revealing the rental car in front that was packed with the essentials. She wasn't sure what awaited her in her home town upstate, but whatever it was, Ruby wanted to have what she needed. Oak Valley, small as it was, was always full of surprises.

Hopefully her childhood sweetheart wouldn't be one of them. Her mind wandered to her strapping first love, his broad shoulders and muscled torso. The way his dark hair burned umber in the sunlight, his dimples that threatened...

"Okay, you ready?" Rachel asked.

Ruby came back to the present. The last thing she needed was to be thinking of her hot ex-boyfriend. There was a reason they'd broken up. Even if it was ten years ago.

She turned to her friend, surprised to see wet eyes. Rachel was glossy, chic. Pulled together, sometimes cold. Ruby felt her own eyes well.

"Stop it. If you don't stop, you'll get me started." Ruby laughed as a tear escaped.

Rachel laughed, wiping her cheeks. "Sorry, I'm not good with goodbyes."

"I'll be back."

Rachel just nodded, heightening the knot in Ruby's stomach. She didn't know when — or if — she'd return. She assumed she'd move home, take care of her mom, who would quickly get better, and before long, be back in New York City where she belonged.

She was telling herself a story she didn't believe the ending to, and Rachel didn't seem to believe it either.

## 2

Colton glanced from his phone to his little sister, shamelessly flirting with one of the other mechanics. His ex-football star status should've been an automatic deterrent for any guy that wanted to look twice at Katie, but clearly that was a boundary that needed to be reset. He was right fucking there, but they were acting like he didn't exist.

Damian threw Katie a wink before taking off, leaving her giggling. Colton shook his head, returning to the small screen. He was a little surprised the only update his dream job posted was that they'd closed applications — he guessed they'd moved quickly with hiring.

It'd been a long shot, applying to work at the new San Francisco restaurant being opened by Pierre Hermé, France's top pastry chef and one of Colton's idols. After seeing the job posting on Instagram a few weeks ago, Colton applied on a whim. There was no way an ex-football star with zero professional pastry training would ever get the job. But Colton had learned the hard way that life was too short. He had to take risks. Plus, the job was on the other side of the country, and at this point, any place was better than Oak Valley. His football stardom had gotten him out, but it had also sent him right back where he started.

"Yo, broski." Katie hopped up on the stool next to him. Working the family auto shop let them both work when and where they wanted — Colton usually stayed in the reception area, but Katie was usually elbow-deep in the hood of a car.

"I'd appreciate it if you wouldn't flirt with coworkers," he said.

She gave him a blank stare before recognition hit. "Damian? Seriously?"

"Yeah, seriously." Colton scowled as Katie laughed, fixing her ponytail. She was pretty — too pretty, with her long raven hair and brown doe-eyes — to constantly be surrounded by the guys in this godforsaken town. While he'd at least been able to get out into the world, Katie had always stayed put. He pushed aside the nagging thought of how okay she was with settling.

"Chill, Colt. It's harmless. Besides, I know not to bring any guy around you. He'd disappear." She nudged him. "You don't need to always be my protector. I'm an adult."

"Barely." His sister was twenty-four but he couldn't help but see her as his little sister. So of course anyone near his age — even his friends — had at one time or another tried to make a move. His blood was starting to boil.

The bell on the front door chimed, and they both looked up as their dad walked in.

Bryce was tall, broad, his beer belly dwarfed by his sheer size. Black hair only just starting to salt and pepper, skin ruddy from a life working with his body. He threw Colton a nod before giving Katie a kiss on the cheek.

"Kids. Katie, what are you still doing here? Take off, go have fun." Their dad smiled at her.

No, beamed.

"Dad, I am having fun. You know I love it here." She beamed right back at him, Daddy's little girl.

Colton had to keep from rolling his eyes. Their dad had never wanted Katie to take over the family business — that was supposed to be Colton's job. Something about how the sons in the four-generation business were supposed to inherit what started as a blacksmith forging shoes for horses and now stood as one of the oldest auto shops in America. But Colton's football career had left Bryce with no choice, and he'd started grooming Katie late to take over.

Until Colton blew his knee out and returned home a year ago.

But what their dad didn't want to admit was that Katie had always wanted this job. While they both used to hang around the shop as kids, it was Katie that asked questions and got her hands dirty. Colton was usually in the corner reading, or finding some excuse to go to work with his mom at For Goodness Cakes Bakery.

"Colt, did you take care of the leak in Roger's Nissan?"

"Yeah, Damian finished this morning."

"What about following up on the Parker's invoice?"

"I called them this morning, Mr. Parker said he'd swing by with a check this afternoon."

His dad grunted. "Good. I'll see you guys later." He gave Katie a hug and took off.

Colton sighed. He watched his sister head into the garage. The window between the offices and the work area was thin, and her laugh traveled as she joked with Damian.

She was going to be the death of him.

His phone vibrated on the counter. A text from one of his best friends, Caleb.

*FYI Ruby's back.*

Colton's vision tunneled as the world spun. Ruby Delacey, the fiery beauty of his youth, had returned.

It'd taken him years to forget the way her hair smelled, splayed on his pillow. It'd taken him years to stop looking for her in grocery stores. It'd taken him years to forget the way her freckles formed constellations only he knew. But the way his body flushed at the sheer possibility of finally running into her after ten years...

He hadn't forgotten a thing.

# 3

Ruby slammed the car door with her foot, arms full with the last remnants of her old life. Turning to her childhood home, she nearly dropped what she was holding and ran.

The sun setting behind the majestic two-story farmhouse made everything feel dramatic. Straight out of a horror movie. Or family saga. It had always been too big for just her and her mom. It served them well when Ruby was in school and she'd host parties to try and make friends, but over the years it began to feel skeletal. Like the walls were caving and the bones were breaking. She ambled up the stone path, careful to avoid the inch of snow no one had shoveled, and took in the faded white paint and the porch with a slight bend in the middle. She set the boxes down, opening the front door and calling to her mom.

"In here!" Beryl's voice echoed from the kitchen.

Ruby sighed, heaving the two boxes from the porch into the foyer. The hardwood had been worn down, begging for a refinish ten years ago. Ruby kicked off her tennis shoes, dropping her keys on the entry table, and poked her head into the dining room. The pass-through between the dining room and the kitchen enabled her to see her mom dancing to Fleetwood Mac, the oven on and the stove smoking.

"Hey, Mom." Ruby smiled, her mom's tangle of curls pulled onto the top of her head with a patterned scarf while she bounced around. While Ruby's were bright red, her mom's were auburn. Stories of her father told her she looked more like him than her mom.

"Oh! Hey, honey." Beryl turned. "Did you have a nice drive?"

Ruby saw behind the wide smile. The deeper crows feet, the dark circles, the thin slope of her neck. Seeing her mom so tired, so flat, was startling.

"Y-yeah. Yeah, it was fine. Everything got to the storage unit and I have everything I need for the time being."

"Okay, well if you decide you want to save money on the unit and move everything into the basement, lord knows we have the room. Are you hungry?" Her mom turned to the stove, her face hidden.

"Thanks. Yeah, I'm starving. You should've waited, though. I could've made you something." Ruby made her way to the other side of the stove, across from her mom. The big pot had seen them through many pasta and soup nights. Tonight smelled like soup.

"Psh, I would never let you cook for me after the day you've had. Besides, you'll be taking on that responsibility soon enough. But in the meantime, I'm making sure you have lots of home-cooked meals." Beryl cleared her throat, fussing with the oven. Cake, from the way her mom stuck a butter knife in the center of two pans.

They didn't usually talk about her mom's cancer. Ruby barely remembered her mom's first bout with it, but she did remember hospitals and grandparents over the course of a few years when she was young. After that, they'd celebrated her cancer-free date and only had one scare.

But this was different.

After almost two decades cancer-free, Beryl had taken a more holistic approach — if she felt fine, she was fine, despite Ruby's pleading, begging, that she go for regular checkups. Just in case.

But by the time her mom started to feel unwell, the cancer had spread from her breast to her lymph nodes. The doctor's were worried about it spreading even more, given the late Stage 4 diagnosis.

Now Ruby watched her mom. Her beautiful, vibrant, funny mom. There was the part of her that intellectually accepted what this next chapter would look like. But there was the other part of her that refused to accept that this was anything more than a nightmare.

Her mom set down the soup ladle, blue eyes meeting Ruby's hazel ones.

"Honey, if there's anything you ever need to talk about, please know I'm here. For you as much as you are for me."

Ruby nodded, feeling the flush reach her cheeks. They had time. "Thanks, mom. Do we need bowls?"

Her mom cracked a soft smile. "Nah, I'll pull them out of the dishwasher. But save your appetite - I made a just-because chocolate cake."

It was one of Beryl's favorite things to do — make a cake just for the hell of it. She always found things to celebrate.

"Are you sure you're feeling up to all this cooking and baking before Christmas?" Ruby wasn't sure of her mom's limits, but judging by the way she looked, Ruby could hardly tamp down the feeling her mom could drop at any moment.

Beryl side-eyed her. "Don't you dare start questioning my abilities, Ruby. I feel fine, and Christmas is weeks away. Speaking of, shall we go to the Christmas tree lighting in the square this weekend?"

Ruby sighed, knowing that doing anything in a small town heightened the chances of seeing people she desperately did not want to see. In high school, Colton had always dragged her to the annual lighting, and despite feeling like she'd break out in hives, she'd gone because it made him happy. Her mom had tried to pick up the mantle after, but with Ruby's work schedule and living in New York City, the timing never worked out. And if going to the tree lighting with Colton was hard, Ruby couldn't imagine what going without him would be like.

"We'll get hot chocolate from the new coffee shop or For Goodness Cakes and we'll stand out in the cold with everyone else, packed like sardines, and then grab takeout and watch a movie." Her mom stirred the pot — Mexican chicken soup — and gave Ruby a look that said there was no room for arguing. "Besides, most of the people who used to live here don't anymore, it'll be good for you."

"Fine." Ruby turned, needing to finish getting her belongings in from the car. Her mom's subtle nod to the anxiety high school brought was one thing, but Ruby knew it didn't include Colton Taylor. He'd moved home a little over a year ago, and as far as Ruby could unearth, he hadn't left.

Somehow, they'd both ended back here after ten years.

The reality of moving home, living in her childhood bedroom, was starting to sink in, and this time there was no way out.

# 4

Colton heard the guys behind him laughing, but he was too far ahead on the hiking trail to pick up what they were saying. The backpack slipped across his winter jacket, his shirt underneath clinging to his back from sweat. He'd more or less stomped his way up the mountain, his five best friends from high school taking their sweet-ass time. But it wasn't their fault Colton had energy to burn — knowing Ruby was back in town was enough to set Colton's body on fire.

"Yo, Colt! Wait up," Liam called out, breathless. Colton let out a long, hard breath and stopped. Their footsteps grew closer, and eventually Dragan brushed past him. But while Colton settled at a solid six-foot-two, his friend was closer to six-five and broad, and Colton almost went down.

"What the fuck, man?" Colton whipped around. There was a gleam in Dragan's blue eyes, a smirk on his stupid symmetrical face.

"It's Ruby, isn't it?"

The rest of the guys — Caleb, Liam, Archer, and Dean — burst out laughing.

"Dude's got his panties in a twist," Liam said, shaking his head.

"They've been twisted since he was fourteen," Dean laughed, pushing past them to the front of the pack.

Colton's face flushed, his hands squeezing the backpack straps until they turned white. They weren't wrong, but that didn't mean he needed to hear it.

"Have you seen her?" Archer piped in, walking alongside Colton as the guys continued along the path.

"No."

"Are you going to?"

"I don't know." *Probably not.*

Archer glanced at him, running a hand through his short blond hair. "You probably should, given how things ended."

"Should he?" Caleb grumbled, pushing his way to the front of the pack.

Colton stopped in his tracks, ignoring Caleb's comment. He was probably right, but he didn't need to know that. Instead, Archer thought he knew everything which only served to rile Colton up even more. "Oh? And how *did* things end, Arch?" Maybe his voice raised, but he didn't give a fuck. He didn't need this asshat reminding him that if he'd wanted to fight for their relationship, he could've. He didn't need to be reminded that Ruby had always been too good for him. That she deserved better.

The guys turned around, giving each other a look.

Dean shrugged. "We just know how much you loved her and how hard it was. You took your football scholarship close to home, she went to New York City."

*Love, not loved.* With all the fame and women he'd had, Colton never had the heart to tell them that part had never changed.

"You were together every day for four years, dealing with the high school b.s., and literally the next week you went your separate ways." Dragan's gaze pierced Colton's. His friend, while sometimes a grump, was a bit of a hopeless romantic and saw right through everyone, everything.

"I wonder if Cara knows," Liam added before continuing the hike.

Colton shivered, and not from the cold. Head-cheerleader Cara Griffin had always had her sights set on Colton. She was bubbly on the outside, but Colton heard stories from some of the other girls — she was a stereotypical mean girl, especially to the girls she had a bone to pick with. Nice to their face, nasty behind closed doors. Like to Ruby, although Colton could never figure out why. As football captain, they'd been constantly around each other, and she'd done everything to make that fact known. He'd been used to shrugging her hand off his arm, taking a step back when she stood too close to talk to him. Occasionally, Ruby saw. And while nothing had happened between them, and Colton did everything to set those boundaries with Cara, he'd seen the hurt in Ruby's eyes.

His heart pained at the memories. When they ended things, even though Ruby hadn't said anything about it, Colton knew Cara bothered her. After the breakup, Ruby went to New York City and Colton stayed in Oak Valley — and so had Cara. He couldn't stomach the way she'd treated Ruby, and even after all these years, it made his stomach drop. So he stayed away from her, avoiding her in town or giving her car troubles to someone else.

It would be the one thing that would completely undo Ruby, and four years with someone as a teenager created a level of loyalty Colton didn't want to — couldn't — break.

Colton tried to focus on the conversation with the guys, but he'd missed the first bit. Archer still walked beside him, silent, while the others were up ahead goofing off. Since his football injury over a year ago, Colton's physical abilities were limited. Going from a competitive athlete to bedridden had done a number on his mental health. But his friends and family had known that, had rallied, and made sure he got outside regularly. Hiking had become one of their favorite activities.

He took in the quiet stillness winter always brought upstate, in the woods and mountains. Ruby had always loved winter — the muffled beauty, the snow, the brilliant clear nights. He could picture her head of fire laughing at something he'd said, when they were seventeen. He could imagine her here, now, giving him that look she'd mastered without saying a word.

The look that said how much she loved him, but how much they'd hurt each other.

# 5

The doctor's office was typical — blue-gray chairs lining the perimeter, a couple coffee tables stacked with magazines, mint green walls with framed watercolor landscapes. The reception area was quiet, Ruby's mom nose-deep in a book on manifesting.

Ruby sighed and looked around. There were only a couple other patients, but she'd been waiting with her mom for what felt like hours. She'd tried reading the book she brought, but couldn't focus. Being back in her hometown was strange and anxiety-producing. Every time she went to the post office or the grocery store, she wondered who she'd run into. If she'd run into any of the ghosts that still haunted the familiar streets.

If she'd run into *him*.

Her body flushed at the thought of bumping into Colton. He'd been built when they dated all those years ago, but she'd seen him age like a fine wine since. Tall, broad-shouldered, having mastered the smirk that unleashed two perfect dimples. In TV interviews, she'd seen him lean into a cocky strut, casually flashing a smile framed by those two weapons at the camera. Ruby had rolled her eyes at the move, knowing what a teddy bear he was underneath the football star persona. After his injury, he'd disappeared from the spotlight. But she knew there was only one place he could go — one place either of them could go.

Tapping her foot, she glanced at the reception desk. Heads down, fingers clacking away. No one in a hurry. Ruby leaned forward, spreading out the magazines. Fitness, fashion, medical, parenting, home. Tiny homes. She smiled to herself. After living in the closet that was a New York City apartment, complete with three roommates so she could pay off her student loans and send extra money to her mom, Ruby could live anywhere.

She flipped through the magazines, surprised at how many cheap, money-pit homes profiled were upstate near her, and how many young couples had bought land to build a tiny home on. But there was one profile that made her pause: a young couple had bought a school bus and converted it.

Not only was it now classified as a motor home, but they could live and work rent-free from anywhere.

Ruby stared at the glossy image of the bright yellow school bus before its transformation, and the one of its hippy-dippy conversion, complete with running water, shower, toilet, kitchen, and bedroom. They'd built a pull-out sofa, included a projector and screen, and lived with their dog. The article revealed they'd known nothing about the project before starting — a mechanic friend looked at the engine upon buying it, and they'd used Instagram and Reddit to piece together the rest.

Something inside Ruby clicked. She looked over at her mom, still buried in the book on manifesting, and wondered just how easy it would be to build a new life. One that factored her independence with taking care of her mom. One that would give her the freedom to leave when it was time.

Placing the magazine back on the table, she pulled out her phone. School bus conversions — or Skoolies, as they were known in the community — were relatively common in the tiny house movement. A step up from van life and a step down from a stable tiny house, Skoolies afforded couples a larger mobile home without the usual cost and with the ability to be off-grid. So long as you could do the work. Ruby saved interior design ideas on her Pinterest and saved a conversion video from YouTube.

She could do this. Even if all conversions seemed to be done by couples.

"Beryl Delacey?"

Ruby looked at up at the nurse and then at her mom, who closed her book and stood. They trailed the nurse into the intake room. While her mom was being weighed, Ruby kept scrolling through conversion ideas. It was easier than watching the nurse's pitying face while she took her mom's vitals.

The doctor came in, dismissing the nurse and shaking their hands, introducing herself as a Dr. Jessica Lahm. Her blonde hair was showing dark roots, pulled back in a ponytail. She had a warm smile, and when she looked at them it was without pity.

Finally.

"So, Beryl. We know from the biopsy that the tumor in your left breast is G3, which is high grade, and we saw from the CT scan that the breast cancer has metastasized to your lungs. These scans also showed some abnormalities in your bones. I won't lie — I'm concerned the cancer has spread, and I'd like to have a PET scan done to check your bones."

Dr. Lahm let the information sit between them. Ruby picked at her nails, staring at the table.

Her mom cleared her throat. "What are my chances?"

"Chances for having metastasized breast cancer in your bones, or chances of survival?"

"Both."

Dr. Lahm sighed. "Chances for the cancer metastasizing to your bones? High. Chances of survival? We'll know more once we conduct the PET scan. But currently, the chances aren't terrible. For stage four breast cancer, the median life expectancy is three years. Some live longer, some not. But that also includes those that don't seek treatment. I'm confident that with treatment, we can get you to over five years."

Ruby glanced at the doctor. She seemed so sure, despite the odds. Her mom nodded and grabbed Ruby's hand. She squeezed back. It had always been the two of them.

Her mom had to fight this.

# 6

The mailbox was tilting, but that didn't stop Colton from throwing the door open, grabbing the stack of paper, and slamming the door shut. The post wiggled with the force, but he was too busy rifling through the mail to notice. The cold air bit into him through his thin henley while he made his way down the long driveway.

Nada.

He slammed the front door shut, throwing the mail on the entry table. He didn't know if he'd hear from Hermé's job via email, letter, or phone call, but that didn't stop him from checking each avenue as often as possible. Or maybe that's what he told himself as he tried to burn off steam, to keep the frustration from seeping in. He didn't know how he'd get through another day at the auto shop, let alone another ten months. It helped having Katie around, and his mom. At almost thirty, being relegated to his childhood bedroom under the thumb of his father made what he'd lost even more unbearable.

Storming to his bedroom, he paced and tried to slow his breathing.

*In, out. In, out.*

That's what his therapist had said. And his football coaches. And his physical therapist.

It's not that his temper was legendary. More that it was just... well-known. It'd seen him benched more times than he could count, and while he'd managed to control it in the big leagues, his injury had sent him spiraling to square one.

He looked around his childhood bedroom, sparse and emptied of items from high school — most of the furniture in Colton's luxury penthouse wouldn't fit in his childhood home, both in size and style. He'd sold off his prized California King bed and was now stuck with a queen, which co-opted most of the room. A skinny IKEA dresser still held up in the corner, dusty and with sun-stains from where trophies had sat for years.

When he moved home, he didn't need any reminders of what he'd lost.

Always back to square one.

His door flew open, nearly bumping his shoulder as his dad strolled in. Colton subconsciously recoiled, left over from his days as a kid with a big mouth. While Bryce had never gotten physical, he was loud and not a small guy. But now Colton was bigger. He stood to his full height, moving toe-to-toe with his dad. Hid dad was bright red, eyes gleaming.

Bryce thrust a large envelope in his face. "You looking for this, boy?"

Colton ripped it from his hands. Return address, San Francisco. Envelope opened. He swallowed, his skin humming. He risked a glance at his dad.

"Where'd you get this?"

"Where do you think? The actual question is what the fuck is a letter from some French chef doing in my home, addressed to my son?"

Colton stepped back from his dad, pulling out the contents. He skimmed the letter — they wanted a video interview, and if that went well, for him to fly out to their test kitchen in San Francisco. An email would follow shortly with details. A wave of hope rushed over him, similar to the one he'd gotten with his first draft. His first paycheck.

This could be his new start.

"Well?"

"Well, I'm a fucking adult and wanted to apply," Colton chuckled, counting down the days until he didn't have to deal with the bullshit.

"Well, smart-ass, so long as you live under my roof you'll follow my rules, and I made it crystal clear when you moved back last year that you were to focus on the family business."

"And I have been. I've been working there almost every day. I brought in Dragan when Dan quit suddenly. I reworked your management system so it's almost all online." Colton bit his tongue from asking what more Bryce could possibly want.

If it wasn't the rest of Colton's life, his dad didn't want to hear it.

His dad shook his head. "You went to college for football. You got a political science degree and a minor in two languages. All of which your mother and I have helped support you through."

"Are you kidding me?" Colton crossed his arms. "My college was paid for by my scholarship."

Bryce laughed. "Oh yeah, big man? And who drove you to football practices? Who spent weekends practicing? Money for camps and training?" He shook his head. "You ungrateful shit. You have everything because of us. Because of me. And you have a responsibility to this family, to your grandfather's legacy."

Colton could always trust the truth to come out eventually with his dad. He didn't mince words, and while Colton was grateful to have inherited that trait, it was hard to be on the receiving end of it. He straightened. This conversation was so over, he needed a new word for over.

"I was never going to inherit the legacy. I went away for football with no plans to come back. It was supposed to be Katie. It was always supposed to be her — she loves the garage. I never did. And I never will."

He pushed past his dad, rushing out before Bryce could fire back. The front door almost hit him on the way out, the cold cutting into him as he nearly ran down the driveway. His dad wasn't a brute, but he was mean. Always had been. Grades were never good enough, performance never good enough. He was never good enough. It didn't matter he graduated top ten in his high school class, set state records in football, helped his dad at the shop, and maintained a long-term relationship.

*Ruby.*

Colton's breath caught. He stood facing the road, memories of her flooding him. He used to bike to her house when his dad got like this. He used to hold her on the couch or in her bed, her fingers stroking his arm while they laid in silence. She'd been his refuge, his rock. She knew him, saw him, in ways no one else had.

But over the years, he'd had to learn to live without her warmth. He'd had to find solace where he could. When he was pro, it was usually women and parties. When he returned home, it was usually escaping by any means necessary to any place. The driveway, the local bar, maybe one of the guys' houses.

A little voice in his head murmured she was back, he could go see her.

Colton shook his head and turned to face his house. He could probably grab his jacket and keys without his dad knowing and drive to Dragan's or Caleb's.

But never Ruby's. There's no way she'd want to see him now.

# 7

She shouldn't have worn her coat in the car, knowing that the drive into town for the Christmas tree lighting would be filling her with a dread that burned through her body. But Ruby had been caught up in getting out of the house under her mom's frazzled insistence, worried that they'd be too late to either get hot chocolate or see the lighting.

The streets she'd grown up on passed by in a blur, changing from spread out farmland to the more closely built houses that indicated their arrival into Oak Valley's suburbs. The streets were already somewhat packed. From farmers markets to tree lightings to the annual Valentine's Day festival, the small-town inhabitants loved all the quaint happenings and usually showed up in droves. Which usually equated to about two hundred of the 1,000 residents.

"I absolutely hate finding parking in this town," Beryl mumbled, inching her way down Main Street. Ruby looked to her right, watching people walk down Center Street toward the tree, trying to see if she could recognize anyone beneath their hats and scarves. The square where the tree was to be lit was really just a square plot of land with a large evergreen in the center, in front of one of the town's two churches. They passed the packed parking lot on the left in front of the middle school, and the packed lot on the right nestled between The Crispy Crust Pizzeria and Joe's Hardware. The lots at the end of Main Street, next to Oak Valley Pharmacy and the new gym, were also full.

Beryl hooked a left down South Street, turning right into the large lot behind the main strip of boutique stores. She pulled into a spot at the far end, behind a yoga studio.

Ruby got out of the car and looked around, staring at the studio.

"They moved in a few months ago," Beryl said, as if reading her mind. "Never thought I'd live to see the day when yoga came to Oak Valley, but I'm not complaining. Things seem to be changing, and for the better. C'mon, let's get some hot cocoa."

Her mom led the way back to South Street, where they walked past the front of the studio, the Little Prince Bookstore, and the thrift store before ending at For Goodness Cakes. Ruby steeled herself, knowing the chances of running into Colton here were almost as high as running into him at the auto shop. But her mom charged ahead, not giving Ruby any time to focus on what it would be like to run into him in such a small space after not talking for ten years.

Thankfully, it was absent of everyone except the owner, Evelyn Dougherty, who was also the mom of Ruby's friend Olive. Another redhead, she'd always been extra friendly to Ruby when she was little, aware of the silly playground taunts that came with sticking out like a sore thumb.

"Well, if it isn't the Delacey women," Evelyn said, untying her apron and coming around the corner to give them big hugs. Ruby viewed her as a second mom, and she was grateful some things hadn't changed in the small town.

"We're just here for some hot chocolate, we're unfortunately in a bit of a rush with the tree lighting," Beryl explained.

"No worries, we anticipated it." Evelyn went behind the counter and pulled two large paper cups out. A lineup of large silver carafes sat in the back corner of the bar area, and one of them Evelyn poured hot chocolate into the cups. The bakery made their hot chocolate the old way — heated milk and sugar and chocolate chips — and when they were feeling creative, they tried different spices or flavors. Ruby had missed the richness and flavor from the shop, and gladly took her cup from Evelyn while her mom tapped out the pay info on the iPad on the counter.

"Thanks, Mrs. Dougherty!" Ruby said between sips.

"Anytime, don't be a stranger! I'm sure Olive will be glad you're back."

They waved goodbye, Ruby and her mom facing the cold as they power walked the ten minutes to the tree, doing it in seven. The crowd around the tree was tighter than Ruby imagined, but in some ways that made it harder to distinguish individual faces. She still didn't catch a glimpse of Colton, or anyone else she knew. She relaxed a little, taking in the hot drink and large tree, a large silver menorah already lit beside it. That was new, and nowhere near as large as the tree. The main attraction was well over a hundred feet tall, a point of pride and joy for the town. It was thoroughly strung with white lights — Ruby remembered one year they boasted using one hundred strands — and she realized she did actually enjoy these moments of celebration. She'd never gone to the Rockefeller tree lighting when she lived in the city, too full of anxiety from her youth, but now she was faced with a pang. She'd left Oak Valley behind, needing something new. But now that she was back, she was wondering if she actually had walked away, or if she'd carried most of it with her this whole time.

"Good evenin', everybody!" Macy Weathers hopped onto the makeshift stage in front of the tree, microphone in hand. The town busybody was also the Town Supervisor — Oak Valley was too small for an actual mayor, and Supervisor was the next best thing — and Macy never failed to find the hottest news before anyone else. Ruby didn't mind the gossip as much, but being in New York, the slight southern accent always bothered her.

"How's everybody doing?" Macy beamed at the crowd, her gray hair curling below her blue Santa hat and above her green scarf. The town cheered and responded as she walked the stage, waving her arms to amp them even more.

"As the kids say, who's ready to get this party lit?" Macy laughed at her own joke before continuing. "Followin' the tree lighting, there will be live music from several local bands and free hot apple cider from Willow Farms. You can partake in the Holiday Penny Social in the parking lot behind the church. Festivities will conclude at 10 p.m. Now are we ready?"

The crowd cheered.

"I can't hear you! I asked, are you ready?" Macy put her hand to her ear in mock-listening. Ruby rolled her eyes. No wonder she avoided this thing like the plague.

Macy picked up the lighting cords and made a big show of inching them together before slamming the plug cord into the outlet cord. The tree burst into tight and the crowd erupted. It really was beautiful, covered in thousands of white lights and casting a soft glow on the crowd. The first band started setting their equipment up onstage while most of those in the front slowly made their way out. Ruby and her mom inched closer to fully take it in.

When they were in front of the tree, a light flurry started. Ruby looked up the length of the tree, feeling comfortingly small in its grandness.

"It's something, isn't it?" her mom asked, doing the same thing.

"It really is." Ruby hadn't been able to be home for the days, let alone weeks, leading up to the holidays. She glanced at her mom, whose pale face was warmed in the light. Ruby didn't know how this next year would turn out, but being here, now, she was filled with gratitude for the time she had with her mom.

"Well, kid. Penny Social or home?" Beryl turned to her, crunching her empty paper cup.

"Um..." Ruby looked around. She hadn't seen anyone she knew, but staying for the bands or milling about the Penny Social might change that. "Let's get takeout before everyone else has the same idea. Here, give me your cup, I see a trash can. You should start heading to the car, it's cold out."

She grabbed the cup from her mom and worked her way through the crowd, tossing both cups into the can. When she lifted her eyes from pushing them down, she caught the one person she regularly dreamed about.

Colton Taylor stood beside his sister, Katie, and a few others Ruby recognized. They were off to the side of the stage, slightly masked by the dark.

But Ruby would recognize those shoulders anywhere, the way his baritone voice filled any space. Katie said something and he laughed, throwing his head back.

Ruby was petrified.

This was it, the moment she'd dreamed and dreaded.

He shifted and glanced around, doing a double take, noticing her.

# 8

No.

It couldn't be her.

Colton kept his jaw from dropping. He knew Ruby was back in town, but it was another thing entirely to see her for himself. A ghost lit gold from the lights of the tree, her red curls loose about her shoulder. Her mouth was slightly parted, a deer in the headlights as she stared back at him.

She was more beautiful than he remembered, even thirty feet away.

He was frozen in place, every way this could play out running through his head. They broke up not because they didn't want the same things, but because she wanted them right then and he needed to stay home, to help with the family shop while he went to the local state college. Sure, he'd gotten a full ride and it helped propel him into professional stardom, but he chose to stay local. The one thing Ruby swore would be the death of her.

Colton didn't know losing her would be the death of him, and at that point, it was too late.

"Is... Is that Ruby?" Katie asked, pushing against him,

squinting as if to get a better look. "Oh, shit," she whispered, turning back to the group.

Dragan and June also peered over, cautiously looking back at Colton.

He faced forward, avoiding anyone's gaze. When he risked a glance back at Ruby, she was gone.

"Well, if isn't Colton Taylor."

Colton tried to shake the buzz from his body, looking around until he spotted Cara Griffin strutting towards them. Her girlfriends tagged along, about five of them if he included every petite woman with glossy, waved hair and full-glam makeup who walked behind her. They were all beautiful, sure. He understood why guys fell over, craning their necks to get a look. But none of those girls had ever done anything for Colton. And the way Cara rested her hand on his bicep only strengthened his aversion.

"I didn't realize you came to these things, Colt." Her hand stayed on his arm, and he tried to catch any of his friends' eyes. When he couldn't, he looked down at Cara, blue eyes smiling up at him. Her gold hair was perfectly styled, draping over her black coat in perfect waves. Her straight teeth were bleach-white, her skin flawlessly tan. If she was taller than 5'3", she could've stood in for Barbie.

"Yeah, I love this stuff." He shrugged, hoping it would push her hand off.

It didn't.

"Me, too! But my god, it's cold." She wrapped her arm under his, huddling her tiny frame against his body.

"Uh, yeah, we were actually gonna head out." He pulled away gently, not wanting to make a scene.

She pouted but let go, putting her hands in her pockets. "I get that. We were thinking of heading to Cheers to warm up.

Maybe..." She looked between Katie and June, Dragan and Colton. "You guys want to join?"

Cheers and Beers was the only bar local to Oak Valley, so it was usually teeming with everyone Colton tried to avoid, including Cara and her crew.

"Oh, thanks for the invite," Katie chimed in. "I think we were gonna go our separate ways, though. Maybe next time?"

Colton knew his sister was just saving face since they lived in such a small town — there would never be a next time. Katie adored Ruby and despite being four years younger, knew all the shit that had gone down in high school. Cara being at the center of it.

Cara shrugged. "Okay, then. Hope you guys have fun. See you around, Colt."

He cringed at her use of his nickname, the way she batted her eyelashes and ran her fingers across his back as she walked away.

"Damn, she just doesn't quit," Dragan said, once Cara was out of earshot.

"No, no she doesn't." Katie watched the crowd part for Cara and her posse like the Red Sea. She turned back to Colton. "Why don't you ever just, I dunno, put her in her place? Just outright say you're not interested?"

"It would certainly be your easiest option," June said.

"After ten years, she should know it's not gonna happen," Colton said. "Otherwise it would've already."

"I hate to break it to you, but that's not usually how women work. They either walk away cold turkey or go for what they want until you say something," June said. "I think we all know which one Cara is."

Colton cocked his head, looking at his best friend's crush. He clenched his jaw, biting his tongue from asking which one she was. How she had no room to talk. She kept playing the friend card when it came to Dragan, even though it was clear as day he would give anything to be with her in a romantic capacity. Colton didn't oppose their being together; he just wish she was honest.

Before he could respond, Dragan jumped in. "I think if she doesn't stop and you don't want her advances, just fucking shut her down, man. It's cold, can we get going? We could do pizza at mine?"

Dragan started making his way to the street, heads above everyone else. His large body didn't need to press through; they parted easily, taking multiple steps away to let him by. Colton sighed and followed, Katie and June far enough behind that he couldn't make out what they were saying over the din of the crowd.

The same crowd he couldn't stop himself from scanning, desperate for one last look at the mirage from his past.

# 9

Ruby exited the highway, anxiously navigating the New Jersey streets for some academy that held her bus.

*Her bus.*

After the doctor's office, she rummaged through her mom's manifesting books and gleaned what she needed. Lo and behold, manifesting and searching brought her to a Craigslist listing for a 54-passenger school bus in New Jersey. The private academy decided last minute they didn't have use for it, despite putting in new batteries and a full tank of gas. They needed the sale, so the price was a steal.

*New year, new you.*

Ruby chuckled to herself, giddy with this next chapter. She was on her way to pay cash and have the bus towed back upstate. She should've asked Olive or Penelope — some of her only friends left in Oak Valley — to accompany her. There was still a part of her that didn't believe this was happening. It didn't help that Craigslist was known for being a little sketchy, and who sold a school bus in great condition for less than two grand?

Some things were too good to be true.

*Shit.* She accidentally passed the left turn to the school, so she made a U-y and entered the empty parking lot. It was a freakin' yellow bus, why couldn't she see it? She slowly made her way around the school, scanning for a bright hunk of metal against the grey day. The front and side lot brought up nothing, so Ruby made her way to the back.

And there, slightly hidden by a back entrance and a tree in a median, was her Bluebird bus.

Of course busses are big, but this was bigger than she'd expected.

She parked the car in a space a bit behind the bus and shot a text off to Jack, the Craigslist contact. A few minutes later, he stepped onto the back concrete stoop and waved before entering the bus. The engine rolled before kicking up, the large diesel engine vibrating the air.

Not only was she big, but she was *loud*.

Ruby got out of the car, tightening her scarf. Jack met her halfway.

"You gotta let her run to warm her up in the winter, but go ahead and check her out."

"Thank you," Ruby said, making her way to the door. It'd been years since she stepped into a school bus. The steps creaked slightly. One of the double doors was rusted through on the bottom, but she planned on replacing that anyway with an RV door in the conversion.

She rested a hand on the driver's seat headrest, taking in the burgundy vinyl seats. 54-passengers. Remnants of its previous elementary school passengers littered the floor — sparkly pencils, candy wrappers, forgotten homework assignments. The bus rumbled around her as she walked the aisle, envisioning the conversion.

Ruby turned around and left the bus, peering underneath.

There was some rust, but it didn't look like much considering the bus was regularly exposed to snowmelt and salt. Her research had told her what to look for in terms of rust, and to hire a mechanic to check the engine, but now faced with everything all at once, she felt frozen by the responsibility. She didn't really know what to look for, and she'd come alone. Besides, the only mechanic she knew was one she never wanted to see again.

But she was good at taking risks — the bus looked and sounded good. How bad could it be?

Maybe she was just desperate enough for a change that this was a risk worth taking.

"You said $1,800, cash?" She turned to Jack.

"Yep. We just want to get rid of it. All the most recent paperwork is in the driver's box."

Ruby pursed her lips. "Okay."

Rummaging in her bag, she pulled out the envelope. Jack pulled out the title and keys.

"Is it okay if I leave it here until the tow comes, tonight or tomorrow?"

He laughed. "Of course, it's your bus now. Pleasure doing business with you, send me pics of the conversion. I've always considered doing one myself."

They made the exchange and he nodded before ambling back into the building, a new spring in his step.

Ruby looked at the bus, the motor still growling in place. Her bus.

The tow wouldn't be able to get to it until the following morning, and then it'd have to make its way from New Jersey to New York's Hudson Valley. There was something about handing over a wad of cash and walking away that made her nervous, and she kept reminding herself that no one would want to jip her of a school bus from 2002.

She really should have asked one of her friends to come, but she was good at being alone. And this was her project, her risk. Her new life.

## 10

Oil changes were the most Colton was willing to do at the shop if he couldn't work reception, and Katie had specifically asked to work the desk. Unusual for her, but he understood needing a change of scenery. He replaced the fill cap on the engine and removed the drip pan, glancing at his sister through the window. Thankfully, Damian didn't work today, so she was bent over the keyboard, furiously typing away. Better that than the so-called harmless flirting she was always partaking in.

Colton started the car, checking the oil light before getting out to look around and under the vehicle. All clear. He turned off the car, settling into the driver's seat to wait a bit before checking the dipstick. He stared out the windshield, wondering what goods his mom was baking at For Goodness Cakes with his ex-classmate Olive and her mom, who owned the shop. He'd have to start preparing recipes, in the off-chance his interview went well.

He smiled; he had an interview.

A rap on the window made him jump. Katie's cackle was on the other side, and she was bent over. Colton threw the door open and slammed it shut behind him.

"What's so funny?"

"Y-y-you." She could barely get the words out. "Your... f-face!"

"Grow up," he huffed, pushing past her to the office. She could deal with the fucking oil change.

"W-wait!" She chased after him, her hand on his arm stopping him. She was still grinning like a goon, but at least she could speak.

"I need you to make a house call."

"We don't do house calls."

"We do for this. Some guy bought a school bus to convert, but it's stranded in his yard. Engine's turning but not starting. I figured you could use a break." Her big eyes softened, the unspoken understanding of their father in them.

"Okay. Where is it?" Colton sighed. At least it wasn't here — he hadn't wanted to come into work, but living with the boss made it difficult to play hooky.

Katie shrugged. "It's down on Cypress, past that big barn that says Ryder's Farm."

Colton stared at her, but she averted his gaze for some papers on the desk.

Ruby lived out there.

"You don't have an address?"

"It's a freakin' school bus, Colt. You can't miss it. I'll finish the oil change." She nudged him as she made her way back to the garage. He watched her go, his skin heating at the thought of being on the same street as Ruby. Katie had said it was a guy, and he took solace in that.

Colton left the shop, hopping in his two-year-old Audi R8. The black luxury sports car was a holdover from his pro days, bought just before his knee injury. It was the one thing he'd held onto, the one thing that still made him feel alive. He revved the two-seater, taking the curves a little too fast but relishing the way the gears shifted as he flew.

He hadn't driven this way since he last saw Ruby, ten years ago. The time they ended things for good. It amazed him how deep the muscle memory to her place was. He knew the old church, the river on the right, the turn that was hidden by trees. It wasn't until he passed Ryder's that he slowed down, engine purring as he crawled along. He was nearing Ruby's, and he'd be lying if there wasn't a small part of him that hoped he'd catch a glimpse of her outside her house.

But it wasn't a glimpse of her that undid him.

It was the bright yellow school bus sitting in her backyard, her mop of red curls burning in the sun as she stared at the monstrosity.

He'd been had.

## 11

Ruby heard the sports car engine but refused to turn around, every atom in her being willing it to not be who she knew it was.

There was only one person in this town who could afford a car like that.

She kept her back turned as she heard the wheels crunch down the gravel driveway. At least he had the balls to continue. The rushing in her ears only intensified when the engine cut, and the door opened and shut, and she heard those familiar footsteps that she'd memorized over years of being near him. It lacked the confidence of the strut she'd seen on television. No, this was his walk, his awkward teenage gait that struggled to catch up to his manly looks, his football stardom.

Ruby turned to face him, this ghost that haunted her every night.

But there he was, real as ever. And way too attractive.

He still towered over her, all broad shoulders and lean muscle. She had no doubt there was an eight-pack hiding beneath his thin green henley, the light jacket more for show than for winter protection. He shoved his hands in his blue jeans, hiding the black grease stains. Her eyes traveled up his chest, well defined beneath the fabric, landing on his eyes. Those deep brown, warm and rich like mahogany. Her face flushed. Those eyes had seen parts of her no one else had seen. They knew her inside and out. They'd loved her, from gangly teen to confident woman. He gave her a small smile, the hint of a dimple threatening to undo her.

This was him. This was the Colton Taylor she remembered, just cocky enough to take a chance. And fuck if she was going to let him back in.

"Why are you here?" She cleared her throat, trying to sound braver than she felt.

He shrugged. "Katie told me some guy had a school bus that needed starting. But something tells me you're not some guy and that this is your bus." He looked at the bus and shook his head, smile spreading. "You sure are full of surprises, Ruby Delacey."

Ruby thought she swooned when he said her name. The way he savored each letter before letting them go.

It shouldn't still feel this way.

"Some things never change."

"Ain't that the truth."

Their eyes met, and Ruby heard everything they'd left unspoken. Maybe she was just reading into his stance, a little too close to hers. Maybe it was the way his eyes delved into hers. Maybe it was the way his breathing quickened since stepping out of the car.

She shook her head and opened the bus doors. "So, it won't start. It started just fine when I picked it up, but now it won't. Hopefully it's a quick job, I just need to move it over." *And you need to leave.*

There was no way she could trust her body if he stayed any longer, even if her heart hurt at the thought of him leaving.

He moved past her, close enough to brush his arm against hers. Goosebumps erupted over her skin, and she pulled her jacket tighter around her. Entering the bus, Colton turned the key, listening to the engine catch and fall. Ruby waited outside, watching the flex of his bicep beneath his jacket, the furrow of his brow as he concentrated on the sounds. He'd never been fond of the mechanic work, but he'd always been good at it. He'd helped more than once when they had just started driving — bald tires, where the brights were located, oil changes. He climbed down the stairs, again too close for comfort but not close enough to satisfy the ache in her. Popping the hood, he went to work fiddling with the wires and tubes.

"Do you have socket wrenches?"

"Um... yeah, hang on." Ruby was lost in the veins of his forearms, revealed from the push of his jacket sleeves. She let out a deep breath, heading into the basement. She'd stocked up on some tools for this project. Finding the multi-piece set, she brought him the wrenches. He smiled at her with those damn dimples and took the case, just barely missing her pinkie with his.

She shuddered. It had been a mistake to call Will's Auto, but Google said they were the nearest diesel auto shop around. When she called, she'd sent a little prayer that Colton had managed to get out of the family business — even if she knew that was a stretch. She'd known he was back in Oak Valley after his injury last year, and she knew how his dad was. Katie had thankfully answered, and Ruby asked for discretion. Clearly Katie had other plans, and while she couldn't blame Colton's younger sister, Ruby was still pissed. Seeing him here was a reminder of so many things, including one of the reasons she'd ended things. While she'd worked to build a life for herself and what she wanted, he had built a life that was so far under his father's shadow, she knew he'd never be happy. Could never be happy.

That wasn't the life she wanted, even though it nearly killed her to let him go.

But he hadn't fought for her, and that said everything she needed to hear.

Colton packed up the wrenches, hopping back into the bus. He turned the key, the engine sputtering before catching. He grinned, dimples on full display.

Good thing he couldn't see the way her nipples hardened when he threw that smile her way, bounding down the steps.

"Okay, you're all set." He ran his tongue over his lips, staring at her. "So."

"So."

"You're back."

"So are you." She didn't know what else to say. She wasn't supposed to feel this way around him. It'd been years, and they'd hurt each other. She thought she'd moved on in college — and based off of his social media and paparazzi photos, it certainly seemed like he had. But just because they were back in the same town, surrounded by the same memories, didn't mean she needed to entertain the idea of them being friendly. They could be civil, and it would have to be enough.

He rocked on his heels. It was a nervous move, one that brought Ruby back to times before he launched into rants about his dad or anxiety before a test. "You know, if we're going to be in the same town again, maybe we should clear the air." His eyes pierced hers.

Ruby held back a sharp laugh. "Yeah, I don't think that's necessary."

"Really?"

"Really." She scrunched up her nose. "Thanks for helping with the bus, I'll see you around." It was dismissive, but his energy was stifling. She wanted, needed to be surrounded by him. Under him.

His eyes softened, the hurt apparent in the disappearance of his dimples. He set his jaw, cheeks flushing.

"Yeah, see you around."

Stomping past, he slammed the car door behind him. The engine revved as he backed down the driveway faster than was necessary. Ruby watched until his car disappeared behind the bend, shoulders involuntarily sagging.

It felt like her heart had been ripped out.

It'd been ten years.

It wasn't supposed to feel this way.

## 12

Colton pulled into the lot beside the abandoned church, head reeling from his encounter with Ruby.

He tried to get as close to her as he dared, even when her lemon jasmine scent became an assault. Even as the urge to cup her face almost overwhelmed him. The way she parted her lips, hazel eyes pleading for him to come closer...

And then she'd frozen him out.

"Fuck!" He slammed the steering wheel with his palm.

*In, out. In, out.*

It's not like he had forgotten what she looked like. He'd followed her social medias, trailing her success in New York City, watching her grow into the beautiful, smart woman he'd seen hidden beneath her teenage skin.

But he had forgotten what it felt like to be in her magnetic field. Forgotten what it felt like to see the slight gap in her front teeth when she smiled at him, to count the stars on her skin. He wasn't even sure if he wanted to be close to her again, but there had been no denying the way his body responded to hers.

He called Katie.

"Are you fucking kidding me?" His blood boiled.

"Oh hey, sunshine. Glad things went over so well," Katie chuckled.

Colton gripped the steering wheel, still trying to slow his breathing. "Why would you do that?"

"Why do you think, you big lunk? You would have avoided her for god knows how long. Better to just rip off the band-aid."

"I'm going to rip something else if you pull that shit again."

His sister barked out a laugh. "What, a new asshole? Jeez, you're so predictable. Such a mechanic. Just come back to the shop, Dad's going to throw a fit if he thinks you're skipping out."

Colton seethed. "I'm on a house call. I'll see him tonight." He hung up the phone, before Katie could get under his skin any further. He worked at an auto shop, but he'd never been a mechanic. His dad wanted him at the family shop, but when the anger threatened to boil over, it was the kitchen he needed.

He threw the car down the road, switching gears and slamming the gas. He should've been a race car driver, maybe then he wouldn't have gotten his stupid injuries and dumped back in this stupid little town. The drive to Main Street was a blur, and Colton squealed into the bakery parking lot. A few people braving the early January cold risked a glance before scurrying along. He watched them, knowing what they thought.

Asshole. Failure.

Probably something about compensation.

That made him snort — he knew the stigma of trucks and sports cars, even if it wasn't true. He had his muscle car because it made him feel alive and in control. He got out, the cold hitting him. It was getting close to Christmas and probably time to break out his winter coat, but there was a point of pride attached to claiming imperviousness to cold. Colton had always waited for his dad to pull out his coat before he did. And his dad hadn't pulled it out yet, so neither would he. Since he got the pride gene from his dad, he was always trying to come out on top. Even if his dad didn't see it that way.

*In, out. In, out.*

He ambled to the bakery, located on the one main street that cut straight through town. Tucked in the scenic Hudson Valley, Oak Valley fulfilled its storybook potential: trees ringed with lights, street posts with glittering wreaths, residents calling jovial greetings as they hurried to their destinations. If he concentrated, he could probably make out the Salvation Army bell from outside the grocery store. It was a cute town with everything anyone could need.

It was just so damn small. Constricting.

Sleigh bells jingled as he opened the door to For Goodness Cakes, overcome with the smell of baking bread, buttercream frosting, and coffee. The narrow storefront managed to fit in a hodge-podge of four vintage tables with chairs that were often being moved to accommodate the large groups of teens or parents with young kids who hid there for warmth during winter or to escape the summer humidity. The new coffee shop down the street, AC/DCafe helped offload some of the cramping — it was large and sleek, and more for people wanting to work rather than people looking to be cozy. For Goodness Cakes had recently started selling their baked breads there, and the added income was starting new conversations on what the future of the little bakery looked like.

There was a binder on the small counter with the wedding cakes and catering options, a glass case beneath displaying scones, breads, muffins, cookies, and tarts. When any of the three employed bakers — or Colton — felt like experimenting, there was a platter left on the counter with the new item and a locked box with accompanying papers for comments. They'd been able to keep the menu updated with items that would be loved, but Colton knew they needed more ways to stand out.

Oak Valley was small, but it was still growing. He sighed, wondering if they had the time or budget to brainstorm and implement new ideas.

Olive Dougherty came out from the back. He noticed the slight hitch in her step as she saw him, but she recovered with a warm smile and leaned forward against the counter. They'd always been friendly, but not friends. Growing up in the same classes could do that, plus her mom owned the bakery and she was good friends with Ruby.

"Hey, Colt. Haven't seen you in here for a bit." She tucked a strand of jet black hair behind her ear, the end of the bob curling around some glitzy dangly earrings. Her bright blue eyes softened. She was Ruby's friend, but he knew she'd always rooted for him.

He shrugged. "Yeah, been busy with the auto shop. Is my mom in?"

"Yeah, in the kitchen." Olive raised an eyebrow. "You going to bake us up a new masterpiece? I still get requests for those orange almond croissants you made back in high school."

He shrugged, remembering how everyone had pushed him to enter a county-wide food contest. But the grueling football practices for state championships — and the hard set of his father's jaw — had deterred him.

"I'm thinking about it. Maybe some rose cardamom eclairs?"

"Oh, don't tease me like that, Colton!"

He laughed. "You guys aren't hiring by chance?"

Olive perked up. "Not unless you want to replace your mom. You could've had one in high school, you know."

"You know that's not true, Olive." He walked past her, not bothering to look her way.

His mom was elbow-deep in dough, kneading and rolling the large ball on the floured counter. Bruce Springsteen was on low, and she was softly singing along. Colton smiled. These were the moments he wanted to remember forever.

"Oh, you scared me!" Cheri jumped, hand resting on her chest.

"Sorry, Olive said you were back here." He gave her a quick kiss on the cheek. "You making sourdough?"

"Always," she laughed. There were stripes of flour on her face, and he saw why when she tried to brush a stray hair away with the back of her hand. "Are you keeping me company?"

"If you don't mind. I might've mentioned some rose cardamom eclairs to Olive and don't want to leave her hanging."

"Well now that you mention it, can't have you leaving me hanging either! There should be a clean pan in the dishwasher, and the rosewater is in the far right pantry." Cheri smiled before returning to her dough.

Colton exchanged his jacket for a navy apron from the hook, looping it over his neck and tying it around his waist. He opened his mouth, wanting to tell his mom about the interview. He'd told her about applying, and she almost started crying from pride — now wasn't the time for more waterworks.

He rolled up his sleeves, his body settling into the rhythm of the kitchen. Baking had always been an escape, first as a way to spend time with his mom. But the more time he spent surrounded by flour and exotic ingredients, the more he wanted to experiment. While football worked his body, baking worked his mind. It allowed him to feel with his fingers, to make mistakes and push the boundaries of what people wanted.

What he wanted.

This was a home he'd never found anywhere else. He'd had so much taken from him, including this once before. He'd be damned if he let it happen again.

## 13

Ruby eyed the aisle of chisels. The more research she'd done, the more she realized how utterly unprepared she was for this conversion.

She'd had the right tools to start on the seat removal that weekend but wanted to jump into the ceiling panel removal immediately after. So long as her body would be up for it. She wasn't unfit, but Ruby certainly wouldn't call herself active. Plus, she enjoyed a large stuffed crust pepperoni pizza and a pint of ice cream as much as the next person. Preferably all to herself.

She let out a huff, lost in how many chisels stared back at her.

"So many options, so little time."

Ruby froze, the deep baritone voice all too familiar.

"Don't you have a car to fix?" It came out icier than planned. She crossed her arms and turned. Colton infiltrated every one of her senses. He towered over her, broad shoulders blocking the outside world so all she could do was travel the planes of his chest — still no winter coat — to meet his eyes. The deep brown eyes that searched hers, the crawl of dimples framing his slow smile.

"Not today, Dragan asked me to pick up some anchors. I guess June's hanging shelves at the book store. What do you need chisels for?"

"The bus. Obviously."

"Smart ass." He brushed past her to grab one of the chisel sets, a wave of earth hitting her nostrils. He'd always smelled like the forest after a cold rain, with a hint of car oil lingering after. Ruby found comfort in the smell, the sheer masculinity of everything it carried.

"It's for the ceiling panels," she sighed. He was reading the back of two different sets, clearly not leaving anytime soon.

He frowned. "You plan on hand chiseling those rivets?"

Ruby shrugged. Ceiling panels were held with rivets, which many a skoolie account said a rather expensive air compressor tool would work best on. But chiseling and popping out the rivets by hand was the most cost-effective method. She was working part-time at Maven Media from home, but the majority of her funds were going into an account for her mom's current and upcoming medical bills. Her mom's job at the town library — while emotionally and mentally fulfilling — didn't offer the greatest paycheck or health insurance.

Colton placed the sets back, running a hand through his hair. Just as thick as Ruby remembered, and she tried to ignore the flush of heat that rolled through her body when his gaze pierced hers.

"I have an air chisel."

Her body buzzed with the unsaid offer. Of course the asshat wouldn't flat-out say she could use it.

"Good for you. I'm going to be the proud owner of a chisel set," Ruby huffed, reaching around him to grab a set from the shelf.

He placed a hand on her arm and shook his head. "Ruby, I

know you like to do things yourself. But hand-chiseling rivets above your head can be dangerous."

"Lots of things are dangerous."

"That doesn't mean you need to go out of your way to be in dangerous situations."

"Skoolie people do it all the time."

"And how many of them accidentally hammer their hands? Fingers? Drop a panel on their heads? And then they're out of commission."

"So what do you suggest?"

Colton sighed, looking around the store before settling on her eyes. "You... You could borrow mine. I could show you how to use it."

Her body buzzed as she imagined Colton coming over and helping her with the ceiling panels. One full day of being in the relatively small space with her ex? Ruby chewed her lower lip. She sighed. He did have a point, even if she didn't want to admit it.

"Fine. But it's only because you may or may not be right about the potential injuries, and I really don't want to be held up for something stupid."

Colton smirked. She rolled her eyes — it was the smile he gave anytime he won.

Cocky bastard.

## 14

Colton looked down at Ruby. Arms crossed, shooting lasers at him. She'd backed him into a corner, but he still won the argument. And she knew it.

He hadn't wanted to offer and almost didn't. But picturing the spitfire before him craning her neck while hammering her ass off on metal studs had involuntarily filled him with concern.

He couldn't let her do that, not when he had easier means.

"When should I bring it by?"

She started down the aisle toward the registers, buttoning her black wool coat as she went. "Well, I'm dealing with the seat removal this weekend, so maybe Monday? I don't know if I'll get to it until next weekend though, so that's fine, too."

"Wait, you're removing the seats? By yourself?" Colton stopped in his tracks.

"Well, I'm going to angle grind - angle grinder? - the bolt heads first. Then I'll need to actually take the seats out of the bus." Ruby kept walking, exiting the store. Colton jogged to catch up, his knee twinging when he stopped short to keep from bowling her over on the sidewalk.

"Those things can't be light." He looked her over, unable to decide between being awed or frustrated at her recklessness. He knew she was a hard worker and few things could stop her, but this conversion she'd gotten herself into — from all the tools to the heavy objects — couldn't normally be a one-person job.

She shrugged. Colton fingered the anchors in his jacket pocket, thankfully bought before he saw her. He didn't know how long they stood there, only that Ruby wouldn't look at him. The cold bit into his skin, even through his jacket. She'd broken his resolve, but at least he knew she wasn't going to ice him out all the way.

"Okay, well I gotta go. Dragan's waiting for me. But I'll see you Monday."

"Okay, thanks." She threw him a half-smile before taking off.

Colton watched her leave, curls bouncing in her ponytail. She glanced at him before getting in her car, no hint of a smile. She pulled out, not looking back.

He shook his head and walked down Main Street to the The Little Prince Bookstore, keeping his head down to avoid the stares from passersby. He grew up in this town, and nothing had changed. All the shops, all the people, all the expectations.

Stay. Good job. Get married. Family.

He'd had a taste of more, and he couldn't forget it.

"Oof!"

The sound came from a middle-aged woman he smacked right into, and Colton managed to grab her elbow before her body hit the ground. He started apologizing profusely before she held up a hand, bundle of loose flyers in the other.

"No, it's okay, I wasn't looking where I was going," she said, brushing her suit off. "You're Bryce Taylor's boy, the football player, aren't you?"

*Great.*

"I'm Carla Lopez, I took over Robertson Realty a few years

ago." Her dark eyes looked around. "I—I heard through the grapevine you like to be in the kitchen?"

Colton started to grumble a non-committal response but she brushed him off. "Look, it's no secret in this town you've got talent — and not just in the field. Forgive me for overstepping, but since you're no longer playing, have you considered what's next?"

He took a step back, taking in her neatly pressed suit and severe bun. Her arms crossed over her chest, eyes piercing his. Who was this woman, digging into his life? Irritation started moving swiftly through him.

"Look, lady, I don't know what this is about but I'm in the middle of something." He pushed past her, not hard enough to knock her but hard enough to send a message.

The last thing he needed was some rando in his business.

His back to her, he didn't break stride as she spoke. "Well, Mr. Taylor, I just wanted you to know we represent several commercial kitchen properties. Just something to keep in my mind."

He heard the tinkle of the doorbell as her words rang in his ears, the idea of something he hadn't considered warming him as he made it to the bookstore.

## 15

Dragan Carter leaned against the counter, eyeing June Beaumont as she shelved the new shipment of Young Adult hardcovers. Her long hair glowed gold in the soft light, delicate fingers tracing the spines. She bit her lower lip, a soft sigh escaping. Dragan knew she was anxious to read each book she hadn't had the chance to.

Being in love with his best friend since kindergarten made sure he noticed every detail.

He sighed and looked to the door for Colton. Dragan had promised June he'd hang her new shelves, and Colton was late with the anchors he needed. Being six foot five lent itself well to those kinds of jobs, but he would've done it for her even if she was taller than her five feet. He'd do anything for her.

"Hey, D?" June's soft voice cut through his thoughts.

He met her green eyes, his heart breaking once more at their wide-eyed, hope-filled forest. "What's up, J?"

"What do you think about us adding a little coffee and tea station over here?" She walked to the back wall, skirt swishing from the sway of her wide hips. June pulled her cardigan around her, crossing her arms over her chest as she turned to him.

Dragan walked over to where she stood, hyper-aware of his proximity to her. It was natural for them to stand close, even if her warm scent made it almost unbearable. She always smelled like vanilla and wood left in the sun, like the summers they spent reading on The Little Prince Bookstore's worn front porch. They grew up there, her because her parents owned it and him because he needed an escape from his own family.

It didn't hurt she was there.

Dragan looked down at June, remembering their 5th grade selves at her parents' funeral. Her grandma Missy taking over the shop, how that summer Dragan brought June to his favorite spot by Beaver Creek to read. Slowly they'd adapted to life without her parents, and the bookstore became a refuge once more.

She was in the process of taking the store over from her grandma, and wanted to make some aesthetic updates.

"Would you charge or would it be free?"

"I was thinking a free drink with a book purchase? Or maybe a coffee subscription-type service. I was thinking of putting an electric fireplace here," her hands motioned against the wall, "and maybe the service bar on top. Shelves above that for the goods and shelves on either side. And then some overstuffed armchairs facing the fireplace and throughout the store."

Dragan smiled as her voice grew stronger with excitement. "That sounds lovely, J."

She leaned her head on his shoulder, a shock of electricity zipping through his body. "You don't think all these changes are... too much?"

"Not at all. Your parents would be proud." He put an arm around her slender shoulders.

The door jingled and Dragan jumped from June. He caught the barest hint of her face falling — disappointment? — before plastering her storefront smile and turning.

"Sorry, did I interrupt something?" Colton stifled a laugh and gave Dragan a knowing look.

"No, nope. No, not at all," June said, her fair cheeks pink as she made her way to the counter. Dragan caught Colton's raised eyebrow and shook his head.

Nothing had happened. Nothing would ever happen. Aside from their friendship, there was no way a woman like June could be with a man like him.

Colton shrugged, setting the anchors on the counter. June set a drill alongside them and leaned over the counter. Dragan shifted his gaze from her cleavage, feeling his body tense with the need to know her body as well as he knew her heart. He turned his attention to his best guy friend.

"Why are you late, Colt?"

He scoffed. "Ran into Ruby at Joe's. Apparently, she's converting a school bus into a tiny home and doing everything herself."

June chuckled. "Yeah, sounds like Ruby."

"Yes, yes it does." Dragan remembered how independent Ruby had been in high school, when she slowly became a part of their friend group as her and Colton started dating. He'd always admired her spirit and had many conversations with Colton on the impact she had on him. Colton never feeling good enough for her.

Colton clenched his jaw. "Well, it's dangerous."

"Careful, He-Man. She's got this. You know she supported herself in New York City, right? And not in a ritzy neighborhood. But in a crime-ridden, one-of-her-roommates-was-a-drug-addict one." June stood, spreading her arms across the counter. She was generally gentle, sweet, but she took protecting women — any woman — seriously. And while Dragan knew June and Ruby were only acquaintances, she'd never let Colton walk his hyper-masculinity over Ruby, even just in conversation.

"I—I didn't know that." Colton looked at Dragan. "Did you know that?"

Dragan shrugged. It was a small town, and what June heard through the grapevine she often shared with him. "It's not my place to tell you what goes on with Ruby."

"I know she can take care of herself, I just..." He ran a hand through his head and shook his head. "Thanks, J."

Dragan cringed at Colton using his nickname for June. When Dragan met her in kindergarten, he was only just starting to learn English. Saying her name with his Polish accent was undecipherable, so they'd settled on just the first letters of their names. But Colton had no way of knowing that her nickname meant more to him than just that. It was a testament to their friendship, to her acceptance of his roughness.

"It's okay, Colt. Just... chill, ya know?" She gave him a soft smile. "She's different than you remember, but I think better than ever. Just be nice to her."

"It's a two-way street."

"One of you could try putting aside your ego," Dragan added.

Colton glared at him. "Let's not forget she's the one who ended things with me. I'll catch you guys later."

Even on the carpet, Dragan could hear his stomps. The slam of the door with the holiday bells was the icing on the cake.

"He's such a... *guy*. And not in the good way," June huffed.

Dragan shook his head. "He didn't have the sweet effects of a beautiful bookworm to help offset the potent masculinity."

June rolled her eyes. "Please, you may not have the undercurrent of traditionalism he has, but you are by no means far from potently masculine."

"Oh, really?" Her words lit a fire in him. It was hard knowing whether she saw him as a brother or a friend, but when she said things like that it answered that question. Even if it left out the one he wanted to ask most.

"Dragan, I'm not blind." She blushed and grabbed the drill. "Can you please help me with these shelves?"

She didn't look at him as she sashayed to the wall. Dragan stared at her back, filled with the most dangerous emotion he'd ever known.

Hope.

## 16

Today was the day demolition started.

Ruby stared at the bus, angle grinder in hand. Somehow, by herself, she'd have to use this thing to get the bus seats out. She'd spent an hour researching what an angle grinder even was, watching many a YouTube video on how to hold it, what the discs were, and what bolts needed to be ground down.

So today was the day.

She took a deep breath and kept staring, nausea rising her throat. If she could just start…

"Honey, are you okay?"

Ruby turned to the house, trying to figure out which window her mom's voice floated from.

"Yep! All good."

"Okay, if you need anything just let me know. I'll be here."

"Thanks!"

Ruby swallowed. Maybe she could trick her mind into having her mom hold her accountable. She turned back to the bus, pulling the angle grinder cord with her. It was a bit of a stretch — the cord was plugged into the basement, extending through a small window and across the width of their driveway.

The bus was off to the side, situated on a patch of grass on the other side of the drive.

Now or never.

She opened the back door, placing the grinder under one of the seats before hauling herself up into the aisle. Which in and of itself was a chore. Ruby chuckled at the absurdity of what she'd done. At the very least, converting the bus would be a gym membership. Standing, Ruby put on her safety goggles and put in her earplugs. The angle grinder was much louder than she anticipated, and the vibration traveled up her arm.

This would be interesting.

Bending down in the aisle, she found her first victim. Sparks flew, and she had to stop several times from the vibrating and sheer overwhelm of what she'd gotten herself into. This was a massive project, and she'd only just started. Ruby tried not to think about all the steps that came after. She moved down the aisle, grinding and cutting each bolt head before moving to the bolts against the wall. She contorted herself into a variety of shapes, folding and bending under and over the smelly — sometimes sticky — vinyl seats.

When she finally stood, she was covered in a fine dust. Curls had escaped her bun and tickled her sweaty neck. And she was dying of thirst.

But all of the seat bolts had been cut. Step one was complete. Ruby smiled at the progress, even though she couldn't really see it. That would come after her quick lunch of leftovers and a million gallons of water. Her body hurt in ways she hadn't known were possible, but there was a sense of pride along with it.

The crunch of gravel brought her attention to the driveway, half-expecting a package-delivery truck and half-hoping her mom had surprised her with food-delivery. She froze at the sight of the black Audi, somehow still squeaky clean despite the country town its owner resided in.

He wasn't supposed to be here until Monday.

Ruby paced the bus aisle, trying to smooth down her hair but knowing that, at this point, the curls couldn't be tamed. She went to wipe her face but her hands were just as dirty. *Fuck.* Just because she couldn't stand him didn't mean she couldn't put her best foot forward. Hell, that was as good a reason as any to do just that.

Sighing, she hopped out the back door. His door swung open, that cocky smirk plastered on his face. One hand shut the door while the other held the handles of a large brown paper bag. Colton Taylor sauntered over, stopping just within reach. If she wanted to touch him, her fingers could graze his chest. Which Ruby definitely did not want to do.

"You're early." She crossed her arms, trying not to count the abs beneath his thin white shirt. Still no coat, his light jacket open and revealing the tightness of said shirt as he brushed a hand over his short hair. His smirk turned to a small smile.

"I thought you might be hungry." He held out the brown bag.

Goddamn him.

Ruby's stomach growled, causing his dimples to come out in full-force. "I was going to have lunch with my mom."

Colton looked around. "Really? Because I'm pretty sure I saw her car at the library on my way over here."

"Either way, you shouldn't have," she said, rolling her eyes. Her stomach grumbled again and she snatched the bag from his hands.

"Clearly someone needed to. Shall we eat inside?"

Ruby glared at him before leading the way. While she appreciated the food, she didn't ask for it. She didn't owe him anything, least of all her company.

## 17

Belly full, Colton followed Ruby out to the bus, almost tripping on a rock because his eyes were glued to her ass in those workout pants.

He could watch her walk away all day, every day. Even if it was because she was pissed at him. Which she was, given her silent treatment during lunch and their slightly heated argument about whether or not she needed help removing the seats from the bus.

And hey, he'd listened to her side. This was her project, she needed to do it, she hadn't asked for his help.

But he was here and those seats had to be heavy. They were both stubborn, but only one of them won this argument.

Colton chuckled to himself as Ruby popped open the back emergency door, hauling herself into the narrow bus aisle.

"Okay, since your stubborn ass insists on being here, I was thinking I'll wiggle the seat out and you can take it to that empty spot?" Ruby pointed to a bare patch of lawn at the front of the bus.

"Sounds good," he said, stripping off his jacket. Colton

caught Ruby's gaze, her cheeks burning red when their eyes met. She disappeared into the bus.

"Ready?" She yelled out.

"Yeah, let's go."

She pushed one of the backseats toward the back, slowly lowering it down as he grabbed one end and pulled it to the ground. The two-seater had to weigh a hundred pounds. Sweat trickled down his spine. Colton put his hands on his hips, looking at Ruby. She was already out of breath, soft lips parted as she panted.

He cleared his throat, wanting to break the ice. "These are heavier than I thought."

She barked out a laugh. "Do you need help moving it?"

"Seriously?"

"I wasn't sure if this was too hard on you." She shrugged, her face softening. "You know, with your knee."

Colton met her gaze. He could've sworn he saw a glimmer in them, one he hadn't seen in over ten years.

*I care about you, I worry about you, I love you.*

He shook his head, trying to rid himself of what he thought he saw, the sickening pit of possibility he felt in his gut. She let him go, all those years ago. It didn't matter if she regretted it now. "Nah, all good. This is nothing. You on the other hand..."

Ruby scoffed. "Please, I was going to do this by myself before you steamrolled."

"I didn't steamroll." *I just don't want you to get hurt.*

Colton swallowed the words before they dug him into a hole he wasn't sure he could get out of.

"Yeah, you kind of did, Colton." She stood in the bus aisle, arms crossed while she looked down at him. "I'm not who I was, I've been through a lot in the last ten years. I can handle myself, and I wanted to do this alone."

Colton remembered what June had said. It was a far cry

from what he'd seen on Ruby's social media. Dinners out, dressed up, laughing on the street. Not that he wasn't sure those things happened, but there was another side he didn't have access to.

He sighed. "Ruby, I know you can do this alone. And believe me, you'll do most of it that way. But it's okay to accept help now and then."

It was a hard lesson he had to learn after his injury. All of the doctors, physical therapy, aid to and from different rooms in the house. He didn't want her to have to learn the same lesson the hard way. He just had to remind himself it in no way had to do with the way his pulse quickened knowing she was back in town. It in no way had to do with the way his breath caught when he ran into her. And it definitely in no way had to do with the ache in his heart when he stood near her.

Ruby chewed her lower lip. "Fine. But you don't show up unannounced anymore, got it?"

"Even if I come bearing food?"

The longer she glared at him, the harder it was for him to keep from smirking. At least one thing hadn't changed.

"Text me first," she growled before disappearing. "You ready to keep going?"

"Bring it on, sweetheart." Colton bit his tongue at the slip of his old endearment for her, grateful she was somewhere in the bus and she couldn't see his face. When she came into view wiggling the next seat, she pretended like he hadn't said it.

They continued removing the seats, taking the occasional break for water or to catch their breath. Each seat was easily a hundred pounds, and while there was a time he could flip tires quadruple that size, the aches in his body were making him hyper-aware of his age and just how long it'd been since he'd done any real physical activity. His knee was twinging by the time they were done, but Colton felt alive in a way he hadn't in years.

And maybe it partly had to do with the satisfied smile plastered on a certain red-head's face, the way she looked at him while she guzzled water.

## 18

Ruby looked Colton over while she finished her water bottle. His skin shone with sweat, hair sticking up at odd angles, his biceps pushing against the sleeves of his t-shirt. She'd had the absolute pleasure of watching his arms bulge as he moved the seats from the back of the bus to the clearing. He still had a cocky bite to his words, one she only learned through his interviews over the years, but there was a softness to him that reminded her of being seventeen, star-gazing from the back of his pick-up.

"Thanks, Colt. Seriously," she said, wiping her mouth.

He shrugged. "You can just say I was right."

"Over my dead body." She shook her head but didn't stop the smile from spreading. "How's your knee feeling?"

"Been better but can't complain. I didn't realize how much I missed really working out." He looked at the bus, and she realized just how big a difference his being there made.

Maybe he was right. Even if she was going to do most of this alone, there was room for help.

"You know, if you have any questions about the rest of the build, don't hesitate to ask."

She started walking to his car. "Yeah, yeah. Are... Are you still coming Monday?"

His steps followed hers and stopped when she turned around and leaned against his car.

Of course his eyes had been glued to her ass. Some things never changed, and Colton being the playboy he turned into after they broke up seemed to be one of them.

"You can stop looking at my ass anytime," she said, fixing him with a glare.

"Not a chance, cupcake." He smirked.

Ruby's cheeks flushed, and she mentally kicked herself. She hated that he could — and did — still do that to her. She cleared her throat, needing to get back on track.

"So. Monday."

Colton kicked the gravel driveway, stuffing his hands in his pockets. He took a long look at the bus before answering her.

"I can stop by around 4 p.m., I think if that works for you. And I really would like to help you, Ruby. With this project. A home on wheels, to travel and see the world... It kind of feels like a dream, you know?"

Ruby would've taken a step back if it weren't for his stupid fancy sports car. A dream? The wistfulness in his voice about anything other than football was new to her, let alone something that involved leaving Oak Valley. Hell, ten years ago wanting to go to play college football was part of why they broke up — and he wanted to stay close to home to help at the auto shop while he pursued his dream at a semi-local state college, and she needed to get out in order to pursue hers.

"Y-Yeah, I do know." She cocked her head, trying to see this new version of him.

"Why do you sound so surprised? You know I've always wanted to build a house. This is kind of like that, only better in some ways."

"I just... I thought you wanted to stay in Oak Valley."

He barked out a laugh. "What, ten years ago? Mainly out of obligation to my family? Ruby, I traveled around. I love Oak Valley but being back here after everything I've experienced... I don't know if I'm ready to stay put."

She let his words sink in.

Ten years was a long time. It was possible that in those ten years Colton had changed, just as she had.

"Earth to Ruby." Colton dipped his head in front of hers, close enough their noses almost touched. A wave of his earthy scent hit her, and she was thankful she could catch herself against the car. His scent, his proximity, did not mean she needed to swoon like a damsel. Or at least not enough for him to see his effect on her.

"Sorry. 4 p.m. works on Monday. We won't have much light but some work is better than none."

He smirked, those damn dimples coming out of hiding. "Great. I'll see you then."

"Great."

He cleared his throat and raised his eyebrows. "You know, if you want me to stay all you have to do is say so."

"Wha— " Ruby realized she was leaning against the driver's side door, but Colton didn't move aside when she pushed off the slick black frame. They stood chest to chest, Ruby's breath quickening. Colton loomed over her, his broad shoulders shielding her from the bitter winter wind. She looked up at him, meeting his brown eyes. She could step around him, but there was that part deep in her body that wanted to go through him. That wanted to merge herself with him until they were one, to remember what it felt like to be his.

Colton swayed closer, and Ruby watched his lids lower, his lips part. She was drawn to him in equal measure, the magnetic force field almost too much to take.

Until she was slammed with cold air, Colton off to her side. He ran a hand through his damp hair, thrusting the car door open. It pushed her forward and Ruby turned on her heel.

"Yo, watch it, asshat!" She wasn't sure about the moment they just had, where it was headed or if she even wanted it to happen. But there was no need for him to sidestep out of nowhere and to throw his door into her.

"Sorry, I forgot I needed to be somewhere. I'll see you around." Colton slid into the car and slammed the door, his face mostly hidden by the heavily tinted windows.

Ruby stood back as he peeled down the driveway, reeling from what just happened.

Colton not knowing what he wanted and being a dick about it were things that clearly hadn't changed, even after ten years.

## 19

Colton sank the red solid in the corner pocket, trying to tune out the din of the drunk patrons at Cheers and Beers. He and the guys were making use of their Saturday night, even if they risked running into Cara and her crew; a guys' night was worth the risk given the distraction it afforded Colton from his day. He could barely feel his arms from the heavy lifting he did that afternoon. Or stop his heart from pounding at the near kiss he'd had with his beautiful, infuriating ex. A cold shower and a nap hadn't settled his nerves, so he was hoping the guys' night would do the trick.

It was him, Dragan, and Archer against Liam, Dean, and Caleb. They'd been friends since the first grade, when happenstance landed them in Miss Morales' class. And unfortunately for their parents and teachers, the bond developed from a sweet reading group to class clowns in no time. Archer and Dragan were always the least likely to get in trouble, but Colton was convinced that had more to do with their acting abilities than their looks. Especially Dragan, who should've played basketball or football professionally but opted to spend his time with his nose in a book. Colton snickered, knowing it probably had to do with June Beaumont more than anything.

He was too distracted and scratched on the next hit.

"Mr. Panties-in-a-twist, what's up?" Dean playfully shoved him while moving into place for his turn.

"Nothing." Colton scowled, downing the rest of his IPA.

Archer raised his eyebrows and tried to hide a smile. "Would you prefer Mr. Pissy Pants instead?"

Liam and Dean burst out laughing, Dragan shaking his head with a smile.

Colton's face burned. "What the fuck's your problem?"

"Did you see Ruby?" Caleb's voice was barely loud enough to hear, but Colton caught the sting. Caleb had never cared for Ruby when they dated and found their break-up as justification to actively make it known.

Colton clenched his teeth, hating how transparent he was. "What does it matter?"

Caleb sipped his rum and Coke. "Just curious."

"Did you?" Archer asked, leaning over the scarred pool table for his turn. Dragan snickered over in the corner and Colton stabbed him with his pool cue.

"Yeah. And?"

"How was it?" Archer hit the ball, narrowly missing the intended pocket. For an ex-military, current firefighter, his pool aim was shit.

"Fine." Colton eyed the bar, thinking his next drink should be something a bit harder. One of the best parts of having money — and his well-off friends would agree — was being able to afford top shelf without thinking too hard about it.

"Just fine?" Dean finished his whiskey ginger, glancing at the bar. Although Colton knew it was the group of women that was next on the menu, not what he'd be drinking next.

"Yep. Who needs another?" Colton asked while Liam took his turn. Everyone raised their hands, stacking empty glasses and handing them off to Colton and Dragan. Dean tagged along, eyeing the girls at the bar. Colton snickered, choosing the space next to them. They were clearly being bothered by a couple of guys, two of the four girls sitting and facing the bar while the other two leaned against their friends and as away from the guys as possible. Colton placed their order, Dragan standing silent beside him. The girls kept eyeing his giant friend, but quickly turned their attention to Dean when he flashed them his pearly whites.

"Hey, ladies." Colton heard Dean start his charm, turning his back to give full attention the women. Colton thought he vaguely recognized one or two of them from high school. They were all beautiful, there was no denying that.

But none of them had a shock of red curls and a sweet gap-toothed smile that made his heart ache.

As if reading his thoughts, Dragan leaned against the bar. "So how was seeing Ruby?"

"It's bullshit, D."

"Remember your deep breathing." His friend gave a low chuckle, broad shoulders pushing between Colton and Dean, who was listening intently to something one of the brunettes was saying.

"Which part is bullshit?"

"All of it. She's pissing me off but I — She's just pissing me off. How's June? Could've sworn I interrupted something the other day." Colton didn't want to admit Ruby still affected him, and instead smirked at Dragan, who'd always had a thing for the sweet blonde. Even if he couldn't admit it to anyone — let alone to himself.

Dragan kept a straight face but couldn't keep the color from rising in his cheeks. The bartender lined their drinks on the bar. "Thanks, man, you can put it on my tab." Colton glanced at his friend while he and Dragan gathered the glasses. They left Dean's on the bar and balanced the other five through the crowd.

"There was nothing to interrupt," Dragan yelled.

"Your delayed response says otherwise."

They reached the guys and a cloud of tension. Handing off the drinks, Colton looked between them. Caleb was sulking, Archer and Liam scrolling their phones.

"Everything good?" Dragan asked. "Who's turn is it?"

"Colt's," Archer said.

Colton tried to dismiss the slight head shake Arch gave to Dragan but he couldn't leave it. "Did we miss something?"

Liam shook his head. "Nope, all good. Your turn."

"Look who I found!" Dean's voice came up behind Colton, followed by the giggles of four somewhat-drunk girls. Dean had his arm around two of them, his hand holding an almost empty glass, the other girls dancing their way to the pool table. "It's Izzie from Chem with Mr. Shapiro!" Dean gave the brunette under his arm a squeeze and made introductions.

Colton didn't give a shit about Izzie from Mr. Shapiro's 9th grade Chemistry class, but he did care about whatever was going on between the guys. And the way Caleb avoided him, the way Liam and Archer hung beside Dragan, made it obvious enough it had to do with Colton.

Or, more likely, it had to do with Ruby.

## 20

AC/DCafe was a newer addition to Oak Valley, and a much needed one. Ruby looked around the expansive coffee shop, filled with large tables, outlets, overstuffed chairs and sofas. For a Monday morning, it was less crowded than she expected. It was the perfect worker's retreat, complete with the delicious smell of coffee and a large milkshake menu. There was a large glass case with baked goods from For Goodness Cakes. When Ruby first walked into the cafe, she had to stop herself from checking the case for one of Colton's signature bakes.

Instead, she ordered a black coffee and checked her phone for the hundredth time.

After fuming all weekend from his storm-off and his stupid proximity to her, she'd texted him yesterday to forget his stupid air chisel and to keep his stupid, hot self away from her. Not in so many words, but still. She wanted to get the point across.

Ruby took a seat by one of the large storefront windows, setting her bag on the chair beside her. She pulled out her laptop, digging for her headphones beneath the bag of chisels she bought earlier that morning.

Which just further fueled her anger. How dare he lean so close and then stomp off?

He hadn't changed. He should've stayed away, and she never should've agreed to let him help her.

Opening her laptop, she logged into the Zoom meeting with Rachel.

"Hey, babe!" Rachel greeted her with a wide, brilliant smile but it fell as quickly as it appeared. "Is everything okay? You look pissed."

"Peachy." Ruby gritted her teeth, even more annoyed that Colton made her reactions so obvious. "How's the office?"

"It's fine, relatively quiet. We miss you." Rachel made a pouty face.

"I miss you guys." Ruby softened, missing the camaraderie she'd grown to love. Even Julie, she missed their easy banter before things got messy.

She hadn't known Anthony was Julie's until after the fact, and while he said they were over, she could tell they weren't. At least not internally. Ruby didn't take it personally, she was used to guys wanting only one thing from her, but that didn't mean she was going to waste her time with a boy.

Not when she needed a man.

"You'll have to come visit! How's your mom?" Rachel asked.

"She seems okay," Ruby said, taking a shaky breath. "We're waiting to hear back on the results from her PET scan to see if the cancer's spread to her bones."

"If there's anything I — we — can do, please let me know. I can't imagine having to deal with that."

"Thanks, I appreciate it. Honestly, being able to work remote is a huge load off. I couldn't imagine having to find a job at the craft store or something while also taking care of… things." Ruby gave her friend a small smile. She hadn't told anyone about why she was home. Not that they'd asked. But saying the words aloud to someone she loved and trusted hurt. They made it real. And Ruby wasn't sure she was ready to face reality.

Rachel cleared her throat and started typing away. "Did you get the email I sent? Lemonade Films and Atlantic reached out, we should have contracts signed by end of week so Friday, you can do your thing. How are the others?"

"Great, thanks! I'm excited to work with Lemonade," Ruby said, pulling up her prepared update on BRICK Talent Agency, B23 Productions, and World Talent. Lemonade Films was the new project of one of the world's biggest pop stars. "The others are fine, we're working on a press pack for two A-list actors under BRICK, and then I'm wrapping up B23's press releases for the next year. They have a few world premieres scheduled in the early summer and late fall for Academy season."

Ruby fibbed a little — she only had outlines for the press packs and half the press releases done. But she knew as long as she delivered ahead of their padded deadlines, she'd stay in good standing with Rachel. Maven Media was the brain child and hard work of her ambitious friend and their fellow coworker Ella Davis — they'd joined forces shortly after college to build a publicity empire that focused on empowering women and underrepresented voices. Ella and Charlotte handled music, Rachel and Winsome handled publishing, Priya was human resources, Phoebe had taken over Julie's legal position. Julie now managed Maven's non-profit branch to provide support and professional counseling to single moms and women in domestic abuse situations, as well as provide child care to their kids.

"Okay great. I heard through the grapevine Lemonade may bring in more clients, so I'm keeping my eyes open for a possible second hire to help you with the media division." Rachel flicked her glossy black braid over a slender shoulder, the gold bracelets from her grandma in Pakistan tinkling with the movement. It was a sound that made Ruby miss the place she learned to call home, the people who'd become her family.

She was used to being alone. Her dad was gone before she knew him, her friend group disappeared as soon as she hit puberty. After leaving Oak Valley for college in New York City, Ruby had to fight for her place as one of many in the rat race.

Other than her mom and Colton, Maven Media was the only place she'd felt safe. Seen. Good.

"Great, thanks Rachel. I'm not sure how things will go with my mom but for now, I'm here for whatever you need."

"Thanks, babe. I do have another meeting I need to get to, but it was nice to see you. Let me know if there's anything else you need." Rachel smiled and gave a little wave before the call disconnected.

Ruby stared at the screen for a while after, trying to will herself to work on the things she told Rachel were already almost done. But seeing her friend, seeing even a glimpse of the life she left behind, had covered her in a fog. This wasn't supposed to be her life. If someone had told her three months ago — hell, a month — she'd be living at home with her mom, converting a school bus into a tiny home, no friends but her ex-boyfriend in sight, she would've called them crazy.

She sighed and checked her phone. Still no response from Colton.

Maybe he got the message and she wouldn't see him again, at least not alone. Her stomach churned at the thought, and she couldn't decide if it was because she won the fight or because she missed him.

## 21

The door slammed harder than he planned, his foot heavy on the gas.

Who was he kidding, of course he planned it.

He needed to hear that bang, feel the car race along winding country roads. His anger coiled under his skin, racing through his body with his blood, every pump of his heart. Ruby's text to not bother showing up was a challenge he happily accepted.

If she didn't want him to show up, that's exactly what he was going to do.

The bus stood out like a sore thumb among the dead and dying trees, barren of leaves but not the glittering dust of snow. Colton pulled into the driveway, having to drastically cut his speed no thanks to all the fucking potholes riddling the gravel stretch. As he came to a stop, Ruby hopped out of the back, curls sticking in all directions out of her messy bun. The absolute scowl on her face was a bonus, her gloved hands on her hips the cherry on top. She was furious in a way he'd only seen a handful of times, but he couldn't stop himself from smiling at how fucking cute she looked. Like one of those tiny ass dogs that follows close on the heels, yipping and yapping like it believed it could actually be a threat.

He kicked his door open, popping the trunk as he went. He leaned against the car, crossing his arms while he looked her over. Long legs perfectly sculpted beneath tight yoga pants, black fleece sweater bearing a hint of cleavage. He could practically see the dragon breath escaping from her nostrils, her ears and cheeks a brilliant pink as she glared.

Which just made him smile, a laugh nearly letting loose.

"Are you kidding me, Colton?" She stomped right up to him, the fierceness of her gaze not detracted from the angle of her chin as she looked up at him. He could smell a slight undercurrent of lemon and jasmine, a scent that took him back to hours of being tangled in sheets, holding her body against his.

He shrugged. "What?"

"I told you not to bother coming. I don't need your help and I certainly don't need your attitude."

Colton leaned forward, tempting her to step back. She didn't, and while he didn't think it was possible, her cheeks went a deeper shade, hiding most of her freckles.

"I don't know if you heard me last time or not, but this part is dangerous. I have means to make it less so, and you better bet your sweet ass that I'm going to do what I can to make sure you don't get hurt," he said before leaning back and going to the trunk. "Besides, how could I live with myself if something happened to you that I could've prevented?"

Ruby threw daggers at him while he grabbed the tool. It was heavy for being essentially a high-powered drill, and when he passed it off to her, her arm dropped with the weight.

"Careful, Sprinkles." Colton smirked at one of the nicknames he used for her in high school, her freckles reminding him of stars sprinkling the sky. He caught the slightest angry shake of her head before trailing the plug to the extension cord leading from the basement window. He squatted and unplugged the angle grinder. When he stood, he caught her checking him out.

"Can I help you?"

"No," she spat. "Since you absolutely insist on being here, let me show you what's happening."

She turned on her heel and hauled herself up through the back of the bus. Colton followed, bringing the chisel with him. He immediately felt too small for the narrow bus. Even without the seats, there wasn't much room to move. It didn't help there were tools littered on the ground, but even so he had to bow his head and was pretty sure he could touch both walls at once.

But seeing Ruby in the space, it was the perfect size.

For her.

"How big is this thing?" he asked, looking around as he made his way to where she stood behind the driver's seat.

She played with her bun, avoiding his gaze. "Um, it's about six foot two from floor to ceiling and about seven and a half feet wide. I'll lose some space with insulation and coverings, but it's fine. So anyway," she pointed to the ceiling panel she was beneath. "The panels are steel and held together with rivets. I've managed to get these ones out by doing this — "she pulled a punch from her pant pocket and a hammer from the ground, and when the punch popped the rivet center back, she pulled a wood chisel from her other pocket. She wedged it under the rivet head, pounding the end until the rivet head shot forward. His ears rang, and Colton noticed she had kept earplugs in.

"Are you trying to make me go deaf?" He wiggled a finger in his ear for added effect, annoyed that she'd cross that line. Whatever the tension was between them, construction was a safety issue. Not a playground for Ruby's petty behavior.

"Of course not. Why?" She crossed her arms and stared at him.

"Ruby, this shit's serious. If you're going to be banging metal on metal — especially in a metal box — I need earplugs."

She shrugged. "You're the construction guru, I figured you brought your own."

"And you're the project manager, I figured you'd take care of your crew."

"Oh, are you my crew now?"

"So long as I know you're doing dangerous shit, yeah. Yeah, I am."

"I told you to not bother coming. I don't need your help, Colton."

"And I don't want you to get hurt, Ruby." Their rising voices settled with his admission, the words shaky as they left his lips. She stared at him, chest heaving from the heated verbal sparring.

She sighed and held out a hand. "Fine. Temporary truce?"

"Temporary truce. Now where are those earplugs?"

## 22

Even though Ruby couldn't feel Colton's skin against her gloves, just the sheer size of his hand around hers was enough to make her breath catch. It didn't hurt he held on longer than necessary, or that it came on the heels of his admission.

*I don't want you to get hurt.*

There was something about hearing him say the words, hearing him announce even a sliver of his feelings, that made her feel less crazy about the tension between them.

She was livid when she heard his car pull in, even more so when he had the audacity to stand there smirking with his dimples and broad shoulders. She'd had to look up at him when they went toe-to-toe, something she hadn't done since high school. Something that was even more dangerous — more tempting — now. That magnetic force between them still pulsed, still called her body to stay as near to his as possible. It had thrown her off so completely she'd forgotten about the earplugs, her defenses solidifying against anything else his presence might throw her way.

Colton released her hand slowly, her gaze even slower, before showing her the basics of the air chisel without turning it on. For being the size of a drill, it was oddly heavy, but it felt good in her hands. Like she really could convert this bus.

"Do you have safety goggles?" His deep voice cut through her daydream of the finished bus, her future home.

"Yeah, here." She dug around in the red toolbox she'd found in the basement, pulling two cheap pairs she'd bought in a multipack online. Ruby handed him a pair and put hers on, trying not to ogle as Colton stripped his jacket, biceps flexing against the tight fabric of his navy blue t-shirt. His jeans hung low on his hips, and as he reached up to start the chiseling, Ruby got a peak of the smooth, tan skin of his stomach. Between that and the way he looked right at home in safety glasses and a power tool, she was pretty sure her ovaries were ready to burst.

He tipped his head at her to join him, and when she stood beside him she was careful to keep enough distance so she wouldn't be enveloped in his man-musk. But that didn't stop him from lightly pulling her sleeve until she was closer, close enough they touched shoulders. Ruby sucked in a breath, careful not to let it out too fast in case he noticed.

"You see how the chisel head fits under? You want to really ground yourself in your legs because the kickback can be brutal if you're not used to it." He reset his position before turning the hand-held jackhammer on. In just a few seconds, the air chisel knocked out the rivet head.

Colton turned to her, beaming. "See? Nice and easy. No risk of hammering your hand. You ready to try?"

Ruby grabbed the hammer from him and edged over to the next rivet head, getting the chisel head in place. His chest pressed against her back, his hands moving to her thighs.

"Bend them like this —" it came out a whisper as he gently pressed his hands down. Her ass bumped against his hips, molding her body to his. It, he, was overwhelming, even more so when his face rested besides hers and his hands moved along her arms, lifting them into position. "— and put your arms here. I know it's heavy but your arms shouldn't be shaking just yet." His laugh was breathy in her ear, goosebumps erupting across her skin.

"It's not heavy," Ruby managed to say as she elbowed him away, needing to clear her head.

"Whatever you say, Bob the Builder. Just watch out for the kickback."

She heard his snicker as she reset, taking extra care to tense her arms. With a deep breath, she pressed the trigger and was shocked at the vibrations rippling through her arm, the heavy popping still infiltrating her protected ears. Thank god Colton had reminded her about the kickback or he might've lost a tooth.

In no time, the rivet head shot across the bus. Ruby turned off the tool and shook out her arms, turning to Colton. He had a wide grin plastered to his face, hands on his hips.

"Not bad, Ruby. See? It's not so bad."

She looked down at the tool and then back at the ceiling. She didn't want to admit it to him, but he was right. She'd had a few near misses with the hammer when she started hand-chiseling before he showed up, and each time had scared the shit out of her. The damage would've knocked her hand completely useless for weeks. Plus, this was much faster.

She gave him a smile. "Yeah, it'll do. When should I get it back to you by?"

"What do you mean?" His brow furrowed.

"When do you need your tool back, Colt?"

The beautiful bastard frowned and shook his head. "Ruby, we're going to finish this now and then I'll take it home with me."

"Oh my god." He was impossible.

Those stupid dimples. "Ruby, you can either fight this or

not." He stalked his way toward her, moving with that bulky grace only an athlete could have. Leaning down so she could smell his aftershave — pine? — he whispered, "If you do fight it, we both know who will win."

Heat coursed through Ruby's body. "You know that's a challenge, right?"

"I wouldn't have said it if I didn't."

His brown eyes were warm, inviting, and Ruby was tempted to let him help without fighting, moving forward. But she caught the glimmer in them, the play, and her resolve stuck. Spending any more time with him was dangerous, and not just because she wanted to throttle him every time he opened his mouth or flashed a panty-dropping smile.

But if he was insistent on helping her — even if it was only to make sure she limited her injuries — then she'd not only push back, but she'd be difficult.

If he wanted to play, she'd play.

## 23

Colton sat outside Will's, thankful for the slow day. And that Damian was dealing with the one car they had on the roster and couldn't flirt with Katie.

Colton side-eyed his sister, who was staring off into space while Dragan sat on her other side reading a book. There was the part of him that was still livid with her for setting him up to see Ruby that first time. But there was the other part — especially after the extended time he'd spent with her earlier that week working on the bus — that fluttered at the thought of seeing his red-headed beauty.

*Ex*-red-headed beauty.

Despite the years apart and the changes that had happened, it was so easy to slip back into their old dynamic. Pushing, pulling, flirting. He'd felt drawn to her the minute he stepped out of his car, a moth to a flame, and had to routinely check himself for being too close. For indulging the part of him he didn't even know if he wanted to indulge, but could hardly help himself stay away from her nonetheless.

"Hey, Colt. Did you hear back about that job?" Katie said, not breaking her stare.

"The one in San Francisco?" He'd applied to several jobs, including sous chef ones he wasn't thrilled about. He preferred baking over cooking. Working in a line under a prestigious but rough chef sucked, and it was easier to tolerate when he did what he preferred. But he'd do anything to get out of Oak Valley.

"Yeah, it was with that bag guy, right?" She poked his leg, laughing at her own joke.

"You mean the world-renowned pastry chef, Pierre Hermé?"

"Sure, whatever you say, Francois."

Colton snorted and shook his head. "They want to conduct a video interview next week. If it goes well, I'll have to fly out to their test kitchen for a few days."

"Oh, shit. So, like, you could actually be moving there?"

Colton shrugged. He knew it was a long shot — he was an ex-football star, not someone who'd been in the kitchen for years on end.

At least they wanted to interview him. Even though it was probably a pity interview, given how his last career ended.

"Sorry to interject but Colton, I just remembered — did you let Mrs. Johnson know about that muffler quote?"

"Fuck." He'd completely forgotten about it. And at the thought of Mrs. Johnson's missed quote, he realized there was actually a stack of invoices he forgot to send out.

He'd finally, fully reached the point of not giving a flying fuck about this job. He didn't need the money, not really — it was more a precaution while he figured out his next step. His football money would last years, his whole life if he was smart. But after his injury... The not working, not having a purpose nearly killed him. At least the family business made sure he got out of bed every morning and talking with people, something his parents agreed on to help keep him from sliding further into the depression that took hold. Even though his mom wanted to have him in the bakery instead, he knew she'd never dare to push it on his dad.

But now? Now he was going to lose his shit if he had to stay here any longer.

"It's okay, I'll take care of it," Dragan said.

Colton returned his weak smile and caught one from Katie. But it quickly turned into a beam, and Colton looked behind him to see what caught her eye.

He'd spot those flames from space.

Ruby's curls bounced along with each step, the slight wind helping their spring, her slender figure hidden by a long black coat. Her eyes glimmered and Colton got a peak of her gap-toothed smile.

But it wasn't directed at him.

His heart sank a little as she focused on Katie, his sister practically running to greet Ruby with a hug. After working on the bus earlier that week, they'd settled into a new version of their old ways, teasing with the occasional heated argument. But they had always been a good team, and the ceiling panels were done fast enough they hadn't needed a construction light to guide them in the setting sun. Sure, being in the bus cocoon, away from the town's prying eyes, was one thing. He didn't know what it would be like to see her in public. But at the very least he thought she'd be friendly.

What was her fucking problem?

Colton clenched his jaw, her mixed messages making his brain buzz as he stared at her and Katie talking. He couldn't hear the words, but when Ruby threw her head back laughing, a fire coursed through his body.

He huffed. Must be so fucking funny to blow off your ex after spending hours laughing together.

Even though she hadn't laughed like that with him. Not since they were teenagers.

Ruby and Kate kept talking and laughing, and all Colton could do was sit and stare. And try not to let the sounds get to him. When they started walking over, Colton clenched his fists in his pockets, trying to steady his breathing.

"Hey, Ruby," Dragan said, closing his book with his finger marking the page.

"Hey, Dragan. Hey... Colton." She gave a slight nod in each of their direction but avoided Colton's eyes. Colton didn't respond but stared at her, willing her to look at him. Willing her to pretend they were back in the bus and the rest of the world — and their history — didn't exist.

"How are you liking being back in Oak Valley?" Dragan stretched his limbs out, finger still stuck in the book raised over his head.

Ruby shrugged. "It's fine."

"Just fine?" Katie bumped shoulders with her, casting a glance at Colton. He shook his head. His sister was such an oblivious idiot sometimes.

"Yep. Just fine. Nice seeing you guys, but I need to get going." Ruby gave a little wave and walked away, still not meeting Colton's eyes.

He didn't look away from her retreating body, didn't acknowledge Katie and Dragan's chatter.

He stood from his chair and stalked after her.

He wasn't going to let Ruby get away with this.

## 24

The wind whipped Ruby's hair as she scurried away from Will's Auto Shop. Of course living in a small town meant running into people from her past.

But it didn't mean she was ever prepared for when it happened.

Especially not when it was Colton Taylor, hanging outside his family's shop like he was fifteen again.

Heavy footsteps came up behind her, and she would've given anything for them to belong to anyone but him. After spending so much one-on-one time with him, it was hard seeing him in public. He wasn't exactly outright friendly with her, and she tried to take that as a cue he didn't want a big to-do about their reconnecting. But that flashback to him doing what he did almost when they were kids… Some things never changed, even if he swore up and down they had.

"Ruby, wait." Colton's strong hand landed on her arm, not quite grabbing her but still forceful enough to stop her in her tracks. She held her ground, trying not to face him. If he wanted to act like he didn't know her, she could return the favor.

"What?" Well, she never promised to hide the venom.

"What the fuck was that?"

"What the fuck was what?"

He barked out a laugh. "Don't play stupid with me, Ruby. You act like you don't know me and walk away?"

"Are you for real?" It was her turn to find this comical. She risked a glance and immediately wish she hadn't.

He towered over her, all muscle and broad shoulders. The winter wind carried his woody scent over her. His face was a particular shade of red, from anger or the cold she couldn't be sure. But the rigid set of his jaw and outline of clenched fists in his jacket pockets told her everything she needed to know about his wounded pride.

She swallowed, meeting his deep mahogany eyes. Beneath the layer of anger was a layer of hurt.

"Colton, I took my cues from you. We don't need to be friends. Hell, it's probably best if we're not." She didn't need to tell him that the picture-perfect replication of their teens was enough to send her in the other direction, away from what she'd already experienced.

"I took my cues from you. You weren't exactly friendly, Ruby." His shoulders relaxed, the bulge of his fists softening.

"Okay well... I guess we both didn't know what to do. But I—I think it's best if we just stay civil. If you insist on helping with the bus, fine. But outside of that..." She couldn't bring herself to finish. To say how being around him was hard enough, that the closer they got the more she felt herself falling into old habits. And old habits with her ex wasn't a place she wanted to revisit.

Colton looked disappointed but quickly schooled his face. This was the Colton she knew, the hard-edged, won't-let-anyone-in, lone-wolf.

Good. Normal. She could work with this this.

"Fine. Civil it is, and you can bet your sweet little ass I'm gonna help with that bus to help mitigate injuries."

She rolled her eyes at his macho, caveman identity while trying not to blush at his ass comment. "Fine, but it's my project and I'll do what I want, when I want."

"Of course. When are you working on the bus next?"

"Oh my god, Colt. None of your business. Thanks for the agreement, I really have to get going." She hesitated before offering her hand in truce.

He smirked, his hand shaking hers. His firm, calloused hand. The simple feel of his skin on hers heated her core, the strength in his shake reminding her biological wiring how safe she'd always felt with him, how protected and secure. He embodied the alpha man and goddamnit if her strong independent self didn't enjoy it.

She released his hand but his lingered, his palm pressed against hers sending warmth through her body. "I'll catch you around. Baby girl." He said it with a smirk before releasing her hand.

When he finally walked away, all Ruby could do was watch.

Until he looked over his shoulder and flashed his dimples. Heat flushed her cheeks and she turned quickly, walking with renewed purpose to pick up lunch for her and her mom.

She might not be able to help being back home in Oak Valley. She may not even be able to help her run-ins with Colton. But she sure as hell could work on a plan to get out of here. Since Colton was insistent on helping with the bus, at least she could use the extra man-power — and boy, what a man with power that was — to hurry her timeline along. She could possibly be done with the bus conversion in six months. Six months until she could travel the country. Six months until she could move on with her life.

Six months until she never had to see Colton Taylor ever again, or deal with the butterflies he sent soaring through her body.

## 25

Colton tried not to slam the door as he entered the house.

He really did.

But there was something about his dad always asking for a family dinner and his mom finally guilt-tripping him into showing up that stung. Like he was fourteen again, which was probably the last time his family had all sat around the worn oak dining table for a meal outside of the holidays.

He traipsed through the living room, passing the dining room and glancing at his mom in the adjoining kitchen. She was humming over a pot on the stove, lost in the way the spoon moved through soup. His mom had realized it was best to not address any slams or shouts, wall punches or attitudes. That's what his dad was for.

Colton pushed aside the sadness that almost always followed seeing his mom in their house and hooked a right down the hall to his bedroom, closing the door gently. He didn't need to remind his mom of the life she ended up living.

He'd tried to buy her a new house when he first hit it big — that one million dollar paycheck was just the start — but his mom cried at leaving the home where he and Katie grew up. So they stayed, and now Colton was trapped in his childhood bedroom with a queen bed and no way out.

The front door opened, Katie's laugh ringing throughout the house while he heard the gruff timber of his dad greeting his mom. Colton sat on the edge of the bed and switched into pajamas. He steeled himself, taking the deep breaths his physical therapist had taught him and the ones Dragan often reminded him to do, and joined everyone in the kitchen.

Bryce had gone upstairs to change into clean clothes, while Katie leaned against the counter laughing with their mom. His mom turned her flushed face to him, tendrils of brown hair streaked gray escaping from her ponytail.

"Hey, honey. How was your day?"

"Yeah, buddy. How was your day?" Katie playfully teased, drawing a smile from Cheri.

Colton couldn't help but return the smile. These women were the rocks in his life. Always had been, always would be. And they knew just how to keep him sane.

"Fine enough. Thanks, Katie-Cat, for sending out those last invoices."

She shrugged. "No problem, Dad was my ride anyway."

Colton's body tensed at the devil's footsteps on the stairs, a part of him wishing he'd put on a fresh pair of jeans and a clean shirt instead of his grey sweatpants and faded Henley. The pajamas-around-the-house thing was a trait he picked up from his mom and one his dad hated in him. But if he was going to have to sit through family dinner, he wanted to be comfortable. And he was a grown-ass man, he could wear what he wanted. He reminded himself of that as Bryce entered the kitchen and glanced at the sweats, his mouth pressed into a thin line. Their eyes briefly met before Bryce gave his wife a side-hug and a peck on the side of the head.

This was a battle they'd already fought — many times —

and if his dad wasn't going to pick up the sword about it tonight, he must be in a decent enough mood.

"Hey there, dear," his mom said, rubbing his dad's arm. "Katherine, could you please get me four bowls. Who wants bread?"

Cheri loved her homemade soup and sourdough and dished out more than enough whenever she made it. Katie dutifully carried the full bowls to the table while Colton managed the plates, avoiding his dad's gaze while he tenderly touched his wife. Even if he was a hard dad, he was a soft husband. Colton didn't believe in a higher power but he thanked the world everyday that was the case.

"So, how was everyone's day?" Cheri asked, buttering her bread. There was silence except for the scrape of the knife, the slurp of soup from spoons.

Katie took one for the team. "It was good, shop's been busy. I'm looking into expanding it into the lot next door. I spoke with Mr. Denaube and it sounds like he'd be willing to sell."

Bryce nodded. "It'll be a great move, especially once Colt here fully takes over. We'll be able to take on more business and might not even have to hire help."

Colton swirled his spoon in the bowl, glancing at Katie. Her cheeks burned, jaw clenched. No matter how hard she worked, their dad would never see it for what it was.

He cleared his throat. "Wow, Kate. That's awesome. If you expanded the business and spear-headed that project, would that make you, like, a boss or something? You pull that off, I know I wouldn't want anyone else running the show."

Katie met his gaze with fire and a slight shake of her head. *Stop, don't go down this road. Not here, not now.*

"Katherine here is an exemplary employee. As the future of Will's, you best take note, boy. I expect the same kind of leadership your little sister's taken."

Colton tried to school his face, catching the look of defeat in Katie's eyes before she turned back to their soup. Their mom kept chewing her food, removing herself from the conversation in every way except proximity.

But Colton just couldn't help it, and he mentally kicked himself as soon as his mouth opened.

"But if Katie is doing all this awesome stuff, how great would it be if she took over? Instead of fighting for me to do shit, why not just... go with the flow?"

Bryce dropped his spoon in the soup with a clatter, staring Colton down. "Don't you dare start spouting that hippie-dippy bullshit. Will's is a father-son shop, has been for over three-generations. That's how we do things around here, and it's past time you got it through your thick skull. You did your football thing, it didn't work out. You're right back where you started. You know why? You were never meant to leave."

The words burned through Colton, racing through his veins and burning the space behind his eyes. The dinner table blurred, truth given to what he'd been thinking since he first moved home.

He was never meant to do anything more than run his family's shop.

He was never good enough to get out.

His mom cleared her throat, a quiet warning. "Bryce, we've talked about this."

"Oh, yeah?" Bryce chuckled. "Have we talked about what a good for nothing kid we raised? How he can't do even the bare minimum of what he's supposed to? I didn't realize asking my son to take over the family business was such a fucking burden, Cheri. You coddled him too much. You filled his head with ideas of everything but his purpose."

"Is that really all I am to you? Bred to take over the shop? You're lucky you even have a son. You're lucky you even have a kid that wants to take over, and she's sitting right there. But you can't even see her because you're so wrapped up in some ridiculous fantasy about how the familial power lies in the men. Do you hear yourself?" Colton didn't look up from his bowl until the very end, shaking his head. "You need a reality check or something. I'm leaving. I'm getting as far away from you and that stupid shop as possible. If anyone takes it over, it'll be Katie. But honestly? I don't blame her if she doesn't, given the shit way you've treated her. She deserves better."

Colton stood throwing his napkin on the table, glancing at his mom and then his dad. "We all do."

He stormed off, grabbing his jacket.

"You walk out that door, you better plan on not coming back."

His dad's voice followed him outside. It was nighttime, and he immediately regretted not grabbing his coat. But it was too late now — he knew he couldn't go back. At least not anytime soon.

His first instinct was to call Ruby. Funny how that never went away and, if anything, had grown stronger since she'd come home.

Home.

This place was no longer home to him. Hadn't been for some time.

He watched his breath puff white against the dark, aimlessly walking toward the main road. He felt better, stronger, both physically and mentally. Maybe now was time to move out, if he could find one of the coveted apartments Oak Valley boasted. But was it worth it if he ended up getting a job in San Francisco? The interview was this week. Slim chance, but a chance nonetheless. And if he found an apartment here, wouldn't that just solidify his place here?

His head hurt with the possibilities, but not as much as his numb fingers. He'd left his car keys in his bedroom, in his catch-all on top of the dresser. His phone hung heavy in his pajama pockets. If he couldn't go home anytime soon, he certainly couldn't stay out here all night. He could try the small bed and breakfast in town, but it was a good four-mile hike. As much as he wanted to, calling Ruby wasn't an option. Which left his friends. They'd all let him crash for a few days, but Dragan was the one he could talk to.

Colton dialed his friend, pacing to keep warm until he heard the sputter of his friend's car come down the road, waving at the headlights that signified his rescue.

## 26

The beeping machines became a kind of metronome while Ruby worked, careful not to take her eyes from the laptop screen. While she wanted to be there for her mom's first chemo treatment, she was having a hard time not breaking down every time she looked over and saw her mom wince or pull the blanket tighter. She shifted in the yellow armchair, body buzzing with the knowledge her mom was stuck with a needle right beside her, that in the coming weeks she'd have to help her through a variety of side effects.

Ruby didn't know what having chemo was like, but she'd heard stories. She had vague memories of the aftermath from her mom's first round, when Ruby was young. It was cold, it burned, it was like a low-warmth spreading through the body. In general, it was only mildly uncomfortable. She'd been a kid when her mom was first diagnosed and was only vaguely aware of the seriousness of it all. It was just her and her mom, and her mom had tried to keep the severity from her daughter. But now that Ruby was an adult, she was a partner in this. She was the question-asker, the hand-holder, the document-carrier. Given the recurrent cancer and the spread, Beryl was set for a 3-month

IV chemotherapy course comprised of six treatment cycles, two weeks each. After that, the doctors would re-evaluate what actions to take next.

Beryl had brought some magazines, a book, her knitting. Ruby turned back to her computer, needing to respond to work emails but searching the various Skoolie forums instead. She hadn't been able to get to the bus since removing the ceiling panels. She tried not to notice the flush coursing its way through her body, the involuntary clench of her thighs at the memory of his body pressed against hers. Remembering how infuriating he was — especially when she ran into him outside the auto shop — only slightly dimmed the reaction.

She sighed, checking her school bus task list. Next up was the floor. The questions and answers she found noted removing the thin rubber layer first helped, and then removing the plywood. Crowbar and a drill should be enough to leverage everything out, an average of four hours with two people. Ruby chewed her lip. She was torn between wanting the satisfaction of doing most of the conversion herself but also wanting to get it done as soon as possible. Torn between putting distance between her and Colton and feeding the craving in her body to spend as much time with him as possible.

"How's work going?"

"It's not, I'm looking at school bus stuff."

"Ah. How is the bus?"

Ruby kept her eyes trained on the screen, not reading what was in front of her. She could sense her mom wanted to say something. After last time when she mentioned Colton had come to help with the ceiling panels, Ruby was on alert for the mom radar for red flags.

"So... Colton."

*Bingo.*

"He's just helping, Mom." Ruby clicked through her tabs, pretending to be busy.

"If you say so. Seems like he's offering a lot of his time."

"Some of the stuff is dangerous, like the ceiling panels. Better to have some help than to break my hand or get knocked out."

Beryl shrugged. "I don't disagree, I only find it interesting that the help is Colton Taylor."

Ruby sighed and looked at her mom, who was casually flipping through one of the magazines.

"He happened to be around and to have the tools."

"Of course. Just be careful, Ruby."

"Of what? Having help?"

"Getting close to him. You and I both know where that leads."

*Disappointment.*

*Heartbreak.*

"I'm not getting close to him." Ruby stared at her mom before turning back to her computer. "Besides, it's been ten years. Maybe we're different people." She knew as soon as she spoke that her mom would take that as an excuse for Ruby to continue spending time with Colton. Hell, when Ruby thought about it, maybe she was trying to find an excuse for why there was no issue with her spending time with the man she once called the love of her life.

Her mom sighed. "Maybe. Just be careful, Ruby."

"Of course." Ruby kept her eyes on her laptop, turning the conversation over in her head. "I mean, I'm not who I was ten years ago. Nowhere close. People can change."

"Maybe."

Ruby mulled, not seeing the screen in front of her. She knew how to read her mom — and the passive, exasperated reply was enough for Ruby to know her mom didn't believe it. At least not when it came to Colton. Her mom had been right about a lot of things before. Paired with the reminder Ruby had when she'd seen him outside the auto shop, maybe people didn't always change.

A knot in her stomach formed in agreement.

## 27

Dragan gathered the tangled sheets from his couch, remnants from Colton crashing at his apartment the last few nights. His friend was out and there was no telling if he'd be back tonight, but Dragan figured three days of couch-surfing was enough for his wealthy ass. Dragan was happy to help but couldn't stop the itch on why Colton hadn't just moved out from under his dad's rule yet. It was bad enough Colt was stuck at the family business, but it'd been over a year since he moved home, six months since he'd gotten most of his old self back from the crippling knee injury and depression.

He sighed, throwing the sheets in the in-unit washer and straightening up the place. He knew how rare it was to find a nice apartment in Oak Valley. Hell, several years ago it'd taken him a year to find this little place within walking distance to Main Street with a dishwasher and in-unit laundry, and he knew Colton would want to wait out for the ideal situation so he wouldn't have to move too much. Prices had also gone up, making Dragan more thankful that he'd secured part-time coding work for an app company based in Australia. Dragan was off work at the auto shop today, and it gave him valuable time to work on the app he and Archer were developing, a side project that could be his way out of the life he'd been born into. At least before June came over.

His heart might've skipped a beat at the thought of her name. His breath might have stopped at the thought of her laugh echoing through his two-bedroom apartment. Whatever it was, he needed to get himself under control. His fingers subconsciously went to his forehead, fingers finding strands to twist until knotted. June was the only one who ever caught him, a soft hand resting on his bicep or gently working the twisted pieces apart. She knew without him having to say that it was an anxious quirk, one picked up from trying to hide from the intensity in his house growing up.

Dragan started loading the dishwasher, conscious of the chip on his shoulder. Being from the wrong side of the tracks in a small town, he knew where his place was in the social hierarchy early on. It didn't matter when he was a teenager that his grandfather in Poland passed, leaving a sizable estate in the name of Dragan's mom. It didn't matter that the sizable inheritance was kept in a fund his parents refused to touch, instead allowing the family to continue living in a house that was falling down or their four kids to go hungry when his dad couldn't make ends meet. As the oldest son, he'd been expected to help support the family — especially during the times when his dad dropped out for several days at a time. Dragan had started teaching himself how to code when he was a young teenager, spending as much free time in the library computer lab when not at June's family bookstore. He slammed a plate into the washer a little too hard, the sound reminding him to take a breath.

He got his anger from his dad but his awareness from his mom.

A knock on the door pulled him from his ego trip, and he dried his hands before seeing who it was.

The door flying open brought a wave of vanilla and wood, the scent reminiscent of being buried beneath a blanket with an old book. He smiled at the ray of sunshine before him, her blond hair brushing against his arm as she barreled in.

"I'm so sorry I'm early, I just needed to get out of that place and I need your help," June said, the words crammed together in a huff as she set her bag down at the dining table and pulled out her laptop.

"Hello to you, too." Dragan shut the door and closed the dishwasher before taking a seat across from her.

She shut her laptop, meeting his gaze. "Sorry, D. Hi. How are you?"

Her eyes bounced the morning light streaming in from the window, deep emeralds that whispered of a forest filled with magic. Dragan's heart definitely skipped a beat, her slightly crooked smile heightening his loss of breath.

"I-I'm fine. How are you?"

June giggled. "So formal. I'm okay. I'm a bit worried about the shop and I know you said you'd help me bounce ideas on promotional stuff but I'm stressed about the financials. So... Hi. Here I am. Sorry for barging in so early."

"Don't be. Colt just left, I was cleaning up. What's going on with the shop?"

"Colton was here? Is he finally leaving his house?" June asked, pulling her laptop open again.

Dragan shrugged. He knew what it was like to need to leave his family home but feel held back by personal responsibility. Whereas Colton initially got out with scholarships and national acclaim, Dragan pulled himself out of the hole his parents had dug with hard work and passing the responsibility torch to his bother, the next oldest sibling, while still contributing when he could. He'd learned the hard way to be a little selfish and put himself first.

"Hm, well he certainly has the means."

"What's going on with the shop, June-bug? Juniper? Ju-Ju?" Dragan teased, trying to pull her smile back out. Since June's parents passed away, her once fanciful upbringing was slowed and the pursestrings pinched. She never fell from her comfortable middle-class status, but that didn't stop her from worrying about it.

Dragan wondered if the nearness to his own poverty influenced her fear, but shook the insidious thought from his mind when she turned her laptop around and showed him The Little Prince Bookstore's budget sheet.

There was a lot of red.

He scrolled through the sheet, mentally crunching the numbers on the fly to reach the sums she had. He may have done poorly in school and not gone to college, but he was smart. He didn't need the colors to tell him where her problems lay.

"This... It's not good, June."

Her face fell, and he kicked himself for being Captain Obvious. That wasn't going to help her.

She rested her chin in her hand, and when she met his eyes he saw tears pooling. "I talked to the landlord about rent. I cut back on over-stocking. I set up a store on the website. I post on social media multiple times a day. I don't know what else to do, Dragan." A tear slipped and she hid her face behind her hands, shoulders shaking in silence.

His heart dropped to the floor. "We can figure this out, June. I'll never let you lose the bookstore. I promise."

Dragan didn't know how he'd keep his promise, only that he would.

If there was nothing else he could do or no other way to be the strapping, wealthy educated man she deserved, he'd at least find a way for her to keep the small town family bookstore.

He'd give his life to make June happy, even if that was all he could give her.

## 28

The bakery was thankfully quiet as Colton cleared papers from the desk in the back room. He'd had to work with Katie on how to call out of work today. Despite crashing on Dragan's couch the last few nights, Colton had still gone to work, careful to avoid his dad. Calling out of work when the boss was your dad never worked out well, but he couldn't afford to miss an interview for his new lease on life.

His redemption.

A pang of guilt swept through him at asking his mom to let him hide in the back room, where it was relatively clean and the steady hum of mixers was still faint. He couldn't risk going home, not yet, and he knew Dragan was off today and needed his apartment to work on his own side project.

His mom had given him a defeated smile, told him of course he could use the back room, and left him to manage the front of the shop.

Colton checked his reflection in the video call preview, adjusting the collar of the ironed button down he'd borrowed from his slightly bigger friend. Thankfully, Dragan took more pride in his appearance than Colton, so the shirt was neat as a pin, the accompanying suit jacket neatly tailored, the navy tie formal but with a playful golden floral pattern. Some of his recipe creations sat in a pile on his right, photographs of his best artistic work resting on his left.

His papers almost went to floor when the ring from an incoming video call nearly gave him a heart attack.

"Hello," he said, smiling at the petite Asian woman and the big black man on the other side of the screen.

"Hello, Mr. Taylor! I'm Annette Li and this is Julien Dubois. We are the sous-chefs under Chef Hermé." Annette's voice was cheerful, held even higher by her lilting French accent. "It is a pleasure to meet you."

"It's a pleasure to meet you as well, please call me Colton."

"Will do. As you know, we wanted to interview candidates before doing a kitchen interview," Julien started, his own French-accented voice deep and calming. "I will not lie, we were both very impressed with the images you sent in with your essay."

Colton chuckled. "Impressed because of my football background?"

"Yes, but also because of the attention to detail," Annette laughed.

Julien cleared his throat. "What struck me most, personally, was your CV. I want you to talk more about what you envision for yourself moving forward."

"Like, in terms of this opportunity? Or like a ten year plan?"

"Both."

Sweat cropped up on Colton's neck, beading down his spine. If he was honest, he'd acknowledge he mainly just thought of what the job could — would — do for him, in the short-term. But what did that look like long-term?

"Would you like to circle back?" Annette asked.

Colton took a deep breath and shook his head. "No. No, it's okay. I'll be honest in saying I don't really know. I've never really had a chance to think about it outside of wanting to be a pastry chef and knowing the only way to become one is to do it. So working under Chef Hermé would allow me the chance to do what I really love. Maybe one day I'll open a shop, maybe I'll find I like working under a coach. But this opportunity would give me the chance to follow my dream instead of my dad's. I thrive under pressure, I bring my A-game to every field, and I'm ready to give my all to the one thing I regret letting go of."

*Ruby.* He didn't need to acknowledge there might be two things he regretted, but right now only one of them saw him getting out of Oak Valley.

Julien nodded his head while Annette scribbled a note and asked more questions.

"We see you deal mainly with desserts and pastries. Do you have a signature creation? Do you foray into the art of cooking, or are you strictly baking?"

"No signature yet, I like experimenting with flavors and sometimes certain flavors work best in different vehicles. I like cooking but haven't had as much practice — my mom does most of it so we worked out a system where she cooks and I bake."

"What kind of flavors work best for different items?"

"I've personally found I prefer more floral or herbal flavors in small doses — rose, thyme, lavender, rosemary, the like — in macarons or miniature eclairs. Whereas there seems to be more area to play with more traditional flavors, like orange and chocolate, in larger items like danishes and croissants."

Julien nodded. "Do you have a kitchen philosophy?"

Colton pursed his lips, thinking back on all the times he'd been in the kitchen. The number of times he'd accidentally swapped baking powder for baking soda and vice versa, or forgot sugar, or doubled the butter. The ways his mom taught him to handle dough or be careless with seasoning amounts. He smiled at the how horrified everyone was when he eyeballed flavors instead of measuring them out, trusting it would all work out. "I think it's a mixture of being playful, trusting yourself and the process, and having a willingness to learn. The great thing about being in the kitchen is you have room to experiment, and if it doesn't work out it's not the end of the world. And you can't treat it like it is."

Annette smiled. "So very true."

"We saw in your resume and in your CV you have more formal experience in the business side of being a pastry chef," Julien began. "Menus, supplies, time management. Do you understand what this job you've applied for would entail, and how do you see yourself fitting into the dynamic?"

"I'm assuming this position is more of a baking one rather than management." Colton swallowed, trying to read their faces. "And I, uh, I see myself learning and growing as a baker but with the ability to step in on any of those management tasks, if needed. Ideally, I would be able to hold this position for a long time and grow within the business, to learn as much as I can from Chef Hermé. It would be instrumental to my future being able to focus on the baking aspect instead of what I've had to do, which was split my time between baking and management."

He hoped that was good enough. That it was the right answer. He still couldn't believe he was interviewing with Hermé' right-hand chefs, that they thought some ex-professional football player from a middle-of-nowhere small town in New York was worthy of an interview.

"Thank you for answering our questions, Mr. Tay— Colton. It was a pleasure speaking with you. We should have a response to you by the end of the week," Annette said while scribbling something down.

"Great. And if you need anything else from me in the meantime, please let me know." Colton smiled at them and they said their goodbyes, hanging up the call. He stared at the computer screen, the sweat still dripping down his back. The tie felt tighter than before, the room warmer.

Had they jumped off the call really fast? It felt like they did. It didn't feel that way immediately following the questions — and it had been a fifteen minute interview, which they'd said in their email would be the length of the interview — but now that Colton was left with the blank screen and the distant whir of mixing bowls, it felt rushed, like they had heard enough.

A soft knock on the door was followed by his mom's head poking into the room, her hair wisping out from her ponytail. Those front pieces that never grew more than a few inches and surrounded her head like a halo she lovingly called her wings. Colton always thought they made her look more like a lion.

She smiled at him and stepped into the room, closing the door until just a sliver remained. "Sorry, honey. I heard the voices stop. Did it go well?"

He nodded and leaned back in the chair, folding his hands in his lap. "I think so. Hard to say, but they were friendly. They said they'd know by the end of the week."

"Oh, good. That's not too bad a wait." Cheri crossed her arms, seeming to shrink even more into her petite frame. It seemed as though she wanted to say something, and Colton sat in the chair waiting, hoping she'd let her guard down and say whatever it was that was on her mind.

Some time passed, and Colton cleared his throat. "How are things at home?"

"Fine." Cheri shrugged. "I miss you, though." Her smile was sheepish, her fingers picking at the edge of her apron. Colton sighed, knowing he'd put his mom first.

How could he not?

Standing, he made his way to her and pulled her into a hug. There were times it felt he could swallow her whole, give her the safe space he knew she needed. Give her protection from the world and its tense elements. This was one of those times. She sank into him and he relished the feel of her solid arms. She may be small, but she was Mom. And he needed a mom hug.

When she pulled back, Colton could swear there were tears in her eyes. She rubbed his arm and fixed his hair.

"My boy."

"Always." He gave her a peck on the cheek and opened the door. "I'll be back home tonight, want me to stop at the store or anything?"

"No, thank you. Just bring yourself. Do you want an apron or are you heading out?"

Colton hesitated, knowing he should probably just head home and pretend he was sick, which had been the reason he called out of work anyway.

A sense of pride rose through him. Nah, fuck that. He was going to do what he wanted, when he wanted. This was his life, and he was tired of tiptoeing around his dad. He owed himself.

"Apron me, let's bake up a storm."

His mom beamed, passing him the only apron he'd ever thought of as his. Its navy was faded, but it was still there. Still his. The one he wore when his mom first showed him her ways, the one he used to fold over his torso as a kid and wrap the waist straps around twice.

In most ways, the bakery was the only true home he'd ever known, made complete with his mom by his side. He tried to ignore the pang in his heart when he thought of leaving her — again — and used her wanting what was best for him as the consolation. She'd want him to follow his dream, even if that meant moving across the country. He'd done something similar once before, although two towns over for school and playing for the New York Giants was a far cry from California.

He could do it again. He knew that. But listening to his mom sing along to Springsteen while she pulled out ingredients instilled doubt he hadn't felt before.

## 29

Ruby looked around her childhood bedroom, the white walls still hung with found paintings and a bulletin board covered in scraps of... wrapping paper? Postcards, ribbon, necklaces. She smiled at the odd assortment of items she'd once found inspiration and, ten years later, had yet to go through. She'd always been a ship passing in the night, coming home for holidays and then escaping back to whatever apartment she was living in at the time.

And now with the bus, she figured she'd just put off the deep clean of her room until it was time to move into what would be her home. Although maybe she should consider a trip to the City to empty out her storage unit, $125 a month was still money that could be in her pocket. She could probably rent a UHaul and get it done in a day, shorter if she had help.

Speaking of. She checked her phone, having sent a text to Colton the night before saying she was working on the bus today. The warring sides of her wanted him there to help while also wanting to keep him at arm's length, so giving him the option of working on the bus during a work day seemed like a good compromise. She could feel okay about including him while knowing he wouldn't be able to show.

But that didn't stop the sliver of hope from creeping into her stomach.

Fixing her ponytail, she scolded herself and went into the basement to get a crowbar. Her mom was resting, having taken the week off work to adjust to the chemotherapy, and hopefully removing the bus floors wouldn't be too noisy. Ruby didn't think she'd need power tools for this part of the job, but with demolishing a school bus, you just never knew what you needed until you needed it.

Ruby opened the back emergency door of the bus and tried to determine the best place to start. The utility knife was in the toolbox she'd left behind the driver's seat, crowbar heavy as she pushed it farther into the bus and hauled herself in. The rubber flooring was nasty, streaked with mud from countless shoes and the occasional dead bug. The floor aisle was striped rubber, and upon closer inspection Ruby found a seam on either side between that and the rest of the rubber floor. As good a starting point as any.

She cut and peeled the rubber flooring, revealing the plywood underneath. It was hard and sticky and exhausting. Some pieces refused to come up, and Ruby had to sit on the ground and slam the crowbar wedge beneath the rubber to loosen it. By the time she took a break, only half of the rubber was removed and she was covered in sweat. Seeing the plywood underneath made her want to stay sitting forever, to pretend she hadn't gotten herself into this mess.

The familiar rumble of an Audi made her smile despite her best efforts to not give in, knowing the sleek black vehicle carried a knight in shining armor. As much as she hated to admit it, she could use a good pair of muscles to help finish this demo job.

The slam of a car door was followed by her name, not long before his chiseled jaw and mop of brown hair appeared in the rear door entrance. He folded his arms in the entryway, all dimples and flexed muscle stretching against his long-sleeve.

"A regular ol' Bob the Builder," he teased.

"Shut up," she smiled back, starting to breathe normally again. "Come on and help if you're going to be here."

"You know I took off work for this right?" He hopped into the bus, effortless despite Ruby cringing at something wrong happening to his knee. But he still moved with the grace of professional athlete, sauntering down the walkway until he reached her. He stood before her, his heated gaze making her hot enough she wanted to strip.

No. Nope. This was not good.

She swallowed and regained her composer. "Congrats, want a gold star?"

Colton shrugged and stood, his dimples still in full force. "I mean, I wouldn't say no."

He reached out a hand to help her stand. Ruby hesitated, but as soon as she shifted and felt her jelly legs, she opted for his hand. His warm, strong hand that lifted her like she didn't weigh a thing. And pulled her a little too close to his chest when she was finally on two feet, trying to find her balance.

Reflexively, a hand went to his chest. The smooth surface of his pec beneath his shirt, the beat of his heart against her palm. She was flooded with her body screaming *more* while her brain screamed *step back*. Ruby was suspended between the two, staring at the space she touched while her breath quickened. His fingers brushed her arm before growing bolder, hesitantly finding their way to her neck.

"Ruby." The whisper of her name on his lips brought her eyes to meet his, something inside her cracking.

All at once, in those pleading eyes, was the fourteen-year-old boy she'd fallen in love with, the eighteen-year-old she'd let go of, and the man he'd become. Ruby felt the world spin, the walls cave in, the need to be wrapped in every part of this person she still so desperately loved without knowing why or how, or even who he was.

Only that the last time she loved him, he didn't want what she did.

She shook her head, or at least thought she did. It was soft, almost imperceivable, but the clenching of his jaw told her he had seen it.

"Not... yet."

It was the best she could do in the space between want and need. She wanted him but needed to trust him. Trust that if they went down that path, she wouldn't be left where she was ten years ago. And if everything she'd seen of him so far was any indication of who he was, it was safe to say he was right where she'd left him.

His gaze softened. "But not no."

Ruby inhaled his warmth and sighed. "I don't know, Colton."

"Okay." He took a step back, her body greeted with the cold he kept at bay. She hugged herself and looked around, not wanting to reveal the wetness in her eyes or the way her knees trembled.

"So. Floor." He cleared his throat and moved around the bus, toeing the stack of rubber mat she pulled up before he arrived.

"Floor," she said, clearing her throat. She hadn't expected her voice to be hoarse. "Um, I've been removing the rubber glued to the plywood — everyone in the forums said it's easier because then you can just drill out the plywood once you can see the screw-heads."

Ruby watched him as he nodded and stared at the discarded rubber at his feet. She stopped herself from asking if he was okay, already knowing what the answer was.

"Do you have a trash pile for the bus stuff?"

"I've just been putting it in trash bags and setting them outside. I need to get a dumpster but will probably wait until the weather gets better."

Colton didn't say anything, but found the box of trash bags and started bagging the rubber flooring. Ruby chewed the inside of her lip before getting back to the rubber removal. Lost in the jamming of the crowbar beneath the rubber and the plywood, she startled at the hand on her shoulder.

"Let me have a go, you start unscrewing the plywood at the back."

His voice was soft but firm, and she rose without replying. She mindlessly took the drill to the exposed screw-heads. The whir of the drill and slam of the crowbar ungluing the rubber was a nice foil for not needing to talk. Ruby lost track of time, not knowing how long they worked without speaking.

When she looked up from unscrewing the plywood and pulling up the boards she could, Colton was done with the rubber and walking towards her with the crowbar.

"Lunch?"

"Sure. Takeout or sandwiches here?"

"Delivery, my treat."

"Colt —"

"Stop."

Ruby looked him in the eyes. Normally his commands would light a fire in her, rile her into pushing back. But there was something beneath her tiredness that kept her from that. Something that echoed the feeling of losing a battle before it'd even begun.

"Okay. But then you choose where from."

Ruby turned and hopped out the back of the bus, needing breathing room from him.

## 30

Colton sat on the grimy plywood floor as the crunch of tires echoed down the driveway. He hopped out and paid the delivery guy, taking the large paper bag with tacos, flautas, chips, and salsa. Ruby had walked out and stayed clear while he ordered and waited, but she had to eat sometime. He knew they were both sending mixed messages. How do you revisit the only love you ever had, and after ten years? He was struggling to fight the magnetic force that drew his body to hers. He wasn't the same person, but he was also having a hard time seeing how she'd changed. She was looking to bolt as soon as she was able to, just like she had when they were eighteen. And she wasn't looking to wait for him to catch up.

He walked to the front door while the scent of Mexican food haunted him. He knocked, and the door flew open to reveal freckled cheeks and hazel eyes shooting lasers. The halo of curls framing her face sparked a smile he tried to hide.

"Hungry?" He lifted the bag, watching her flick her eyes to the grease forming on the outside.

"Fine," she grumbled, rolling her eyes and walking further into the house.

Colton stepped inside, still startled at how very much the same everything was. Even when they ate inside last time he was here, he could've sworn even the books on the old shelves hadn't changed. Like he'd been shoved into a time capsule from his adolescence, and wasn't sure if he enjoyed the nostalgia or felt suffocated by it.

Ruby set two plates on the table — an auctioned picnic table painted black with the benches removed, a project of her mom's that Colton helped with when he was sixteen — and he started removing the food items from the bag. They plated and sat across from each other, the gnawing hunger so bad that Colton dug in quickly.

When he took a breath from inhaling his food, he saw Ruby had barely picked at hers.

"I thought you liked tacos?"

She shrugged. "Just trying to go over the bus timeline, figure out when it'll be done."

Colton set down his food, wiping his tongue of his teeth while he thought. "Well, if it goes according to plan, we could probably have it finished by June."

Ruby didn't flinch at his use of *we*. But what he said was dependent on how his interview went, if he'd be flying out to interview in San Francisco or even moving there.

"Why are you helping me, Colt? And don't give me the bullshit, '*I don't want you to get hurt.*' Give me honesty."

The look she gave him cut to the bone, as if she put up a wall he missed the construction of.

"I don't know, Ruby. I just couldn't... not. And I know it means you'll be out of here faster than if you did it alone, but I can't seem to stop myself."

"Better than staying here for god knows how long."

He felt the sting, knew it was intentional. "Yeah, now that my knee's healed more, I'm itching to get out."

"Oh, yeah? Is that way you've been stuck here, your knee?"

Colton shrugged. He didn't know how to explain his sense of pride and responsibility. How living with his family had enabled him to heal, how he felt staying and helping around the house was a way of repayment. Plus, it had brought him and Katie closer, and as much as he hated the auto shop, it had saved him when he was on the edge of despair.

"So what's next for Colton Taylor?" she asked through a mouthful of food.

He met her gaze, her smirk, knowing he couldn't tell her about San Francisco. Not until it became something.

Not until he became something.

"Anything but being here." He picked at his food some more.

"I get that."

"I bet. You just itching to take off in that school bus?"

"You know it." She smiled at him. "If you could go anywhere in the world right now, no holds barred, where would it be?"

It was a game they'd played when they were teenagers, with everything that informed what they wanted their lives to look like. Colton thought of the dreams they'd had, which ones had come true and the ones that hadn't. He'd gotten out of Oak Valley, but his traveling had been limited to the continental U.S. Better than nothing, but he'd had bigger dreams than that.

"Hmmm maybe Thailand? Or India? Morocco. Some place that's the complete opposite of here."

"Oh yeah, all of those would be awesome. I think I'll have to second your choices. Why haven't you gone yet?"

He shrugged, her question inadvertently reminding him of all the ways he'd failed. His career, his dad, even maybe his mom if he didn't get the job. Ruby.

"You have a lot of money, life's too short. Take the trip." Her voice took on a hard edge, one he recognized from her insistence he go to school far away from home. It was a tone that had built up when he accepted the full ride football scholarship at the good — not great — school a few towns over, so he could live at home and keep an eye on his mom and Katie.

It was the tone of the beginning of the end.

"I'm saving." He cleared his throat, the food not as appealing as before.

"Ah." She visibly relaxed, digging into her food a bit more. "Are you finally going to open up your own pastry shop?"

"What? Where did that come from?"

She scoffed. "I mean, Colt... You can't play football anymore and you love being in the kitchen. I just thought —"

"Well, you thought wrong, Ruby."

"Jesus, no need to be a dick."

"You don't know me anymore. Stop pretending you do."

She shook her head and pushed her chair out from the table. "I was just asking." She not-so-quietly took her plate into the kitchen, banging around while Colton sat under his cloud of defeat.

## 31

The slam of the trash can lid and her plate in the sink should not have been so satisfying — Ruby wasn't an inherently angry person — but in the face of Colton being an asshat, it was.

It really was.

She banged around while cleaning up, slamming things just hard enough to get the satisfaction without actually breaking anything. If Mr. Touchy Pants wanted to have an attitude, fine. She could, too.

He meandered into her peripherals, and the call his body had on hers only fueled her anger. She slammed the contents of the fridge onto the counter, making room for the takeout containers full of tacos. Rearranging the fridge gave her an excuse to not look at him.

"What do you want, Colton? You wanna leave this town? You want to isolate yourself, live with your family for the rest of your life? You have your whole life ahead of you and yet you're right where you were ten years ago." She didn't mean for her actual thoughts to slip out, but the heat in the room must have made her woozy.

"Why does it matter to you so much, Ruby?"

Where she'd expected the booming thunder of his voice, it was instead a rolling growl. Low, soft, but she knew it carried the storm. Her hands stopped, breath shaking. She couldn't tell him the truth. Couldn't tell him that despite ten years, despite not knowing him all that time and even now, despite how often and how much she wanted to strangle him, she still loved him. That there was a part of her that had never stopped.

His footsteps crept behind her, the heat from the wall of his chest filling her.

She definitely didn't trust herself to turn around now.

"Colton, I care about you. I want what's best for you — always have, always will. You and I both know that isn't living at home, working at the auto shop for the rest of your life. I just... I want you to see what I see."

"And you think that's me opening a pastry shop?"

His low voice sent a tremor through her body, and she resumed her fridge organization. Anything to keep him at bay.

"I—I think it should be something in the kitchen. You've always loved it, and you kind of have a new lease on life right now. You have money and time to invest in whatever you want that to look like."

The cold air from the fridge filtered through her cotton long-sleeve, an indication to close the doors and face him.

"Ruby, look at me." His voice, husky, bordered on commanding.

She took a step back to close the doors, almost stepping on his feet. Her back pushed against him, the hard muscle, his hands going for her hips as the doors closed against the cold. Her breath caught — it'd been awhile since a man had touched her.

But it'd been forever since *this* man was the one who had the honor.

She turned, goosebumps erupting over her skin as his

fingers lightly grazed the skin under the hem of her shirt. Ruby's eyes travelled the length of his torso, over the defined pecs pulling the fabric of his Henley, the way his Adam's apple moved as he swallowed. Her breath caught when she met his brown eyes, wanting to sink into their depths just as she had so long ago. It'd been so easy then, she knew it was just as easy now.

"Colton..." Faced with him, she let his name dance in her mouth and roll off her tongue, savoring the way it felt like home.

"We don't know each other anymore, but that doesn't mean we can't learn," he whispered.

"T-That sounds like a bad idea," she said, breathless. One of his hands trailed up her side, skimming her breast before landing on her neck. His fingers cupped her neck, thumb pressed behind her ear. Her body immediately responded to the almost-forgotten touch, a gasp escaping. It'd always been one of her favorite placements, and Colton had always had a way of holding her that lit a fire she hadn't felt with anyone else. Like he owned her, but would see that she was taken care of before anything else.

"I think I'm the king of bad ideas." He dipped his head, slowly, as if to give her time to stop him. But maybe he did still know her, even a little, because the way his lips met hers said he knew she wasn't going to.

The hard press of his mouth released a wave inside her, and she welcomed him in. She wanted, needed, to drown in everything he had been and was. He pressed his body against hers, pushing her into the fridge. Her arms snaked around his neck, desperate to pull him closer while their tongues danced in heated fervor.

He tasted like the warmth fall brings, sunny and gold before the crush of hibernation. It was crisp but still felt like home. Colton's hands held her face, firm, the hard length of him pressing into her belly. The insistent reminder of what loving him felt like barreled into her, the wave now a tsunami. She crashed around him, pulling and drinking and following the way her body remembered his.

When he finally released her mouth, they were both panting and clinging to the other. Colton rested his forehead on hers, and she breathed in his scent. Wood and grease, sweat and the unmistakable musk of him. It was a smell she'd only encountered once since their relationship, when she passed someone in a mall in Midtown. It had thrown her body into a tailspin, not only when she frantically looked around to see if it was him, but for days after when the memories haunted her. It had played a part in her fling with her coworker's ex — his smell was almost as intoxicatingly masculine as Colton's was, and it dragged her in.

But faced with the real man before her... Ruby wasn't sure if she was ready for what doors this could open. Would open, given how her heart responded as quickly as her body had. She cleared her throat and placed her hands on his chest. His perfectly defined chest, her hands slipped down slightly to feel the abs she knew lay beneath his shirt. His breath caught as her fingers went to his waist, his impressive member straining against his jeans.

"Ruby." His breath was hot on her face, eyes closed.

She removed her hands, folding them behind her in an attempt to keep them off him. Colton opened his eyes and let go of her face, taking a step back and clearing his throat.

## 32

Colton stared at the woman before him, red curls framing her angelic face. Her spattering of freckles was hardly noticeable in the low-light of the fading sun, hazel eyes staring at the floor. She was reminiscent of a Raphaelite beauty, his heart ached.

"You called out of work to help me?" Her voice was soft, a breath in the space between them. Only a step, but still farther than he wanted. But he'd put that space between them partially to respect her cue, partially because from the way her body was still pressing towards him, he wasn't sure she could be trusted to not take things further. Hell, he wasn't sure he could trust himself.

She raised her gaze to his, and he nodded.

He knew it was a risk to get close to her, knew it had the potential to break him. It had once before, and being surrounded by her brought everything back. Like she was a stronger, more confident, beautiful version of the woman he'd loved so fiercely. Like she'd found herself, and he'd been the thing holding her back.

"A—And you're leaving Oak Valley?"

The question gave guidance on where her head was at. If she

was asking, she wanted to know how what just transpired would fit.

"Planning on it, within the next six months." He still didn't want to drop San Francisco to her — if it didn't pan out, it didn't matter. He knew he needed to get out before he was smothered. But he couldn't ignore the little voice in his head that told him it wasn't just about failing the interview. He didn't want to give her specifics, in case she invited him along in her bus.

Ruby bit her lower lip, eyes never leaving his. The move transformed her, and he got a flash of her at sixteen.

"Okay."

"Okay?"

She nodded, taking a deep breath. "I—I trust that that's true. You've never lied to me before, I don't think you'd start now. So... What did you hope to gain from..." She waved her hands between them. "That? This?"

"You mean, what do I want?"

"Yeah."

As far as he'd known, Ruby had always been a serial monogamous. She had been serious about wanting to find her person, The One, when they were young teens. After they broke up, her socials had boasted a few back-to-back relationships in college, and then went dark on men once she moved to New York City. While there was a part of Colton that also hoped to find his person — and had been convinced for the better part of four years it was Ruby — he'd enjoyed his freedom after to learn more about himself and to explore dating. Now he just heatedly made out with the only person he'd ever saw himself building a life with, and knew there was a tightrope they needed to walk in order to preserve... Well, anything.

He sighed. "I want to relearn you, Ruby. I know it's tricky, revisiting what we had. I know we drive each other up the wall. I know we're different in some ways. I don't want to rush anything, and I don't want any weird, I don't know, expectations?"

"Let's just see where things go?"

He searched her face, anxious to find any sort of approval or disappointment. He was met with a blank stare.

"Yeah. Let's just see where things go."

She smiled and stuck out her hand. "Deal."

He gripped her hand and she pulled him forward, pressing her cheek against his.

"Don't fuck this up." Her words haunted him, sending chills down his spine. He knew he was playing with fire.

But that only made him want it more.

"Over my dead body," he growled in her ear, teeth nipping at her earlobe. She sighed against him, neck arching in the most delicious, inviting way. His mouth traveled down the alabaster slope, kissing and licking down and around her collarbone. Her moans were music to his ears, a lost soundtrack he had forgotten the words to. Her nails dug into his shoulders as his arms wrapped around her waist, pulling her into him.

"Oh, hello."

Colton dropped her, Beryl's voice firm behind him. He glanced down at Ruby waiting for her to finish fixing her skewed shirt and wiping his saliva from her skin. There was nothing to be done about her flushed cheeks, but he had to face Beryl sooner rather than later.

"Hi, Beryl." He turned, choking out the words and running a hand through his hair, thankful his boner disappeared almost immediately with her arrival. He'd been a teenager the last time he'd been caught by her, necking her daughter. Somehow it was made even worse that it was the same situation, ten years later.

Maybe some things really didn't change.

"Ah, the prodigal son returns not only to his hometown, but to his ex-high-school sweetheart's house. And how are you,

Colton?" Despite the colorful scarf covering her bald head, her pallid face, she spoke with conviction and stared up at him with icy eyes. She pushed past them to open the fridge, her slippers shuffling along the hardwood floor.

"I'm well, thanks. How are you?"

She turned to him, half-and-half in one hand while the other shut the refrigerator doors. "I've been better. Are you staying for dinner?" She glanced at Ruby.

"N-no, we just finished eating lunch but I think Colton needs to help his mom with something." Ruby crossed her arms over her chest and gave him a pleading look. He sighed, knowing that even though he wanted to pretend they could fall back into old habits, there were some things they needed to work up to.

Dinner at the Delacey's was one of those things.

"Yeah, I told my mom I'd help her close the bakery today. Actually, I should probably get going." He glanced at the time on the oven, making a show of running late. "I'll see you around, Ruby."

He stepped forward, impulsively wanting to give her a kiss, but she turned her head so he got her cheek.

Right. Probably best to not actively kiss in front of her mom. At least not while they sort out whatever their situationship was.

"See ya, Colt. Thanks again for the bus help and the tacos."

She followed him to the door and gave a little wave as he left. He flashed her a smile, hoping it was as cheeky and salacious as he felt. Getting caught by a parent was thrilling, and as an adult the anxiety of it disappeared and was replaced by that special voyeuristic feeling of doing something potentially dangerous.

And based on how Colton's heart and body reacted to Ruby, if there was anyone that was dangerous, it was her.

## 33

It had been about a week since Ruby was caught in the kitchen basically with her shirt off, pressed between Colton and the fridge. They hadn't seen each other since, but that didn't stop their brief texting from turning into a voracious stampede. They hadn't crossed over into sexting, more general friend chats. But on Saturday morning when she opened the front door to take her mom to chemo, there was a beautiful bouquet of wildflowers on the porch. No note, but finding wildflowers at the end of January was difficult and expensive — and only a select number of people knew Ruby's love of the burst of sunshine from goldenrod, the sweetness of Morning Glories and the delicacy of Queen Anne's Lace.

She glanced at her mom behind the library desk and willed her cheeks to not display the residual embarrassment of feeling like she was sixteen again. Beryl had yet to fully comment on the compromising position, but Ruby knew where she stood from their previous conversation. Part of growing up and becoming an adult was losing the incessant *what are you doing* talks from her mom. Without them, most times Ruby felt like she was doing something wrong, but there was a sense of freedom at making her own choices and facing the consequences herself. Even if she knew her mom would have to pick up the pieces where Colton Taylor was concerned.

Beryl rested her head in her hands, bleary-eyed as she looked around the room. She was insistent on working until the very end, and Ruby felt the familiar tingle of anxiety mount when her mom announced she'd still be working at the library that week. It didn't matter her second treatment had been two days ago, it didn't matter that her mom walked with a cane when she wasn't in public. Beryl felt that the proximity of the front desk to the employee bathroom was a justifiable reason to still work, and since Ruby couldn't change her mind, she decided to bring her laptop instead.

Rachel and the others at Maven Media were being incredibly understanding of Ruby's situation, but after last week when she had welcome meetings with six new clients, she was beginning to feel the inkling of doubt. She wasn't good enough, couldn't keep up with the no-sleep-New-York-City lifestyle in her sleepy hometown.

"Well, don't y'all look cute today." Macy Weathers' voice cut through Ruby.

"Hello, Macy," Beryl said, sitting up a little taller. The smile didn't reach her eyes.

"Hi, Ms. Weathers," Ruby grudgingly offered. Her need to be called by her last name also got under her skin, like Ruby was still ten years old.

"Well, don't you seem too weak to whip a gnat. What's got you down, Miss Ruby?"

Ruby tried to keep her eyes from rolling and nearly failed.

"Nothing, Ms. Weathers. I'm working and keeping my mom company. How are you today?"

"Just dandy. I'm getting the town all situated for the Valentine's Day Festival in a couple weeks, we decided to incorporate different Valentine fun facts from different countries. Just need to do a little research. Could y'all be dolls and direct me to where that info may be?"

Macy's bright blue eyes bounced from Beryl to Ruby, her silver curls flashing more white-gold in the dim library light. She'd been around for as long as Ruby could remember and while she loved trying new things, technology was not one of them.

Ruby sighed, typing in a quick Google search and turning her computer around. "You can just search what you need, Ms. Weathers. See? All sorts of traditions from around the world. You could maybe even turn the fun facts into little kissing booths. Maybe have one for flowers, chocolate, stuffed animals, and have different questions. If the person guesses the right country, they get a kiss or maybe a chocolate or flower or something."

Macy stared at the computer screen with her mouth open before fixing her gaze on Ruby. "Oh, my. Aren't you just full of good ideas. We need you on the planning committee, especially with so little time left. Would you be able to also get the word out to the town? We want this to be the biggest festival Oak Valley has seen to date."

Ruby tried not to laugh — big for Oak Valley was about two hundred people. But publicity was her literal job, and while she loved coming up with big ideas, she rarely had a chance to implement them due to client and Maven's restraints. She didn't know how she could juggle the bus build, her day job, and taking care of her mom, but it could be an opportunity to let her creative flag fly.

"Let me think on it. I'll get back to you by tomorrow." Ruby gave her a genuine smile while Beryl softly told Macy where the computer lab was. Once she left, Beryl went back to laying on the desk.

"Mom, you feeling okay?"

Slight nod.

"Do you feel sick?"

Slight shrug.

"Maybe we should go home, I'm sure you're tired."

Beryl tilted her head without lifting it, the spark gone from her eyes. Ruby hurt with the diminishment of her mom, who was generally feisty and full of life. It'd been silly for her to think she could ever leave Oak Valley in six months. Even a year was probably unlikely. A stone in her heart sank to the pit of her stomach.

If Ruby had to stay in Oak Valley for at least the next year, what did that look like?

Anxiety gripped her as she watched her mom heave herself up, grabbing the walls and shelves as she made her way to the bathroom. If Ruby stayed, at the very least she had to check on her mom, if not continue living with her — depending on how her treatments went. They'd know more at the end, in six months.

Either way, something was changing. Ruby could only hope it was for the best, and that her days of traveling and being free weren't completely over.

## 34

Over the course of the last week, the incident in Ruby's kitchen had burned itself into Colton's body. Now that they'd answered the primal call in their bodies, he couldn't get enough. She was the last thing he thought of before calming himself enough to go to sleep and first thing when he woke up. Morning wood certainly didn't help, but it was more in how he missed waking up to her, wrapped in her warmth and gentle hands, hair of fire spread across his pillow.

He'd tried to keep the texting relaxed, staying true to his word of relearning her. But the more they talked the more he wanted her. All of her. Like the floodgates had been opened and if he didn't die by her waves he'd never be satisfied. The most he felt he could do without coming on too forward was leaving her favorite flowers on her doorstep. To let her know he never forgot the details, that he remembered everything. Even if they were just seeing where things went, he wanted her to know he wasn't just in it for physicality.

He sighed, wishing he was wrapped up in her instead of at the auto shop. It was fairly quiet today. Katie's laugh from outside drifted in, Damian's low voice following. Another burst erupted from his sister. Colton ran his hand through his hair. He didn't know if Katie and Damian were harmlessly flirting or if there was something more, but he didn't trust it. Damian had always been a little too smooth, too cocky, for Colton's liking. And roping Colton's sister in with charm was a surefire way to get him to put a target on Damian's back.

His phone rang, a California number. His heart jumped into his throat. There'd been no word of the interview and Colton was sure they'd passed him up.

"Hello?"

"Mr. Taylor?"

"This is he, may I ask who's calling?"

"This is Annette, I'm so sorry for the delay in communication. I wanted to call and formally invite you for an interview at the test kitchen in San Francisco next week."

Despite the rushing in his ears, he could hear the smile in her voice. He felt confident that if given the chance, he could prove himself worthy of studying under one of the world's greatest chefs.

This was it. This was his dream.

"Oh, wow. Thank you. Yes, I will be there."

"Wonderful. The entire process will be for one day. We will be testing four others, and only three of you will be hired. Is the email we have on file still the best one to reach you at?"

"Y—Yeah. Yes, that one is good." Colton could hardly think straight.

"Great, if you haven't received an email by end of day tomorrow, please let us know. We look forward to seeing what you can do."

"Okay, thank you. Thanks so much, Annette."

They hung up and Colton stared at the desk. He wanted to walk out the door, book his ticket, not look back. He wanted to start this new life, one he wasn't scared of, one that maybe, just maybe, included the one woman he regretted losing.

"Yo," Katie popped her head in, cheeks flushed.

Probably from laughing with Damian.

Colton clenched his jaw at the thought. He lived at home during college, but away games gave him a taste of what his life could be. Once he was drafted to the Giants, he took off as far away from Oak Valley as he could. Which, evidently, was still only an hour and a half away. Katie had been eighteen; he thought he'd done enough to keep her from douchebags like Damian. But he'd be lying if he said he wasn't worried that he hadn't done enough. That he had and would never do enough to keep his family together. To keep them okay.

"Yo," he sighed, leaning back in the desk chair.

She took big steps into the reception area, a goofy grin on her face. No matter how old she was, she'd always be his little sister.

"Hey now, is that a smile I see? Who were you talking to?" She leaned against the desk, her smile even wider. "Was it… Ruby?" She drew out the name, making little kissing noises. Colton couldn't stop his smirk from turning into a full on smile, and he turned away, pretending to dig for something in the filing cabinet behind him.

If the mention of her name gave him no control over himself, he was in trouble.

He cleared his throat and took a deep breath, sad attempts at diminishing the heat flowing through him. "If you must know, it was the French pastry people. They want me to fly out to San Francisco next week for a kitchen interview."

When he finally risked looking at Katie, her jaw was practically on the floor.

"No! Colt, that's amazing. I… I'm speechless. I'll cover for you next week, and with Dad." She bounced on her feet. "Wow, I'm so happy for you. This is huge. We should go to Cheers to celebrate."

Colton shook his head, anxious to not feed into something that wasn't a done deal. If it got around he went but didn't get the job, he'd just be a failure. Again.

And that was all the ammunition his dad needed.

"It's just an interview, I'm just going to see how it goes. There's nothing to celebrate."

"Psh, you're such a downer," Katie sighed.

"Speaking of downers, did you talk more with Mr. Denaube about us buying the lot next door?"

Katie hesitated before walking into the back office, dragging him with her. Colton almost tripped getting out of the desk chair to follow, his knee twinging. He almost said something to her, but when she turned to face him after closing the door behind him, he saw tears in her eyes.

Katie didn't cry.

"Yeah. I think I need your help, Colt."

She crossed her arms, her lip quivering. Colton put his hands on her shoulders and pulled her into a hug.

"Anything, Katie."

She took a deep breath, her voice muffled against his arm. "I had plans drawn up for what the extension would look like, I've submitted to the Town Planning Board, I have cost and potential income. Everything except the actual purchase of the land. But every time I bring it up to Dad, he finds some silly way to tell me it's a bad idea. And then he tells me to run it by you, and get your approval. And it just feels like I have nothing that's mine. He won't let me. And I don't know what to do."

Colton stood holding her, silently fuming over what she said. He wanted to just sign his approval to whatever she needed, but he also wanted to make the old man hurt.

"Give me a couple days to look into some things. And send

me all your paperwork. But trust me, Katie-Cat, we'll get this squared away."

She nodded against him before pulling away, wiping her eyes as she moved around him and opened the door. "Thanks, Colton. Seriously. I owe you." She gave him a small smile before heading out.

"Consider you covering for me next week repayment," he called after her.

She giggled and left the shop, while Colton looked around the office. He thought of all the money sitting in his various accounts. He needed her paperwork, and someone to bounce some ideas off of, but his brain was starting to find ways to give Katie what she wanted, needed. He ran a hand through his hair. He was going to help her. He didn't know quite how, but he'd find a way. He wanted his sister to know she had the power to live her life. Even if that was not going to college and running an auto shop instead — if that's what made her happy, so be it.

## 35

The bus was stacked full of lumber, and Ruby was careful not to trip as she made her way around. Olive and her dad drove her to the closest Home Depot in the family pick-up truck and Ruby had stuffed the bed full of plywood, foam insulation, and wood for framing. Having treated the bared bus floors a few days ago — sanding the rust and patching holes and painting with an insulating sealant — Ruby was anxious to get the subfloor laid and have the materials needed to build out the inside while simultaneously working on replacing unnecessary windows with sheet metal. Having a big metal box for a home meant it was naturally terrible at staying warm in winter and cool in summer, so every inch of insulated wall space helped.

But maybe she over-bought on materials.

She sighed, not looking forward to having to move all the wood every time she needed to get to the space beneath it, but knowing that the sooner she started, the sooner the wood would start to disappear.

The familiar crunch of gravel brought a smile to her lips and a clench to her thighs. Ruby anxiously peered out the window. While she knew she would normally be angry he showed up without notice — how dare he just expect her to be around — she also couldn't help the flutter in her belly at him showing up, in clothes fit for construction and a tool box in hand. He squinted his eyes and looked around, noticing her car and clearly trying to decide if he should try the bus or the front door.

But he must've caught her peeking, sending her a dimpled smile as he walked to the back door. She had closed it behind her, not wanting to let any more January air in than was necessary, so she tried not to trip over the stacks of wood to open it for him.

And as luck would have it, Colton opened the door right as her toe caught a corner, and before she knew it she was falling headfirst right in front of him.

Until she was wrapped in his arms, the wall of his hard chest keeping her stable. It took Ruby a moment to realize how fast he reacted, how if he hadn't she could've been severely injured on any one of the tools or building items left lying about. She wrapped her arms around him and held him tight against her. He was so big, so safe, so warm.

"Whoa, there." He pulled back, looking her over. His hand brushed a stray curl from her cheek, thumb cupping her jaw as he lifted her face towards his.

"What would you do without me?" His cocky grin and raised eyebrow made her roll her eyes, but she couldn't hide the smile.

"I guess I'd just lose my head without your big, strapping manliness to save lil' ol' me."

"Let me nick some sug, sugar."

He pulled her face to meet his, wrapping her lips in a kiss filled with heat. His tongue swept her mouth, and Ruby sighed into him. She'd never forgotten what it felt like to be kissed by Colton Taylor, but she sure did love the reminder. Even if the feeling of home was met with one of caution. She'd fallen for him once before — hard — and couldn't allow herself to do so again. Not when they had decided to see where things went.

When she pulled away, Colton went in for another kiss.

Ruby laughed and playfully swatted him. "You know, I actually have work to do." She tried to pull out of his grasp, but he held her tight.

"I know, I know. I just... I missed you." Colton's face turned red, his gaze shifting away from her.

She cocked her head. "Oh, did you now? The great Colton Taylor missed me?"

A cloud of insecurity swelled around them, and Colton dropped his arms. "I'm not all that great, Ruby. Now what are we working on today?"

Ruby didn't know how to address his comment, and stood with her arms crossed as he walked around her, the bus, picking up the plywood sheets and leaning them against the walls. He took the space heater Ruby had put in the front of the bus, the extension cord pulled through the mostly closed front doors, and moved it to the middle.

The floor was cleared, and having the blank canvas reignited her excitement.

"Ruby?"

"Oh, yeah. Sorry, um I need to glue the insulation to the floor, and then the plywood to the insulation for a floating subfloor."

"You don't want to grid it for more stability? You don't want the floor to shift with you driving it around everywhere."

"Honestly, I don't think it's worth it."

"Worth it?" He looked at her, realization dawning in his eyes. "You mean you're not going to be driving this thing more than necessary? Are... Are you scared? Is Ruby Delacey scared of driving a school bus?" He burst out laughing, bending over his knees and slapping his thigh. She rolled her eyes, knowing some of the theatrics were in jest.

Even if most of it was genuine.

Why did he have to know her so well?

"Maybe I am. So what? It's a big bus."

"Yeah, leave it to you, Miss It-Took-Me-Three-Tries-To-Get-My-Drivers-License, to clean all the mailboxes in town with your converted school bus." He tried to calm his laughter, barely able to get the sentence out.

"Oh my god, you're insufferable." Ruby shook her head. "Are you going to help me? Because if not, I'm going to need you to move your ass from the center of my work zone."

He came up behind her and pulled him against her, nuzzling her neck and grinding his hips into her.

"I can definitely move my ass somewhere else, if the lady wishes."

Ruby's body involuntarily responded, moving in time to his thrusts. She leaned her head back, arms wrapping up and around as he bit her ear, licking her neck, hands pawing under her shirt. Colton flipped her around, his muscled biceps holding her close. His hands squeezed her ass, running down her thighs until he had enough leverage to throw her up and around his waist.

God, she missed being tossed about by him.

He pressed her back against the window and she shivered from the cold glass, causing his kisses to become more fervent. His hard cock pressed against her core, and Ruby felt the wetness between her thighs flood her thin yoga pants at the way he fit her.

One hand wrapped around her waist while the other went under her shirt, his need to get to her breasts evident. Ruby gripped his hair in her hands, pulling and moaning while he continued to grind and his hands found its goal. He kneaded her breast, fingers lightly pinching and tweaking her nipple beneath her sports bra while his tongue tore through her mouth.

She whispered his name, and he moaned into her.

"I need you, Ruby."

His voice was music to her ears, a dream she'd been trying to keep hold of for ten long years. But he was here, and god forbid she didn't take every advantage of this opportunity.

"Condom?" she panted, legs and arms still wrapped around him.

He smirked and laid gentle kisses along her collarbone, stoking the fire he'd ignited.

"Of course."

Ruby playfully pulled his head back by his hair, making sure his eyes were locked on here's. "Then what are you waiting for? I need you to fuck me, Colton Taylor."

He wasted no time diving his mouth to hers and setting her feet back on the ground, hands pulling her shirt and sports bra over her head and peeling the yoga pants around her ankles until she was left standing in her black lacy thong. She couldn't help the unsexy bra, but at least she thought ahead on the underwear.

And the shaving.

She returned the favor, removing his shirt but allowing her hands and eyes to travel the contours of his defined body, the corded muscles beneath golden skin. Her breath shook, torn between wanting to free the god in his pants and wanting to admire the one standing before her.

Colton stood back, a familiar look in his eyes. The one he'd given her when they first made love all those years ago, and every time since. Like he had the world before him and knew it.

"Hey, baby girl." It came out as a whisper. Colton placed a hand on either side of her hips, leaning into her and giving her a languid kiss. "We have all the time in the world. But I need to worship you. It's been far too long, Ruby."

His brown eyes held hers, and she wanted to drown in their depths. In the truth she saw in them, in the way he held her name between his teeth.

Ruby was overcome with overwhelming trust in and love for the man before her.

She didn't have time to think about how she should tell him about staying in Oak Valley because Colton went straight to work fulfilling his need.

## 36

Colton couldn't believe his luck.

He was running his hands along the hips of an alabaster goddess with a head and heart of fire.

*His* goddess.

He kissed his way down the soft plane of her belly, listening to her moans for guidance. Her body was fuller, more lush, made of curves that fit his hands perfectly. Like they were made for him. But he still knew this path. He knew every inch of smooth skin, what every mewl and sigh meant, the way her body moved in time with his.

She was his, and always had been.

His tongue carved paths along her long legs, fingers caressing the lacy band of her underwear over her body until they fell at her feet, until her precious center was bared to him. He breathed in her scent, relishing the way she pushed his head even deeper into her, and he teased with a lick. Her knees buckled, and he chuckled into her core, relishing the way her fingers pulled his hair.

"Shut up and get to work."

Her voice was husky but had the desired effect, Colton's cock twitching at the need to be enveloped in her warmth. He'd missed the commanding way she wanted to be loved, how she took charge of her pleasure.

He drank her nectar, her moans and gasps becoming a soundtrack to his movements. He teased her folds with his fingers, playfully inserting just the tips before using his tongue to swirl around her clit. Ruby hooked a leg around his shoulder, her heel pushing his arm. He knew she was aching for more, but he didn't want to give in just yet.

Colton flipped her other leg over his shoulder, until she was straddling his face and he could bury himself in her. He may not be able to play football anymore, but he could certainly throw his girl around in the bedroom. Or the school bus. He slammed three fingers into her center, her hips bucking against his tongue as he lapped the heaven before him.

Her panting became more frantic, her legs tensing and shaking against his neck. He strengthened his motions, quickened them, needing to feel her release against him. Needing to drink her, let her inside him, become one with her.

As much as she was his, he wanted to be hers.

When the river came, the cliffs of her legs breaking against him, it was greater than his greatest dream. It was both a memory and a premonition, a gift he knew he not only had to work to have, but one to keep.

He drank her slowly, hands rubbing against her skin as she came down from the high, his hard cock insistent it be somewhere warm.

"I need you inside me," she gasped, hands grasping at him, clawing at him to stop kneeling.

Colton unhooked her legs and kissed his way up her body. He took his time, giving little bites and licks as he went, savoring the sheen of sweat on her skin, honeysuckle mixed with salt. His hands caressed her full thighs, her hips, her soft belly, her full chest. His mouth captured a perfect rosebud nipple, the other hand relishing the weight of her other breast, the hard peak of her arousal.

"Colton, please."

He chuckled, nuzzling his face between her chest.

"Are you begging, Ruby?"

"Obviously." Her hands went to his cock, the cold of her skin bumping against his stomach, his balls, sending goosebumps over his heated skin. He clenched his jaw and shuddered against her, her firm grasp on his sensitive member forcing him to find his way to her full lips.

He leaned back, taking in the wild woman before him. Blaze of red-gold curls catching the cold light from the windows, a wild frame around her angelic face, freckles muted by the shadows they cast. He wanted to find each perfect dot and pull it into the light, give them their own show. Her hazel eyes were a rainbow of colors, but the honesty in their depths was what took his breath away. She saw him, still, for everything he was. But more than that, the love in them was that of acceptance.

Despite ten years, that look hadn't changed.

The welling in his chest was too strong, too familiar, and the words on the tip of his tongue almost broke free.

But it was too soon.

He stopped himself with a kiss, wanting her to know the wave crashing through him without saying the words that belonged to her.

## 37

Ruby felt the urgency in his kiss and mirrored it, desperate to have him in her and her in him.

But he was taking too long.

"Condom," she breathed between kissing, her hands fumbling at the button and zipper of his blue jeans. His washboard abs, the smooth V leading to his hard length, the strength in his arms as he held her, was all new. Gone was the bulky teenage body she'd known and loved, and in its place was a cut, strapping man who knew what he wanted and took his time getting it.

His hands fumbled through his wallet while she pulled his jeans down, trying not to show the rejuvenated heat coursing through her body at the sight of his long cock straining against his boxer briefs. Even hidden by the fabric, it was impressive. Ruby fingered its outline, the hard insistence at wanting to break free twitching against her fingers. She smiled at Colton, playfully tapping the head of his cock while he flinched, ripping the condom wrapper. She pulled the briefs down, his cock springing free and brushing her belly. A wet streak marked her and her body responded in kind.

Colton slipped the condom over his length, growling as Ruby tried to touch. Her mouth was salivating, missing him, every inch of him, anywhere she could fit him.

"You want this?" He gripped his cock and rubbed it against her, and she whimpered.

"Spread your legs."

Ruby loved taking control, but equally loved being bossed around. His words filtered through her, wetness pooling at her center.

Colton took those large muscles and hoisted her up, positioning his head at her entrance before slamming his shaft inside as he did. She cried against him, nails digging into his shoulders at the burst of pain and pleasure coursing through her body. He stretched her, filled her, in a way no one else ever had. He touched every crevice, every hidden space inside her. He held her tight as her body accommodated him. He slowly pulled out, easing himself back into her folds, continuing the motion until he slipped in and out with ease.

Ruby gasped at the fervor, the rhythm, the way he knew to keep a thumb on her clit while his hips bounced her up and down on his cock, one arm wrapped so tight around her waist she knew she'd only go where he wanted her to. Ruby got lost in the sensation of Colton, of his grunts and the way his face squeezed tight before pulling completely out. But his thumb kept working her clit, and Ruby came on his fingers.

He set her down and spun her around, pushing her back down as he pounded his dick into her center without wasting time. His fingers dug into her hips while Ruby kept her hands pressed against the wall, the window, the force of him a storm begging her to break once more. The pressure built inside her easily, quickly, a response to his primal call. He was picking up speed, his fingers finding their mark on her sensitive bundle. Ruby was hyper-aware of every movement he made, every grunt, the way his body bent over hers as he released, his teeth against her skin, her body clenching around his as she met his internal force.

They stayed that way for some time, Colton's hot breath slowing against her skin. Ruby's hands were still pressed against the wall, window, of the bus, and without the primal heat of their bodies moving, the cold was settling on Ruby's skin. She slowly rose, her body stiff in a way it hadn't been in some time. Colton slipped out of her, and when she turned to face him, he was pulling the condom off his cock. It was still hung like a horse, and when Colton caught her staring, it twitched.

Maybe his quick recovery time also hadn't changed.

"What's that smile for, sweet cheeks?" His voice was soft, tired, but laced with a sweetness reserved for intimacy. His free hand went to her neck, his thumb rubbing against her cheek. Ruby kissed his palm, reality settling in.

She'd just had sex with Colton Taylor.

"Ruby, you okay?"

When she met his eyes, they were filled with concern. "Was... Was that okay? Too much, too fast?"

She shook her head, not knowing how to tell him it was absolutely perfect, that she'd needed that rushed, wild fuck. And she'd needed it from him. So she kissed him instead, pulling him into her. Releasing him, she rested her forehead on his. His shaft pressed against her leg, already hardening at the contact.

"It was perfect, Colton. I think you're ready for round two but I'm a bit cold," Ruby said. Now that they'd gotten ten years of backed up sexual frustration out of their systems, Ruby wanted to take her time with him. He'd kissed every inch of her body, but she wanted to do the same. She wanted to relearn every mountain, every valley of his muscled body. And there was only one way to do that. She took a deep breath and looked away from him, hugging herself. "Wo—Would you like to spend the night?"

Colton started passing her her clothes, and Ruby took them but avoided his gaze while he kept trying to catch her eye. It was a risk, asking for that kind of intimacy. Especially given their history and how they decided to just see where this went. And while she was close with her mom, she knew how Beryl felt about their closeness and didn't want to risk her mom running into Colton at an odd hour.

She was finally dressed when she looked at him. He still hadn't answered, and that in and of itself was all she needed to know.

"Sorry I asked. Thanks for coming. We can finish the floor another time." She tried to push past him, but his hand on her arm stopped her. She looked into his eyes, almost black in the fading winter light.

"Ruby, I would love to spend the night. You just seemed uncomfortable asking and I didn't know what to say. I want you to want me to stay the night."

*Oh*. She had a habit of jumping to conclusions, or of pushing too hard. Ruby stood tall, looking him square in the face.

"I want you to spend the night. Although you may have to sneak in and out because... Well, I live with my mom and I don't need her to see... this."

Colton chuckled, his dimples already sending her body into overdrive. Yeah, wanted him in her bed — but she needed him more than that.

"What a thrill, to be sixteen again." He pulled her into him, planting a kiss on her cheek. "Lead the way, sweetness."

Ruby shivered from pleasure at the thought of falling asleep next to him and waking up beside him. At the way she knew their bodies would tangle together, moving as one throughout the night. She shivered being so close to someone so dangerous for her.

As she unplugged the space heater, shut all the doors behind them, and led the way up to her room through the basement, Ruby shivered at what would happen if she actually allowed herself to fall into him again.

## 38

The morning light streaming through the blue room was disorienting, and it took a minute for Colton to figure out what time and space he was in. The room was familiar, too familiar, the warm body pressed against his one he instinctively didn't want to lose. But he shouldn't be here, why was he here?

When he remembered the day, night before, he realized he wasn't supposed to be anywhere. He breathed in Ruby's hair, lemon and chamomile, his arm under her neck wrapped around her shoulders. He pulled her closer, and she burrowed her face into his chest.

His dreams had come true, his wishes answered.

Colton turned on his side, keeping her pressed into him. He peppered kisses along her forehead, wanting to capture every inch, every freckle in his mouth and never let it go. Her hair splayed out on the pillow behind her, copper in the light from the window behind her bed. Her breath was soft against his chest, skin glowing white against his tan.

He went over last night, the way they'd spent hours catering to every need, every whim, enjoying every sloping curve and flat plane on each other's bodies. There hadn't been much talking, but what they'd exchanged said everything he needed to hear.

While they were just seeing where this went, Colton didn't want to play games. He didn't want to play with either of their hearts, and his stomach twisted at the thought of him not telling her about the interview. He reminded himself it was just an interview, that it wasn't worth talking about until it became something. Because if he didn't get it, it would reinforce to her that he wasn't leaving.

And if he did...

How could they make it work while she traveled in her bus and he worked long, rigorous hours in a San Francisco pastry shop?

Colton swallowed, not wanting to entertain the possibility that he could lose her again. Not when he'd just gotten her.

Except she wasn't his.

He involuntarily tightened his hold on her, and she kissed his chest.

"Good morning, hot stuff," she mumbled into him.

"Good morning, sweet cheeks."

Her fingers trailed along his skin, sending goosebumps along his arm and back.

This was too good, too perfect, to last.

"What have you got going on today?"

It took Colton a minute to make out the words, and he realized he'd probably overslept for work.

Fuck it. Katie would cover for him.

"Well, looks like I'm playing hooky. What about you?"

Ruby stretched away from him before sitting up on arm. Her hair fell around her shoulders in perfect coils. Colton tucked a strand behind her ear.

"Um, well I should work on the bus some more, answer

some emails. Will... Will you be okay to miss work today?" Her voice was edged with concern.

"Yeah, Katie will cover for me."

Ruby nodded but didn't say anything, her hand still tracing his skin.

Colton took a deep breath, wanting to bring her into his life like she was before. "Actually, maybe you could help me with something. Well, Katie."

"Of course. Anything."

"You know how my dad is, right? Well, Katie has this awesome plan to expand the business by buying the plot of land next door — you know the one, right? — but my dad doesn't like that she's spearheading it. He wants me to. And I don't know how to help."

Ruby pursed her lips. "He still expects you to take over?"

"You know it. Even though — as you know — Katie is the one that should."

She sighed, rolling onto her back and staring at the ceiling. It was Colton's turn to explore her body while he waited.

"Honestly, I think Katie should find a way to buy the land herself. If it's in her name and she can secure a business loan and build out her own business, maybe then your dad will take her seriously. You know?" Ruby turned her head to his.

"That's... that's not a bad idea."

He scrolled through the numbers from the paperwork Katie had shown him. She wouldn't even need a business loan, not with what he had stashed away.

Ruby rolled back on her side and snuggled into him. "I'd love to help in any way I can but I think this might be on you, babe."

"I think you're right. And she needs to get out." Colton's throat tightened, surprising him. He'd been stuck here almost his whole life, mostly through some fucked up need to appease everyone around him. But it wasn't actually there — his mom and Katie would've been fine if Colton had gone to school elsewhere. If he moved to another city, or country, or built a different life. His dad had constructed a veil around him, so Colton would feel responsible if anything went wrong and he hadn't been around.

But Ruby had seen through that and had gotten herself out, offering Colton a ticket to join.

And he'd said no.

But this was Katie's chance. Even if she didn't want to leave Oak Valley, she could still get out from under their dad. And do it in a way that would hurt his pride in the process, maybe help teach him a lesson.

"What do you think you're going to do?"

Colton hesitated. He didn't like talking about money — especially his money — and with women he could play up the football star without going numbers. He knew what those women were after, but he wasn't interested in sticking around long enough to confirm his suspicions. But Ruby was different. She'd seen him when he was a gangly teenager, when he had so much baby fat after he second gross spurt it was easy for him to fulfill his dad's dreams of football stardom. She'd been there for family fights, B-plusses on papers instead of As, the way his dad stormed through the house like a hurricane. How his mom and sister made themselves scarce when the yelling got too loud.

"I'll just pay for it. Invest in her business until she gets her feet under her. Maybe gift it for all the brotherly bullshit she has to put up with." Colton chuckled, trying to offset the way Ruby stiffened — briefly — in his arms. He knew she was going over the potential costs of buying land that wasn't for sale, for building a new auto shop. And the fact he was so comfortable spending that amount of money... Colton knew she had a good idea how much he was worth.

He wasn't that broke, scared teenager anymore. And while he wanted to use what he could to help Katie, there was a piece of Colton that wanted to do the same for Ruby, and for himself. Like he was finally ready to move forward from his past and into his future.

## 39

Ruby did some quick calculations in her head — his draft contracts were somewhat public knowledge — and while she didn't place any value on her ex being a multi-kajillionaire, it was still shocking to run through the numbers.

He so casually said he'd just... buy his sister this land and build her business.

"Why do you still live at home, Colton?" She said it softly, not trying to accuse but ask out of curiosity.

It was his turn to roll onto his back, away from her, a hand resting in his hair while he stared at the ceiling. Ruby watched him, giving him the space he needed to answer.

"After my injury, I needed rehab. It was hard for me to move around, so it made the most sense for me to move home. My mom and Katie saved my ass, in more ways than one." He paused, his eyes glassy, and took a shaky breath before continuing. "Ruby, I have never felt like how I did then. I was reliant on everyone around me, my career was over, and all I heard was my dad talking about me taking over the shop. And I just... I saw the rest of my life just drift away. When I could go about on my own,

I couldn't face getting a job in the town. And my dad wouldn't let me — why would I get a job elsewhere when I had one waiting for me? So they put me to work there, to keep me from truly drowning. And because I still lived at home, I could help my mom and Katie."

"So you stayed because…"

"To help my mom and Katie. I just said that," Colton said. He turned to her, confused.

"Yeah, I'm just trying to figure out the how. How did you staying help them?"

"What do you mean?"

Ruby sighed, trying not to get frustrated. It was so obvious, why didn't he see it?

"Colt, you stayed because you thought they needed you. But they were fine before you moved home. So why did you stay there instead of moving out?" Ruby winced at the sharpness of her own words, hoping they wouldn't cut too deep. While she knew core things about Colton, there were some things she was still learning.

He stared at the ceiling, his breathing measured.

Okay, that was new. Ruby thought back to all the times his anger reached out or his anxiety overtook. That was something that had changed, a pleasant surprise. Ruby relaxed, seeing that maybe they could have a calm, honest conversation.

"You're right." He said it so softly, Ruby almost didn't catch it. But he turned to her, and said it again.

"You're right, Ruby. They were fine before me. But being there, every day, feeling the tension in the air with my dad around, I couldn't leave them in that alone."

"Not after how they helped you."

"Yeah. And you know how hard it is to find good apartments here, it's a tourist trap."

Ruby laughed. "Colt, not to be insensitive, but I don't think money's the issue here."

His face didn't change, and she quieted down.

"Please understand that when you realize your career is over, everything you've worked for, any money you have is supposed to last you until your next job. And I didn't know how long rehab would last, or if I'd always have certain issues or if there were certain things I'd never be able to do."

"I—I'm sorry, Colton. I didn't mean anything by that."

"I know, Ruby. It's just... It's been hard. Really fucking hard. And I'd really like it to be easy for once."

She laid a hand on his chest, watching his hand run through his hair. His eyes were welling, but she didn't want to address it — if he was feeling vulnerable, it would only twist the knife.

She thought about how she still hadn't told him about staying in Oak Valley, how much that would twist the knife. How he was trusting her with some of his innermost thoughts, and she was withholding information that could change the course of their situation.

Information that could turn his back on her, and this time for good.

"Well, Colt, I think it will get easy. Just focus on you, what you need and want. The rest will fall into place. And I know how lucky Katie is to have you."

*I was once even luckier.*

He pinched the bridge of his nose, wiping his finger tips on the sheets. A subtle way to remove tears, but one she knew from way back when.

He was still hers, even after all this time. And she wanted hm to feel as loved and seen as he was back then. She kissed his cheek and snuggled into him, happy to accept whatever he would give her.

Colton kissed the top of her head and held her tight. "How are you doing? How's your mom?"

Ruby sighed, not exactly wanting to get into it. But he'd been so forthcoming, and there was one thing she couldn't be honest about. So she could tell him what she could.

"My mom is... okay. We're still waiting to see the effects of treatment — it's been about a month and she has two more to go before we can reevaluate her treatment plan. I'm... I'm okay. Working part time has been really helpful, and Macy actually asked me to help with the Valentine's Day Festival."

"Wait, what? Macy Weathers?" Ruby felt Colton shift under her, his body turning her way.

"The one and only. I was at the library and helped her with a game idea, and then she found out I worked in publicity."

"So naturally she wants a front page New York Times article on Oak Valley's Annual Valentine's Day Festival."

"And the First Annual Arbor Day Carnival," Ruby giggled.

Colton laughed, and Ruby shushed him. She didn't need her mom knowing he was in her bed and stayed the night.

"You know my car's in the driveway, right?"

*Oh, shit.*

She dropped her head onto his chest and moaned.

"Yeah, I realized it this morning. So... sorry, not sorry."

"Don't be." Ruby gazed at his body, gold in the morning light, the way his muscles flexed with every movement. She traced the space between his abs, his pecs, watching as goosebumps rose across his skin. He smiled at her, dimples coming to life, a light in his eyes she hadn't seen in years.

This was it. This was everything she'd been waiting, hoping, for, without even realizing.

"I should get going, but I'd love to see you soon. Maybe this weekend?"

"Sure."

His hand cupped her neck, pulling her down into a kiss. She drowned, mouth and body and heart opening to him. Ruby didn't care that she had fallen, had never stopped. He was here, and right now, that was enough.

## 40

Cheers and Beers was filled with the usual town patrons, plus a small group of co-eds celebrating a twenty-first birthday. Colton was starting to settle into his role in Oak Valley, sending slight nods to the people he recognized and desperately trying to ignore the ones he didn't. He knew he stood out — pro-athletics would do that — but he was getting comfortable with the fact he didn't have to address it all the time.

Liam bounced the blue stripe into the pocket, aiming for the yellow stripe next. Archer had pulled him and Dragan out to meet the other guys for Taco Tuesday. One nice thing about being in his hometown was knowing who his friends were, that they didn't just want him for association or money. They'd been with him since the start, and had proven they'd be there until the end.

Like Ruby.

His heart swelled at the thought of her in bed, legs wrapped around his. The way she moved pulling clothes on — or off, the way her nose crinkled when she laughed or her slight gap between her two front teeth made him fall for her all over again.

"Colt, you're up," Caleb nudged him.

"Sorry." Colton stood, surveying the table. Liam knocked out a total of four stripes in his turn, which fortunately left a lot of open room for him to hit several solids. He saw the paths in his head and went to work.

"You could just pay attention," Archer laughed.

"How's Ruby?" Liam teased. While Colton didn't kiss and tell, his friends knew what games were being played.

Colton noticed Caleb's jaw clench.

He chuckled, keeping his eyes trained on his disapproving friend. "You know what, it's... Amazing. Better than amazing. It's like, we've been able to grow separately and change, but who we are now still fits like it did before. If not better." He said the last part with a touch of anger, needing Caleb to look him in the eye. To see that whatever he disliked about Ruby, it didn't matter. She was back.

The white ball followed the green solid.

"What does she think about San Francisco?" Dean piped in, taking his turn on the striped balls.

Colton caught Dragan's eye, the only one of them who knew Ruby didn't yet know about his plans. He knew if he told them the outright truth, they would call him out for being dishonest with her. And he didn't need that right now.

"Well, she's planning on traveling around and leaving Oak Valley, so she's cool with it."

Dean missed a ball, passing the torch to Archer.

"You haven't told her." Caleb's voice was soft, but the strength was unmistakable.

The guys stopped drinking, eyeing the pool table, and looked at Colton.

He sighed. "No. I haven't. It doesn't make sense to until I know for sure the interview will come through."

"Oh, dude," Archer said, shaking his head. "Don't you think you should at least give her a heads up? With your history..."

"I think you're kind of leading her on, man," Liam finished.

"Well, we agreed to just see where things go. I have the interview in two days, I'll know by the weekend. Then I'll cross that bridge."

The tension was palpable, obvious that all of them disagreed with how he was going about it and one of them disagreeing on the person.

Cara Griffin was the last thing they needed, interrupting their night. And yet, here she was. She popped up behind Dragan, sliding a manicured hand across his shoulders but keeping her eyes trained on Colton. Her four inseparable girl friends were close behind, everyone pairing up with a guy while Cara made her way to Colton at the other end of the pool table. They all had drinks in hand, but given their slightly smudged eyeliner and ruddy cheeks, the girls were clearly already a couple in.

"Oh hey, Colt," Cara said, sidling up to him with a coy smile.

He pressed his lips together and mustered a smile back, but alarm bells were ringing. After the time he'd spent with Ruby, despite their somewhat casual agreement, he knew he was playing with fire.

"So what are you boys up to?" Cara looked around, smiling sweetly at everyone. They'd all gone to school together and were civil, if not somewhat friendly. And the guys were happy to have the attention from pretty girls like Cara and her friends.

"Just hanging out. What about you guys?" Dean asked.

"Same," Juniper Cruz said, smiling across the table at him. They had been in almost all the same classes throughout high school and always had a slight flirtation.

Cara turned to Colton, talking softly so the other couldn't hear over their own convos and the din of the bar.

"Maybe we could do something... after?" She batted her

wide, blue eyes at him. It was the most straightforward she'd ever been, and there was no mistaking what she was implying.

Before, he'd been able to play off her advances. They were never propositions, they seemed harmless enough. But here she was wanting a check he wasn't willing to cash. His mind flitted to the Rubenesque red-head, the way her laugh warmed him from the inside out. How he'd dreamed of their future over ten years ago and had caught himself doing it again.

Colton faced Cara straight on.

"Nah, I'm good. Actually, Cara, I think I should just set the record straight. Thanks for asking, but I'm not interested. If I was, I would've let you know. Friends is all we can be." Cara's mouth dropped before she quickly schooled herself, but Colton still caught the fire in her eyes has he crossed his arms and turned back to the table.

"You're loss." She turned on her heel, the ends of her pin straight hair lightly whipping Colton's shoulder. The girls saw her attitude from a mile away and said their goodbyes to the guys. Juniper was the last to leave, giving Dean a little arm squeeze.

He looked hurt when he turned to Colton. "What was that about?"

Colton shrugged. "I just... I had enough?"

"I don't get it." Caleb mumbled, taking a long drink from his glass.

"Don't get what?" If Caleb wanted to go at it, Colton was in the mood. He was sick of dancing around people, sick of not getting what he wanted at the expense of other people's bullshit.

"You know what."

Colton stalked around the table until he was chest to chest with Caleb. "Say it. If you're my friend, you'll stop acting like a little shit and actually tell me what you mean instead of hiding behind your little wallowing pity party."

Caleb squared his shoulders, jaw set as he met Colton's stare.

"Why are you so fucking stuck on this one girl? It's been TEN YEARS since you broke up. She wasn't good for you then, she's not good for you now. You can barely look at anyone else even when they're right in front of you. What the fuck is it about her? Can't you see what I see?"

"Well, Caleb, you seem to be the only one who sees whatever bullshit you're talking about." Colton looked around at the other guys, awkwardly shuffling their feet and sipping their drinks. "That's what I thought. So tell me, Caleb, why isn't she good for me? Then and now." Colton widened his stance, daring his friend to have the confidence he'd need for this conversation.

He shrugged. "I— Well... She's just so... soft. In high school, she kept to herself and allowed you to just... follow. And now, she's doing the same thing. Colt, you haven't even told her about the interview because you're scared to lose her."

"And if you'd ever experienced a love like ours, you'd know why." Colton couldn't bite his tongue before the flames licked out. "Have you ever considered that she gave me a safe space in high school? You know my dad. You know my dreams. Did you ever think that maybe, just maybe, she allowed me to fully be myself and pushed me to do more, be more, than what everyone else wanted for me? No, you didn't. Because for some reason, your weird ass locked onto the fact that my life became football and Ruby, which was far different from how we all used to hang out by the river and go for hikes, occasionally spoke pot and sneak drinks from our houses. And you hated that, didn't you? Didn't you?" He tried to keep his voice from yelling, but some of the bar patrons nearby awkwardly looked their way. Caleb kept his jaw set, cheeks red.

"So you know what, Caleb? Think what you want. Nothing's stopped you, and you haven't bothered to actually ask me anything or include Ruby in anything. Everyone else has. When you date someone for four years and plan to marry them, they become a pretty fixed piece of your life. And just because you didn't want that, doesn't mean it didn't happen for me. And I'm sick and tired of your bullshit, your attitude."

Colton took a deep, shaky breath, steeling himself for what was to come. "And, quite frankly, if you can't find a way to accept or work through that, I don't know if this will work. Friends support each other, and at the very least bother to understand a situation before questioning it. You can't seem to do either. I've supported you when you wanted to go into metal work and design architectural sculptures. I've supported you in your string of one-night-stands. I've even sucked it up through your attitude towards the only woman I've ever loved. And I'm done."

Colton downed the rest of his top-shelf tequila, the burn slicing his throat. Making him feel something other than the anger pounding through his veins.

"I'll catch you guys later," he threw over his shoulder as he walked away.

It was past time he put his foot down with Caleb, and it had come out in a long stream. Everything he had quietly sat on the sidelines for came pouring out, and Colton was riled up. He wanted to scorch everything else he'd spent years letting slide.

But first, he wanted to find a way to show Ruby that — no matter what happened between them or with San Francisco — she was his everything, and he needed her to know that.

## 41

Dragan watched Colton's back as he exited the crowd, Caleb slamming back the rest of his rum and Coke before heading to the bar. Liam, Dean, and Archer pursed their lips and looked at one another but didn't say anything.

Dragan sighed, trying to decide if he should follow after Caleb or Colton. He was closer to Colton, but knew his hot-headed friend needed time to walk off his anger. Caleb tended to wallow, and even if Dragan approached him, he'd greet him with an icy silence.

There was no winning.

"Exhausting," he grumbled, slamming the pool cue on the table. "I'm closing out, are you guys done?"

The guys nodded, and Dragan made his way through the crowd. Normally Colton covered everyone's drinks, but Dragan was well-off enough that he occasionally did it. And tonight was one of those times. Even though he came from nothing, everything he had now was his. And if the app he was working on with Archer panned out, he'd never have to worry again.

But in the meantime, he worked two part-time jobs and had a side hustle that paid for his nice apartment and overall lifestyle. He occasionally gave money to his mom or younger brother to help with the other two siblings, especially when his dad decided to dip for a few days. He had a flush savings, an IRA, money in stocks.

Dragan didn't like to play.

At least not when it came to being secure.

He waved the bartender down and paid the tab, covering everyone's drinks and giving a nice tip. Having worked shitty service jobs, he always found a way to tip extra, even when money had been tight.

Checking his phone, he figured Caleb and Colton had probably both cooled down by now and he could risk a phone call with each.

Caleb didn't answer, so he left a voicemail, and Colton picked up on the third ring.

"What?"

"First, chill. Don't take that out on me," Dragan huffed. Managing Colton's moods was sometimes like dealing with a toddler. "Second, where are you? I just closed out and the guys are dispersing."

Colton sighed on the other line. "I'm sitting in my car with the heat on."

"Want company?"

While Dragan was usually the more silent of the friends, Colton met his question with a lengthy quiet before agreeing. Dragan hung up and left Cheers. Since the bar had two entrances — what they considered the front, facing Main Street, and the back, facing Elm Street — he knew Colton would be parked across the street from the front, in the Oak Valley Middle School parking lot. Dragan looked both ways before crossing, noticing someone had started decorating the lamp posts with red tinsel hearts for the Valentine's Day Festival. He grunted. Valentine's Day was all a sham, a Hallmark holiday. Of course, he always celebrated it — it was June's favorite holiday, and while they'd both dated people over the years, they had always been single on Valentine's Day. It was her favorite holiday, and over his dead body would she be left alone without a valentine.

He heard the purr of Colton's ridiculous car before he saw it. Dragan pulled on the passenger handle and slid into the cramped vehicle, Colton just staring through the windshield. They sat in silence for awhile until Colton cleared his throat.

"You don't... You don't think he'll let our friendship, I don't know, die? Do you?"

Dragan stared out the windshield, pondering before shrugging. "Hard to say. I don't think so, though. He's had that stick shoved so far up his ass it's coming out his eyes, at some point he needs to remove it. Before, he didn't think anything was at stake. Now, he knows."

Colton nodded and sighed. "How are things with you?"

Dragan shrugged. While Colton knew him better than almost anyone, he still didn't like to share more than he had to. In his experience, knowledge was power. And in the wrong hands, that could make someone worthless.

"You know you can talk to me, right?" Colton pressed.

"Sure, just nothing new going on."

"June, that secret project you're working with Archer on, nothing?"

Dragan sighed. "Fine. The project is good, we should be able to pitch the idea for sale or to investors in the next month or so. June's... June."

He hoped Colton couldn't hear the pounding of his heart at her name, and was thankful the darkness in and around the car masked the flush coursing through his body thinking of her bright smile, her curvy hourglass figure. He smiled at her various cardigans, a collection bigger than any eighty-year-old woman he'd ever met.

"D, you know I know that you've been madly in love with her since you were five, right?"

"I don't want to ruin our friendship. You know this." Dragan looked out the window. He didn't need Colton to try and read his face, to see that Dragan would be willing to risk it if she felt the same way.

But he knew she didn't. Girls like her didn't fall for guys like him.

Maybe once he had a good job or found a way to get a college degree. Maybe she could see him like that. But Dragan knew that no matter what suit he wore or degree hung in his office, she would always see his scars, his rough edges.

And she deserved better.

Colton tsked. "I just think if you saw how she looks at you, you might consider it."

"No. And she has enough on her plate, she doesn't need me throwing that on top," Dragan sighed.

Colton turned and looked at him. "Is she okay?"

He hesitated, not wanted to share her business that wasn't his to share, but also wanting to talk to his friend. "She's fine, just dealing with the shop and her grandparents' retirement."

"Oh, I meant to tell you, apparently Ruby is doing some publicity or marketing work for some of the local businesses. Maybe she could do something for the bookstore, off-load June a little."

Dragan stared out the window, mulling over what Colton said. That could definitely help alleviate the pressure, at least be a finger in the dam while they figured out how to raise money for the back payments. Dragan had enough he could cover most of them, but it wouldn't be a long-term solution. He'd be cleaned out and in six months June would be right where she was now. No, whatever he came up with, it had to last.

His mind went to the app. If he could just sell it...

"I'm good to drive, Dragan. It's too cold for you to walk, I'll drop you off," Colton said, cutting through his thoughts.

"Thanks," he managed. He loathed the way Colton drove — even two minutes in the car was enough to send Dragan stumbling out the door, clutching his stomach. He never understood why Colton splurged on such extravagant items — his apartment in Englewood Cliffs, New Jersey had been an unnecessarily posh four-bedroom penthouse with a doorman and valet parking — but also knew it didn't hurt anyone and if it made his friend happy, he might as well spend his money how he wanted.

The drive was short, and Dragan considered what it would cost to buy the bookstore flat out as he made his way up to his apartment. He knew he could ask Colton for the money and he'd give it, but there was no way he could put that pressure on their friendship.

No. He needed to talk to Ruby about a long-term business strategy for June. But first, he needed to convince his stubborn, happy-go-lucky crush that she needed help from someone other than him, and that even if she fought him on the expense, he would cover it.

## 42

For Goodness Cakes was locked, the clear hanging lights the only thing illuminating the bakery while Ruby added more Bailey's to her coffee, giggling at something her friends said while they topped up their White Russians and Cosmopolitans and Irish Coffees. She quickly checked her phone for a response from Colton to her last text but put it away when she saw the blank screen.

She tried not to let it bother her it'd been a few hours and it was the time of night when people generally ate dinner, especially if that dinner was part of a date. They weren't technically together — he could do what he wanted and didn't owe her anything. She took a sip of her coffee, catching the end of a dad joke from Penelope and smiling at the robust laughter coming from every side of the round table.

Olive loved to shut everything down in the shop and invite their old friend group — Anna, Penelope, Vivian, and Rory — for drinks in the warm back corner of the sitting area. Now that Ruby was back and the holidays were over, Olive was getting back to scheduling them regularly and invited her to the next one.

It was odd and refreshing hearing everyone talk about their lives — so much had changed, but they still got along as if nothing had. They'd stayed in loose contact over the years, between school and internships and out-of-state job placements, but somehow, all of them had landed right back where they started.

Ruby was the only one who questioned if she was ready for it.

"Yeah speaking of the Valentine's Day Festival, can you believe Macy actually asked my family for more free hot cider?" Penelope Willow shook her head, sipping her cocktail. "It's like, the audacity of that woman. She just expects the farm to give everything for free for every event she wants to host."

Olive shook her head. "She did the same to us — she asked my mom for free heart shaped treats."

"See, that's where working at the DIA comes in handy — she can't pilfer from an art museum," Vivian mused.

"Or a craft store," added Anna.

Rory laughed. "I'd love to see what she could come up with from the elementary school."

"Just wait, she'll enlist all the kids to make a paper chain or heart snowflakes," Ruby said, laughing.

She couldn't remember being this relaxed with anyone. Even in New York City, her friends were pavement-pounders, running to and from either one long-houred job or multiple low-paying ones, all to keep the roof over their heads and bare minimum food on the table. No one had time for relaxed drinks and small-town gossip; they were too busy surviving.

And it's not like the City has gossip. That was unique to small towns, and for once Ruby was grateful to be in Oak Valley where she could talk about something other than deadlines and dating.

But they'd already covered what movies they'd seen, what

books they'd read, what artist or poet deserved what award. Moving into town gossip, of course they'd have to touch on dating. As soon as Penelope mentioned a good first date she had, Ruby tensed. She wasn't ready to talk about Colton. Not with what they shared, not with the uncertainty of where it was going.

Olive also gave her input, talking about the lack of available, upwardly-mobile men in Oak Valley or any of the neighboring towns an hour in any direction. The girls nodded in agreement — it didn't matter the job he held, they just wanted to see some ambition. Goals, plans, good relationships with their moms and sisters. But the middle of nowhere tended to nurture some level of laziness.

Anna pursed her lips. "Maybe it's the dating apps."

Penelope shrugged. "Maybe. I met my good first date on the farm, he runs the cattle farm we buy stock from."

"Actually, you might be onto something," Olive said, mouth open. "I just realized my last good date was someone I met while sourcing new kitchen equipment."

"Oh, are you renovating?" Ruby asked.

Olive shrugged. "Not just yet, but we're trying to figure out how to better our brand and business, potentially expand."

"Olive, you know that's kind of my job, right? I'd be happy to help you out." Ruby smiled at her friend, a little surprised she wouldn't have just said something.

"Ugh, I know," her friend sighed. "Just between the bus, and your mom, and... Colton —" she side-eyed Ruby, "— I wasn't sure if you had enough time."

Ruby's face went hot, and she looked away from the shocked stares coming from the others. Their voices jumped over one another.

"Wait... Ruby, are you seeing Colton Taylor?"

"No way."

"How did that come about?"

She shrugged. "We're just... seeing how it goes."

"It has been ten years," Vivian said, pursing her lips.

"What's wrong, Anna?" Olive asked.

She kept staring at her drink.

A stone formed in Ruby's stomach. "Anna?"

Anna sighed. "I'm telling you this because I love you, but I've seen Cara around Colton... a lot, over the last ten years. Even last night, I was at Cheers, and she was kind of rubbing against him. I left with the friends I was with before I saw anything else."

The stone dropped, a wave rushing through her ears. Cara had always been that way with Colton, ever since middle school. It became worse once they started dating — Ruby had always chalked it up to Cara not getting what she wanted — but still. She thought back to the time she'd spent with the Colton, how they loved on each other the night he stayed in her bed.

But last night, Cara was with him at Cheers. Rubbing up on him, according to Anna.

After all this time, why *hadn't* he shut her down?

"I'm sorry, Ruby," Anna whispered.

She shook her head, wishing the tremors in her hands to stop. "No, no. It's okay. Some things never change. In any case —" Ruby cleared her throat and turned to Olive. "— let's set up a time to chat about the bakery. Macy has me working on the Valentine's Day Festival, and she linked me with Deborah from the Oak Valley Historical Society. And, you know, I still work part-time for the company I was at in the City where I manage TV and media clients."

"Oh, you might be too fancy for these parts now, Ruby!" Penelope laughed, and the other girls chimed in. They changed the topic to some new social media trend, and Ruby tried to follow along, their voices going in and out.

Maybe it was good she'd have to stay in Oak Valley while Colton left.

## 43

Colton looked at his phone, the airport calling for his gate to board. His heart hurt, seeing Ruby's name and responding to her text without any indication of where he was. He pocketed the device and looked around, more people boarding than he would've liked. At least he was in first class — when he spent his money, he liked to spend it on his family, his car, and travel — so he'd be able to stretch out a bit and catch some Z's before landing in San Francisco the next morning. Flight times were weird, and he was leaving the night before his interview and would stay in a hotel until his 5 a.m. report time to Pierre Hermé's kitchen.

Between dealing with the auto shop and his surprise for Katie, helping Ruby with the school bus and spending time with her, he hadn't had any time to practice in the kitchen. Maybe for the best, so he'd be raring to go once he saw the competition. He made his way onto the plane and found his seat, popping his carry-on into the overhead and taking his window seat, grateful he had the extra elbow room and champagne to calm his nerves. He never had nerves before a game, but this was different.

Everyone would know who he was and it'd be easy to be passed off as a fraud.

Colton popped in his Airpods, tapping on his river nature sounds. After his injury, one of his physical therapists had turned him onto the sounds during rehab. He'd carried it into his bedtime routine, and now couldn't sleep with it. Even that night at Ruby's had been difficult, despite being absolutely wiped. But he'd also wanted to savor every second he could with her, not knowing how it would end.

The flight attendants started closing up, the pilot making his announcement. No one had taken the seat beside him. Colton sent a little thank you out into the void, closing his eyes and settling in. The plane started rolling, and Colton concentrated on the vibrations as they took off.

The rest of the six-hour flight from east coast to west went in a blur, Colton waking as the plane landed. Bleary-eyed, he looked around the plane, the sound of passengers already unclipping their seatbelts. He fucking hated this time change. A six-hour flight and arriving three hours after his plane took off always messed with his schedule. His phone said it was almost 1 a.m. A missed phone call from Katie, a 'safe travels' text from his mom, nothing from Ruby.

Fine. That was fine. Given the time change, maybe she was out with friends. Or having dinner with her mom. Or out with... No. Colton shook his head, anxious to get off the plane. He wouldn't allow himself to think of her out with another guy. Wouldn't allow himself to think of her dressed up, laughing at something he said, a glint in her eyes while they gazed at each other over the dim light of a candle. Of course she'd be glowing fucking gold in that low light, like the goddess he knew she was.

Colton threw his bag over his shoulder, almost knocking someone behind him. He didn't give a shit. He couldn't stop his mind racing with thoughts of her with someone else.

And he hated it.

Maybe he couldn't run anymore, but he sure as fuck could speed-walk. And that's just what he did as he made his way into the brisk San Francisco air. He found his Uber and gave the address of a small boutique hotel he'd found close to the kitchen. He watched the dark waves of the San Francisco bay roll beneath the full moon as they made their way up the 101 to the Mission District. The driver turned down several side streets, the famed murals popping up in flashes beneath the street lamps, before he stopped in front of the Parker Guest House.

He got out, adoring the yellow paint that must be soft and bright in daytime, a garage nestled between the two guesthouses turned into bedrooms. While Colton would've preferred something a bit more large, a place easy to disappear among other vintage celebrities and unidentifiable tech tycoons, the privacy this place afforded might work. So long as he kept on his baseball cap and sunglasses, at least during the day.

Walking up the steps, he slowly pushed open the front door. Colton had called ahead to tell them about his late arrival, and a young woman put her book down when he walked up to the reception desk. She checked him in, giving the occasional batted eyelash and shy smile, before sending him on his way. The house was just that — an old house, with hardwood floors and a staircase that creaked under his weight. Opening the door to his room, he was greeted with soft carpet and a king-size bed.

Ruby.

He immediately regretted not inviting her on the trip, despite the entire reason he was even going. Having a deluxe hotel room and a that bed all to caress her body and make her feel every ounce of pleasure he could give her...

He filed it away. He could always take her on a nice trip to New York City, put them up for a night or two in the fanciest hotel he could find. She deserved that. But first, shower time.

Before he went to sleep, Colton still hadn't received a message from her. He tried not to think about what it meant, especially as the clock dwindled until his alarm would go off.

When he woke, there was still no text.

He couldn't let his bad mood — or his three hours of sleep — ruin what slim chance he had of getting this job. And the little voice in his head asking if he even still wanted the job could just shut right the fuck up. Colton pulled on a pair of comfortable grey slacks, a black button down that he'd bought designer and had tailored, and made sure his apron from the bakery back home was folded in his bag. He didn't care about getting flour or butter on his clothes, but he needed a piece of his mom with him.

Looking around room one last time, he made sure he had everything and was disappointed he couldn't stay even one more night, just to get away. Maybe watch some bad television, order all the room service. And he was even more disappointed he didn't have someone to share that with.

Colton sighed, shutting the door and creaking his way down the old staircase to check out. He adjusted his hat, sunglasses, avoiding the stares from a couple guys while their girlfriends chatted to one another. A car was waiting for him outside, the sun just starting to peek above the horizon and cast everything in a cold orange and pink glow. The murals on the way to the kitchen danced in purple shadows, breakfast and coffee shops opening for the day. It was cute.

But it wasn't Oak Valley.

The thought hit him as they pulled up outside Sucre, the new pastry shop owned by world-renowned pastry chef, Pierre Hermé. A skinny man and a small woman knocked on the door, and Annette let them in. Colton could think about Oak Valley, Ruby, after he gave his all to this. He followed his competition, and Annette gave him a big smile when she opened the door.

"So glad to see you, Mr. Taylor. Please, come with me."

She led him past rows of glass display cases with dark wood stands, almost like this was a high-end, vintage jewelry shop instead. The white walls and There were few tables lined against the walls, plenty of space between each one for comfort and privacy. The white walls were covered in mirrors, the floor dark slate. Everything had a sense of gold dust on it, a slight shimmer. Colton looked up at the ceiling, an intricate mural that belonged in Versailles adorning it. Annette pushed the door into the kitchen, and Colton stood before four other contestants, Julien, and his idol.

Julien and Pierre both shook his hand and gave small smiles.

"Thank you for joining us today, Mr. Taylor," Pierre said, his accent thick. "You may stand beside the others."

When Colton was in line, Pierre stood before them, framed by Annette and Julien. "Welcome, everyone. Today the five of you will work in the kitchen on a series of tasks — some individually, some together — to determine which three of you will get a permanent, full-time position under my instruction here at Sucre. You may put on your aprons and will have access to the commercial fridge, freezer, and supply closet. Please make your flavors your own when possible. The first task will be to make three sets of twelve macarons, each set a different flavor combination. Second, six eclairs, and lastly, three identical mini tarts. I do not care which of these you partner up on, but you must partner on one task. Because there is an odd number of you, Julien will team up with the remaining chef. You have until end of day to complete your tasks, in any order. Please let us know when you are done with each task."

Pierre turned on his heel and left while Annette went over where everything was located. Colton was only half paying attention, trying to determine which task he'd pair up on and which of the four people would be his best bet. They started donning their aprons, and he decided to start on the tarts first while he watched his teammates, settling on the macarons as his team task. He slipped his apron on, catching a whiff of home, and got to work.

He settled into a rhythm, creating mini lemon tarts with white chocolate meringue and a dusting of mixed nuts. Annette put them inside in a temperature-controlled case by his work station, giving him the go ahead to move on. Pierre occasionally walked around the room, silently watching. Keeping an eye on those around him, Colton settled on asking the guy who he'd seen walk in to work on the macarons together.

Adam was tall but skinny and came with a southern drawl. Texas, maybe Louisiana based on the way he said 'sugar'. Since they needed a total of six macaron flavors, they agreed on raspberry and hibiscus, raspberry and honey, chocolate and earl grey, chocolate and chai, rose cardamom and pistachio, and orange and pistachio. That way they could make double the cookies and just change out the creme center, saving time. They decided to triple the cookie dough to account for mess-ups and tastings. They moved efficiently and worked well together, almost like they were on the same wavelength. It was a feeling Colton had never experienced in the kitchen before — he'd never baked anything with another person before. At least not since he was a kid and his mom showed him how. But this unspoken choreography was something athletes talked about, how finding that kitchen partner was a special feat. They busted the macarons out, and Annette put their finished products in their respective cases.

Colton took a breath, wiping sweat from his forehead with his arm. The small woman who he'd seen come in was young and running around like a little rabbit, here one moment and over there the next. A third player, a middle-aged Black woman, had a smile on her face while she casually checked her oven.

And the fourth was an older Middle Eastern man, his face stoic while he bounced from one bowl to another. Adam had started his tarts, working just as efficiently alone as he had with Colton. He made a mental note to connect with him outside of this, in case they didn't end up in the same place.

It was time to start his eclairs. Almond choux pastry with a black currant filling. It was a flavor combination he'd only played with once, years ago. He recalled his mom's notes on the flavor strengths and tried to adjust accordingly, so one didn't overpower the other. Sweat ripped down his spine as he piped the pastry, waiting for them to finish in the oven and then to cool. He had no idea how long it'd been or how much time was left, only that it had been hours. His knee was starting to twinge, his back getting stiff. Filling the pastry with the filling, he had to keep breaking to steady his hands.

This was not the kitchen work he was used to.

When his pastries were done, Annette put them in his case. She went around to the other chefs, putting away the last of their treats or speaking to them in a hushed voice. Julien brought stools over to each work station, and Colton sank into its metal seat, grateful for the relief. Adam, also done, took his seat and looked as bad as Colton felt. They exchanged small smiles, the black woman also sitting and resting her head on the table in front of her.

Annette went to the front of the room. "Fifteen minutes chefs, and then we will critique your creations and announce who will be offered the positions."

Colton's travel the night before and the three hours of sleep met with the long day on his feet, and he took a page out of the woman's book, resting his head on the cool stainless-steel table. His nap didn't last nearly as long as he wanted, thanks to Annette and Julien rustling in the cases and putting the finished items on the tables in front of the chefs.

He was up first.

Pierre, Annette, and Julien took bites from each task before Pierre spoke, his eyes piercing Colton's.

"It was a pleasure watching you work in the kitchen, Mr. Taylor. You moved efficiently and worked well with your fellow chef. Communication and attention to detail was not overlooked by speed. I was most impressed with the decision to triple the macaron batter to ensure extras. As for your flavors. The tart was well-executed, although I would've liked a little less meringue. There was white chocolate in there, yes? Okay, a nice way to offset the acid but just a touch too much. Each of your macaron combinations were impeccable. And the eclairs... Quite frankly, Mr. Taylor, I've never had anything like it. The black currant had the perfect bite and sweetness to cut the almond, while still allowing the depth of the almond to highlight the fruit. The pastry was light and full, and there was the perfect amount of filling." Without so much as a smile, Pierre walked on to Adam.

Colton was reeling from what he said and unable to listen to what Pierre told his fellow chefs. He might actually do it. He might actually be offered a dream job under his idol's tutelage. When the head chefs resumed their positions at the front of the room, he was only slightly prepared for Pierre's announcement.

"You all showed immense amount of skill and understanding of the work in being a pastry chef. However, we would like to extend the full-time positions to Mr. Adam Clarke, Mr. Colton Taylor, and Ms. Eliza Williams. Ms. Maria Petrov and Mr. Ali Khan, thank you for joining us and we do look forward to seeing what you do in the future."

Annette extended an arm and gently led the young woman and the Middle Eastern man from the room, while Julien went about cleaning the tables. Colton looked at Adam and Eliza, who were as stricken as he was. The announcement hit him square in the head, and the consequences: leaving Oak Valley, leaving his mom and sister, leaving Ruby. But also... working under a famed pastry chef, working *as* a pastry chef, following his dream. And, of course, leaving Oak Valley.

This is what he'd dreamed about since he was young.

So why wasn't he crying and laughing with joy like his peers?

## 44

Beryl sat in the chair with the tubes attached, napping under a couple blankets, knitting needles still loosely held in her hands. Ruby considered moving them so they didn't fall, but didn't want to risk waking her mom up. They were on week eight of twelve in the first three-month chemo course. Only two more cycles before they could determine the next course of action. They spoke to the doctor before this session and Ruby didn't want to get her hopes up, but his language, his attitude, was better. The cancer had metastasized to her bones, but they caught it early and the doctor alluded to it receding, along with the cancerous cells in her mom's breast.

Ruby wasn't hopeful, but she wasn't not hopeful.

She opened her laptop, forcing herself to look at the unanswered emails. But first her texts. After Colton had taken awhile to respond, she waited until the following morning to respond to his text. But that was yesterday, and it'd been a full twenty-four hours.

Something was wrong, this wasn't like him.

But Ruby caught herself — did she really even know him? Sure, old Colton would've ben glued to his phone to respond to her. Even Colton three weeks ago was more like that. But whatever this Colton was doing had started after they'd slept together. Ruby's heart sank at the familiar realization that maybe this man she really like — especially after years of being a sought after, rich, play boy celebrity — had only wanted one thing from her.

Well, that was beyond disappointing. And when paired up with Cara's weird closeness to him, even after all these years... Ruby shuddered at the thought, her stomach roiling with nausea. Maybe she should get to those emails. She worked through the ones she could somewhat focus on, that were easy to swallow. A couple easy responses about deadlines for Rachel at Maven Media, a couple easy answers for some TV clients, and one very lengthy one from Macy about being two weeks out from the Valentine's Day Festival, complete with a checklist for Ruby's tasks over the remaining period. No mention of what Ruby had already gotten done — press releases in newspapers outside of the local gazette, a thirty second radio spot, the kissing country booths halfway built and ready to go. She was still hunting down kissing volunteers, but worse case she knew her friends would step in.

Ruby smiled at the thought. She'd been able to build real friendships after moving home. When she first moved to New York City, a boss she was friendly with had told her it was the busiest, loneliest city in the world. She hadn't wanted to believe it — how could a city so filled with magic be so lonely? — but that was almost entirely her experience. And it had become easy to settle into it, accept it for what it was.

But here? She'd finally found her tribe. A group of women she could laugh with, gossip with, who all supported and challenged one another. Hell, someone could make a movie or TV show from how perfect the dynamic was, and probably already had. And all it took was moving home.

Was she really ready to leave?

A tiny voice in her head argued she would always be ready to leave, if it meant following Colton. But Ruby had never been — nor wanted to be — the woman that followed a man. And if she was honest with herself, she would really hate to leave the new life she was building for herself here. That realization hurt, sending a sinking feeling through her body as Olive's name popped up on her screen as a phone call, and she answered it.

"Hey, babe! I was just thinking about you. How's the bakery?"

"Good! I was actually hoping maybe I could take you up on that offer for marketing the bakery. Or just some sort of business savvy plan to spruce things up."

Speaking of building a new life. "For sure. I'm with my mom right now but I could come by in a couple hours?"

"Oh, of course. Give your mom a hug for me. I'll see you in a bit. Thanks so much, Ruby."

They hung up and Ruby glanced at the time. Her mom's session was about over, and she caught the eye of a nurse in the corner. Ruby carefully grabbed the knitting needles from her mom, taking them and the yarn and placing them back in Beryl's purse. Her mom slowly opened her eyes, a small smile on her face.

"Hey, honey."

"Hi, mom." Ruby held her mom's hand, the skin translucent and crepey. The nurse finished unhooking her mom, letting them know they could take some time before leaving.

"Psh, I've spent enough time here. I want my bed," Beryl said, chuckling and moving to stand. Ruby helped her rise, handing her the cane just in case and throwing her bag and her mom's over her shoulder. They slowly made their way out of the clinic and to the car, taking care to pause for breath. Ruby helped her mom into the car before driving home, careful to avoid going too fast or hitting any potholes.

She managed to help her mom into bed, and she promptly fell asleep. Ruby left a note for her on the nightstand but knew her mom would sleep for the next three hours, at least. The treatments were definitely taking their toll on her — she was so thin, so pale, always tired and weak. But maybe if the cancer really was receding, they could lessen the dosage in her next cycle. Because Ruby had that sinking feeling there would be another cycle, if not two or three. She pulled the covers up around her mom before giving a soft kiss on her temple and creeping down the hall. They'd decided to move Beryl's room from the second floor to the first, close to Ruby's room, so she wouldn't have to deal with so many stairs and so Ruby was close by if Beryl needed anything.

Beryl hadn't said anything about Colton's car being in the driveway the morning after he stayed over, and hadn't hinted at them being too loud during the night. Ruby blushed at the thought as she started the drive into town.

It really was like being sixteen all over again, staying up late and sneaking around and filled with that youthful, naive hope.

That stupid hope.

She pulled into the bakery parking lot, scanning for his black sports car, releasing a sigh of relief when she didn't see it. She didn't think she could handle seeing his stupid face right now. Grabbing her laptop, she was tempted to walk through the back instead of walking all the way to the front, but their back door opened into the kitchen. No need to disturb whoever was back there and in the process, get herself covered in flour.

Olive was leaning against the counter when Ruby walked in, the sleigh bells at the top of the door announcing her arrival. The went up on Thanksgiving and didn't come down until Valentine's Day, and Ruby always figured they should just leave them up at that rate. But Olive had always insisted that taking them down made them special again when they went back up.

Ruby smiled at her friend, setting the computer down on the table in the back where they had their drinks the other night.

"Figured we could use some hot chocolate," Olive said, coming around the counter carrying two mugs topped with whipped cream and set them down.

Ruby licked some of the homemade whipped cream off the top, savoring the sweetness.

"So, tell me what's going on, Olive."

Her friend sighed and dramatically laid across the table. "I don't know, we just... we need something. New life breathed into this place."

"A—are you guys... you know, are you... okay?" Ruby eyed her friend, hating to talk about money but needing to fully know what she was working with and what the goals were.

Olive sat up and looked earnestly at Ruby. "Yeah, yeah. We're okay. We have noticed a slight drop in customers and we still make most of our money from catering and weddings. I just... I can kind of see the end and need to nip it in the bud now."

"And dreams of all dreams, where do you want the business to go? What do you want for it?"

"I want to expand. Maybe franchise."

Ruby nodded and pursed her lips, thinking. She opened her laptop and started making notes. "How do you handle holidays?"

"How do you mean?"

"How far in advance do you prepare, do you do any special promotions or creations, etc. Particularly in regards to the impending Valentine's Day."

"Not really, they tend to be the busiest season so all our focus goes to that." Olive sank down in her chair, an air of defeat around her. "And honestly, we're tapped on manpower."

Ruby looked at her friend. "Depending on what strategy I

devise, would you be able to hire a new person — even for a finite period of time — to just help bump sales?"

"Um," Olive bit her lower lip. "Yeah, I think depending on the length of time we could work something out."

"Okay great. I'm going to think on this, I may have some more questions but I think I have what I need."

Right then the kitchen door opened, and Colton sauntered out. His head was turned and he was laughing, yelling something back at whoever was in the kitchen. And when he turned around and saw Ruby, he stopped dead in his tracks.

It was unfair for him to look so good, his hair perfectly messy, button down pulling at his shoulders and at his chest, where the buttons met. The deep emerald worked flawlessly against his tan skin, the bulge of his forearms tight against the rolled-up sleeves. His black slacks hugged his tree-trunk thighs, the hard curve of his ass. Ruby gulped, not wanting to give him the satisfaction that her jaw was trying to drop. She couldn't remember the last time he dressed up, but he sure didn't look that *that* when he did.

"Hey, Ruby. I'm sorry I haven't texted you back, I —"

"Save it, Colton. It's fine."

Olive snuck behind Colton and went into the kitchen.

"No, it's not. I've been... running around, I can't tell you yet but—"

"Just stop okay? You don't owe me anything, it's fine if you're seeing someone else, but just... stop." She closed her laptop, more of a slam than she was hoping for, and put it back in her bag. She stood to leave and when she dared to glance at him, his face was a mix of shock and anger.

"Whoa, whoa, Ruby," he said, placing a hand on her arm. "For one thing, I have absolutely no interest in seeing anyone but you. For another, I really hope you wouldn't actually be okay with me seeing someone else, but the way you flippantly said that makes me think otherwise. And lastly, I have a really important errand to run — I'd love for you to join me, and I can tell you... everything."

He was pleading, in his tone and the way he looked at her, but Ruby was still pissed. If he cared so much about her, he would've texted her back in the last two days instead of essentially ghosting her. She took a deep breath and stood her ground, fighting the want to give leniency because this wasn't just some guy — this was Colton Taylor.

"Look. I know we're figuring this out, but I won't be made to feel like a hook-up. You started dropping off after we slept together, so I'd rather just stop it here if that's going to continue. And if you didn't mean for that to happen, fine. But actions speak louder than words — I need to see and feel it. So thanks for the invite, but I have other things to do."

She shook his hand off her arm and left, greedily taking in the fresh air. Being near him always intoxicated her, but she managed to think straight and tell him what she needed. If he didn't like that well... Okay. Too bad. She'd been okay without him before, she would be again. Hell, she'd probably have to be, given how swiftly her plans of traveling the country were going out the window, and still with no clear idea on what his plans were.

Ruby had tried to make plans for her life with Colton in mind, and that hadn't worked out. Now, trying it again, it was like deja vu.

She needed to focus on herself and however he fit into that, well... it would have to be enough.

## 45

Colton watched his spitfire leave, fighting the urge to chase after her. She'd laid the ground rules, set the boundary, and he wanted to respect that. If she needed to walk away, he'd let her.

That didn't mean he wouldn't find her later.

He ran his hand over his face, pressing his fingers into the bridge of his nose. He needed to do something to reiterate how he felt about her — not matter what happened with San Francisco, that would never change.

But first, he needed to finalize the sale with Mr. Denaube.

Colton had crashed at Dragan's since his flight got in late, and he walked back there to get his car. He was meeting the old man at his house on the other side of town, past the church where the Christmas Tree Lighting took place. Telling his mom about the job had been his first order of business, and while he drove to settle this next affair, he imagined how he'd tell Katie and the guys. And Ruby.

He still had to tell her, and while finding space for s converted school bus tiny home would be hard to find in San Francisco, he was sure they could make it work. If she wanted to at least.

Passing all the familiar shops on his way through town, a wave of sorrow passed over Colton. Traveling around the world had been one thing, but Oak Valley had always been home base. Even when he lived in Jersey, that penthouse had never been home. And now he'd be setting up shop across the country, working long hours and hard days. He realized he probably wouldn't get to come back except for holidays, if he even had time off.

He passed the giant tree, white lights still strung but not on. They usually weren't until it got dark, but the town liked to keep things festive as long as possible. Lamp posts had their holiday wreaths swapped out for red and pink tinsel hearts, the trees in the die walked still laced with their own lights. The slight covering of snow on the ground helped it feel festive, and he knew the Salvation Army collector would be ringing their bell until the Festival — just with a springy heart headband instead of a Santa hat.

He slowed down, looking for the long drive that Mr. Elio Denaube had marked as his house, complete with a Beware of Dog and Trespassers Will Be Shot sign. Colton found the drive and turned, curling through the woods before lighting upon a grand estate. Elio's family went way back in Oak Valley, and it was rumored his ancestors were some of the old French settlers that had claimed this spot as theirs. Colton wasn't sure what he did — he was more a town hermit than the involved type — but he knew Elio had something he wanted, needed.

The drive had been gravel, but the path winding through a wild, landscaped garden was paved in blue stone. The front exterior was old stone, with clear additions behind the facade. Colton tapped the lion head knocker against the large wood door and took a step back. A woman in all black opened the door, and it took Colton a moment to recognize Caleb's mom.

Her strawberry blond hair was pulled into a loose braid, a simple elegance to her he'd never seen.

"Colton! What a pleasant surprise."

"Hi, Mrs. Walsh. I wasn't expecting to see you," he chuckled as she let him into the grand foyer.

"You can place your shoes there, or use the booties over them." She pointed to a place for the shoes and where a box of blue shoe covers sat. "I'm Elio's house manager, he said he had an in-person meeting today but didn't give me a name. No one comes down the drive, so it's rare to have a visitor. Especially when it's my son's friend!" She rubbed his arm, and Colton could only answer with a weak smile. He didn't have the heart to tell her the status of his friendship with her son was in question.

"Wait here a moment." Mrs. Walsh took off down the center hallway before disappearing. Colton looked around. Everything was made out of stone, marble, or wood, with ceilings that had to be at least thirty feet in some placed. While the front of the house was clearly original, the rest of the house had been updated and added to over the years. The foyer had a large lantern chandelier, a staircase curving from one side of the room to the other. Beneath the second floor was a hallway down the center, with a hallway to the right and a wood paneled door to the left that almost disappeared into the wall.

Mrs. Walsh came back, waving her hand for Colton to follow her. The rest of the house — at least from what he saw — was less imposing and more cozy but bright, with plush Persian rugs lining the floors, soft light filtering through open doors and windows at the end of every hallway. The walls were bare except for antique mirrors that bounced the light, the wide hallways occasionally boasting beautiful restored antique cabinets and sideboards. She stopped in front of a door, gently knocking so it slowly opened. She pushed it all the way and led Colton into an office.

Mr. Denaube stood from behind a large desk that looked straight out of the 1950s, framed by built-in wood bookshelves spanning the wall behind him. Two mid-century modern, black leather chairs faced the desk, with a furry white rug — sheepskin? — laid beneath everything. No art adorned the white walls, but photos of family were littered everywhere, including ones that looked like Elio with a family. Colton had to keep his brow from furrowing — he'd never heard much of the Denaube clan, had never seen any kids or members with the last name about town. He'd always assumed it had just been Elio, the town hermit, who based off the entrance to his drive lived in a house falling down despite the rumors of old money. The patriarch took his time coming out from behind the desk, dressed in a suit but with the top two buttons of his shirt undone. For an eighty-something-year-old man, he moved like he was ten years younger and looked ten years younger than that. He held out a wrinkled hand. While it shook slightly, when Colton grasped it his grip was firm.

"A pleasure to meet you, Mr. Taylor." His blue eyes twinkled, white hair carefully combed back.

"Likewise, sir."

"Thank you, Carolyn." Mrs. Walsh smiled and left, closing the door behind her.

Elio waved at the seats in front of the desk, taking the chair behind it. Sitting, he folded his hands on top of the deck and regarded Colton.

"I must say, your sister is something." A smile played at the corners of his mouth.

"She sure is. She's busted her butt, she's really worked hard to get where she's at."

Elio smiled. "I appreciate a man that knows what language to use, but I'm not some uptight gent. Sometimes we work hard and get fucked, sometimes things work out. The main thing is to keep going."

"Ain't that the truth."

"I imagine you do know a bit about that. It's a hard lesson, but a necessary one."

Colton nodded. "As long as my family is taken care of, I can figure the rest out."

"A man after my own heart." Elio cleared his throat, shuffling some papers and pushing two documents bound in a plastic covers. "I had my lawyers draft a contract for the sale of the land — and a copy — please feel free to read it over or have an attorney read it over on your behalf."

"To be frank, Mr. Denaube, I need to finalize the purchase today."

He waved his hand and leaned back in his chair. "Whatever you need, I think you'll find the language reasonable and the sale fair. It's fairly straightforward, since you're buying it outright."

Colton nodded and started to read the paperwork. It was pretty straightforward — two million five for the five-acre lot in the heart of town, deposit of five hundred thousand now with the rest due upon signing and deed transfer. There were no variances or hiccups attached to the land — Katie would own everything.

"Seems fair to me." He opened his jacket, pulling out a pen and the cashier's check for two million and five hundred thousand dollars made out to Elio Denaube. He always thought it would hurt to spend that amount of money all at once, and while it definitely dipped into his savings, it felt good to do something for someone who deserved it. He passed the check and one of the signed contracts back to Elio, who presented him with the deed.

"You'll need to register the deed transfer yourself with the town, but since you were planning on putting it in her name you can do it all at once. She'll need to be present. Oh," he said, holding up a finger and opening a drawer. "One last thing."

Elio pushed a thin paper across the desk, and Colton realized it was a check.

A check written out to Katie for one hundred thousand dollars.

"I—We can't —"

"Please." He held up a hand, silencing Colton. "I've spent my life surrounded by stuff, money. And the rumors that come with it. I don't need public approval — how I spend my money is up to me. And — coming from the family I have and having raised four children — I know a good person with a great work ethic when I see one. And not only are you one such person, Mr. Taylor, but so is your sister. She may even have you beat." He winked at him before continuing. "Consider this a gift for her to really start her next venture. I won't hear anything more on the matter."

Elio stood and stuck out his hand. "A pleasure, Mr. Taylor. I do hope we meet again, and best of luck to you and Katherine. I look forward to giving her my business."

Colton stood and clasped his hand, giving him a firm shake. "Thank you, Mr. Denaube. I hope we have the pleasure again."

He gathered the documents and gave Elio a smile as he exited the room. Mrs. Walsh stood at the end of the hall, beaming, ready to lead him out.

Tapping the paper against his palm, he chewed the inside of his mouth.

If he was going to leave those he loved behind, he'd make sure they were taken care of. The giddiness rising inside him only reiterated that he did the right thing, that Katie would be okay if he wasn't here.

## 46

Ruby closed her laptop, still debating on whether she should reach out to Colton. He'd left voicemails apologizing, ones of him tone-deaf singing love songs, wildflower bunches on her porch for the last three mornings. She'd slowly started texting him back — but not regularly — not anxious to get wrapped up in some bullshit dating game.

But she was going to IKEA today and would like some company. His company.

Especially since it was the weekend, and Ruby stressed out anytime it was crowded while she shopped. She could use his strength, the way he made her laugh. He had an intensity about him, but he also knew how to make her feel calm. It was last minute so the chances of him going were slim, but when he responded he'd pick her up in half an hour, the seed of hope she'd secretly been harboring bloomed.

She fixed her hair, owning the curly mess. When she was younger, she hated how wild it was. She hated the freckles posting her fair skin, the gap between her front teeth begging to be teased. And they did, in school. It didn't help Ruby had been tall for her age and relatively thin. Until she was sixteen, she bordered on looking sickly even though it was just genetics and she ate everything in sight. But that hadn't stopped Colton from calling — and treating — her like a goddess. Over the years her body morphed. She remembered when she was twenty-five her metabolism slowing down almost out of nowhere, the soft curve of her belly now complimenting the width of her hips. Her legs were still long and lean, but toned from years of hiking through Manhattan and Brooklyn to save money on subway and bus fares. Ruby adjusted her simple black blouse, knowing the lacy sleeves probably wouldn't make an appearance unless she took her coat off. But the V-neck highlighted her ample cleavage, and she figured if she left her coat open it'd be a good tease for Colton.

The rumble of his car in the driveway sent her heart into overdrive, and she did one last check before leaving. She assumed her mom was sleeping, despite the low sounds of the TV coming from the room Beryl was sleeping in, so she sent a text letting her know where she was going. Colton smiled at her through the windshield, and when she opened the door there was a heart-shaped box of chocolates waiting for her in the seat.

"You know there's almost two weeks until Valentine's Day, right?" she asked, trying to mask a chuckle while she held the box on her lap, Colton navigating his way around the potholes in her driveway.

"Doesn't mean I can't start celebrating a bit sooner," he said, grabbing her hand and bringing it to his lips.

Ruby squeezed his hand. "I'm pretty sure you're supposed to ask someone to be your Valentine, not just assume."

"I was under the impression I had to ask on Valentine's Day. So I figured I'd start celebrating now to heighten my chances of getting an enthusiastic 'yes.'"

"Ah, so you don't want just any ol' yes?"

He scoffed and looked horrified. "Of course not. Not for as important a holiday as Valentine's Day."

Ruby laughed and rested her hand on his knee while he drove. Together, they'd been the most hopeless romantic couple — putting even classic rom-coms to shame with their ability to gift-give and compliment. But they'd never placed an emphasis on any singular holiday. Since the days of her youth, Ruby had never felt as compelled to celebrate any holiday with anyone, the way she had with Colton. Especially Valentine's Day, which she'd always somewhat considered as *his*.

"Well, thank you. You really didn't need to."

"I wanted to."

"Still." She looked at him, his strong profile. Cut jaw, broad shoulders, hair falling across his forehead. She giggled and pushed aside a stray lock

"What?" He turned to her, dimples on display, and Ruby could swear her panties melted.

"Nothing."

"You know it's going to be like, an hour drive, right? You might as well tell me."

"Nah, I'd rather sit with my secret knowledge and watch you sweat."

He rolled his eyes but the smile never left. "Have it your way, but the only way I'm sweating is if I have you in the backseat or if we're dancing so hard to music."

Ruby blushed. "I'll raincheck the backseat, and second the dancing."

Colton scrolled through his Spotify quickly and tapped on a playlist, setting his phone down and focusing on the road. Ruby watched him, and other than occasionally singing to a familiar song or playfully dancing to the ones she didn't know, they drove in relative silence. It was comfortable, and Ruby found herself glancing at him in awe. How they'd been able to be apart for ten years, having ended on not the best terms, and come back together again even better than before... It was one of those weird life happenings that made Ruby believe in magic. Like maybe, just maybe, everything had and would work out the way it was meant to.

He turned into the IKEA parking lot, slowly hunting for a space. Even though they had only just opened for the day, the place was crowded. Ruby spotted an empty place in a far corner, and Colton managed to speed his way there without hitting anyone.

"You know you drive like an absolute maniac?"

"You know I don't allow backseat driver in my car?" He unclipped his buckle and landed a kiss on her cheek. "Come on, sweet cheeks. Let's go shop for your bus."

Ruby grumbled as he exited, and she tried to fix herself before following. "It's just window shopping, I need to check measurements and prices. It's easier for me to see things in person than on a website."

"Okay, but lunch is on me and in the meantime, keep a detailed list of must-haves and maybes."

"Colt, everything's a maybe until I can measure it out."

He rolled his eyes, grabbing one of the large plastic bags held at the front. "Okay, but still. No need to argue. Even though you look adorable when you do." He winked at her and started following the arrows on the floor.

Patronizing asshole.

But Ruby smiled at his back, knowing he was teasing. Knowing that she didn't have to prove to him how strong or cute or funny she was. He saw and accepted her, and he always had. He started sitting down on every sofa he came across, looking like a little boy he was so excited.

"I fucking love IKEA," he said, grinning as he started on a second row of couches. "What kind of sofa are you looking for?"

"Small and narrow," she laughed. "Although I'm kind of hoping to find a sectional that could work. I figure since the kitchen will be next to the living area, I could put a short peninsula along the short side of the sofa. Here, hold this." She passed him one end of a tape measure and started measuring potential candidates, writing down names and sizing, before continuing on the path.

They occasionally point out various items, measure other ones, test out beds and chairs as they came to it. It was easy to dream of a real home instead of a tiny one, but Ruby glanced at every price tag before allowing herself to envision the item in her school bus or in a future house.

"Did your mom ever say anything? About my staying the night?" Colton asked, opening wardrobe and storage doors as he went.

Ruby shook her head. "Did yours say anything about you being gone?"

He shrugged. "I sometimes stay at Dragan's so as long as I touch base with my mom or Katie, no one really asks questions."

"A-and your dad?"

Ruby watched him, not sure if it was a topic to bring up. Colton stopped and met her stare. "We don't really talk like that." He cleared his throat. "How's your mom doing?"

Ruby sighed, grabbing a stuffed animal from the kid's section to hold while they made their way through the mini desks and bunk beds.

"She's okay. It sounds like the treatments are working, but not very fast. She'll probably need at least one more three-month cycle of chemo after this, if not two or three. We'll know more in about a month." Ruby fingered some bed spreads. She'd always wanted a family, and while she had started to feel the biological clock pressure a tad over the last year, it just now hit her how badly she wanted her kids to have a grandma. Her hand reached out to stabilize herself against a large wire bin filled with cute throw pillows.

## 47

"Ruby? You okay?" Colton watched her stumble, her breathing quicken. He tried to keep his voice strong, his hand firm but gentle on her arm. She nodded, but he didn't let go. He could only imagine what it would be like for her to watch her mom in so much pain, and not knowing how it would end.

Colton knelt to her eye level. "I know this is hard, I know this is scary. But if there's one thing I know about the Delacey women, it's that you guys are fighters. You're motherfucking bulls who don't stop until they get what they want. Your mom will be okay. And either way, you will be, too. That doesn't negate or invalidate how hard this is. And I'll always be there for you, in any way I possibly can." He knew it sounded a bit corny, but it was inspired by something his coach had told him shortly after Colton learned he would never play football again. And as much as that hurt to hear, it had been helpful for him. Maybe it would be for her.

"Even if I have to stay in Oak Valley?" It came as a whisper, and Colton hesitated. He'd known with her mom being so sick it was a possibility, but facing it hit him square in the chest.

But he nodded. "Oak Valley is home. So even if I get out and you stay, I'll be back. I promise."

Colton pulled her into a tight hug, unable to tell her about the job offer. Not now. Now wasn't right. He flexed his chest, his arms, trying to be a rock she could hold onto during the storm. Her arms snaked under his coat and around his waist, and she breathed deeply against him. He buried his face in her hair, relishing how the curls kissed his cheeks and surrounded him in brightness. She didn't cry, but he felt a few tears release on his soft tee. He rubbed her back with one hand and held her head with the other, his fingers slowly massaging her temple. He wanted to release every ounce of worry and tension she held. Ruby relaxed into him, and he held her for as long as he could, wanting to remember the way she fit him. Wanting her to feel that no matter what happened, everything would be okay so long as he was there.

When they finally parted, he brought his lips to hers in a gentle kiss.

"I've got you, Ruby Delacey. And that also includes providing you with Swedish meatballs and mashed potatoes, or anything else you desire."

That brought out a smile, and Ruby squeezed his arm. "You know what? I'm gonna let you." She set the stuffed elephant she'd been carrying around in the wire bin with the pillows, and grabbed his hand on her way to the food line.

They stood in silence except for placing their order, managing to grab a two-seater by the large windows overlooking New Jersey shopping strips.

"So," he began between bites of food. "You're thinking of staying in Oak Valley?"

Ruby pushed her mashed potatoes around. "Not so much a choice. If my mom needs me... my mom needs me. I left before because she was okay, but now she can barely move around the house without getting exhausted. And I know it'll get better, but if she needs another cycle, I — I need to be there."

He looked at her, her hazel eyes a yellow-green in the right from the windows. "I get that. If there's anything I can do to help, please don't hesitate to let me know."

"Okay, thanks. A—Are you still planning on leaving?"

It was his turn to push his food around. Colton couldn't lie to her, but now was definitely not the time to bring up San Francisco. They'd given him a week to accept or decline the offer, and while he'd talked to his mom as if he was taking it, there was still that nagging voice telling him it wasn't right.

So he was as honest as he could be.

"Yeah, I think so. At some point, anyway. But I'm not sure when, or how. I—I'm still thinking things over."

He shoveled meatballs and lingonberry sauce into his mouth, avoiding her gaze.

"I think Olive's looking to expand the bakery. Maybe... Maybe you could open your own shop, in a different town. Different state, even."

"Like, as an off-shoot of For Goodness Cakes?"

She shrugged and dug into her food. "Sure. Or even open your own spot."

"Ruby, I wouldn't even know where to start with something like that. Sure, once it was running, I could manage it. But it wouldn't make sense for someone like me to start their own business." Colton shook his head. Why did everyone want him to open his own shop? He tried to keep the frustration from his voice, but based off the set of her jaw and the rising color in her cheeks, he hadn't succeeded.

"It's just a suggestion, Colton," she gritted her teeth. "If you worked with For Goodness Cakes, they'd take care of all that starter stuff. If they franchised, you would. And at that point, maybe it'd be worth opening your own shop. You have the business and baking aspects down, everything else you can ask for help or hire people."

Hunger had left Colton's stomach, the food on his plate becoming nauseating. He didn't know how much longer he could put off telling her about San Francisco, even though he hadn't officially accepted. But it had to be the right time, and in the middle of IKEA after she had a slight breakdown about her mom followed by a tense convo on what his next plans were was not it. He took a deep breath, swallowing his pride.

"Okay. Okay, you're right. I'll keep it in mind. Are you ready to go look through the Marketplace?"

She cocked her head, surprise in her eyes. "Oh — Um, yeah. Sure, that sounds good. Here, I got these." She leaned over and picked up their food trays, giving Colton a nice eyeful of her cleavage. His cock immediately twitched, and as he watched her walk away, he tried to keep the thoughts of those hips around him from causing more damage he'd have trouble hiding. He adjusted his pants, annoyed that even after she irritated him he could still want to throw her on a surface and fuck her until she screamed his name. He rubbed his hand over his face.

"I'm sorry, did I do something?" Her voice was behind him, low in his ear, as she pressed her chest into his back.

She knew exactly what she was doing.

"Nope." Too husky. He cleared his throat. "All good. Shall we?"

He avoided looking at her, trying to think of all the boring things in IKEA. Which led to thinking about Ruby home, which led to thinking about taking her to bed. He sighed and switched tactics, thinking about owning a business. Okay, better.

When he did finally look at her, he could see she was torn between laughing at his reaction and wanting to tease him even more. He shook his head, placing a light hand on her arm and guiding her to the stairs.

"Come on, you brat. Let's go look at dishware."

Ruby threw back her head and laughed, the sound echoing in the large dining hall. It made him smile, and Colton wanted nothing more than give her everything she wanted.

## 48

IKEA had been fruitful, if not for actual items then for information. And not just for her bus — the time spent with Colton doing something a normal couple would do was refreshing, and she felt had brought them closer. Over the course of several hours, they'd goofed off, had a little tiff, and worked well together in measuring and envisioning interior designs for the bus. Looking over at him in the car, singing through a classic, while he drove them back to Oak Valley felt like a dream.

And — miracle of all miracles — he actually gave in a little and said he'd consider his own pastry shop. One thing about knowing someone from being kids was truly knowing their dreams, even if they'd forgotten them. And she'd known from their early conversations that Colton dreamed of opening his own bakery. But that had been so long ago, and then football happened, and then pressure from his dad doubled down.

But hey, at least he'd think on it. Ten years ago, he hadn't believed in himself enough to follow his dreams. He still didn't, at least not fully, but he was open to it. And that was something.

He pulled into her driveway, the car jostling no matter how slowly and carefully he went over and around the potholes. She tried not to laugh at his grimace — she knew it was a bit frustrating, especially with such a luxury car instead of her mom's older sedan — but Ruby thought it was a little funny he cared so much.

When he parked, she unbuckled but didn't move to get out, turning to him instead.

"Stay with me tonight, Colton."

He releases a slow breath before catching her eye. "Are you sure?"

"I wouldn't have said it if I wasn't."

Colton chuckled. "As you wish. You go on up, let me call my mom."

Ruby pecked his cheek and obeyed, trudging through the old snow up the slight hill to the front door. She took off her coat and tip-toed down the hallway. Her mom's door was shut, the TV still going. She knocked first and turned the knob, opening it slowly and calling fro her mom.

Beryl was buried under many blankets, remote in hand. Ruby froze but noticed the soft rise and fall of her chest. She crept over to the bedside and gently sat down, pushing a sweaty strand of hair from her mom's forehead. Her mom cracked her eyes and gave a pained smile.

"Hey, baby."

"Hey, mom."

"Everything okay?" Her voice was hoarse, and Ruby handed her the glass of water from her nightside. Beryl weakly pushed herself into a more seated position, Ruby fluffing the pillows behind her while she helped settle her mom.

"Yeah, everything's great. Colton drove me to IKEA, we just got back." Ruby winced at the use of Colton's name, knowing her mom wasn't his biggest fan. But she just pressed her lips together and gave a tight smile.

"That sounds nice. Want to do takeout tonight?"

"We were thinking pizza, but that might be hard for you."

Beryl managed a weak laugh. "Oh, they have soup. I'll have some pasta e fagioli, although it won't be as good as mine."

"Other people's food never is," Ruby chuckled. It was something Ruby had always said and her mom always denied, and it was nice to hear her mom play around despite looking so worn. "How are you feeling? Can I get you anything else?" She placed the back of her hand on her mom's forehead. No fever.

Beryl shook her head. "I'm okay, just tired and sore. Maybe some more water in a bit, but I'm enjoying just dozing. You'll let me know when the food gets here?"

"Of course."

"Thanks, Ruby. Tell Colton I say hello, and apologize to him for me I can't come out."

"I will, but no need to apologize," Ruby said, patting her mom's arm. She knew sometimes rubbing could make her feel nauseous, and she was sure if her mom was oscillating so fiercely between being hot and cold, and in pain, she probably didn't want to be hugged. Ruby closed the door softly behind her, hearing kitchen cabinets open and close.

"What're you looking for, Chef?" she teased when she entered the kitchen and he was rummaging through the fridge.

He whipped around. "I figured I could make dinner or something."

Ruby shook her head. "I'm too tired, let's just do take-out. I told my mom pizza and she asked for soup. Oh, and she says hello and sorry she can't come out."

"She shouldn't apologize, she's sick. Is there anything I can do?" He closed the doors, his bulging arms finally free from his winter coat.

Ruby licked her lips.

She wanted, needed, a distraction.

And the hunk of a man before her would do just the trick.

Ruby kept her eyes on the ground and walked toward him, taking her time, ensuring extra hip-popping along the way, before stopping right before him and lifting her to his. Her hands teased the waistband of his pants, her fingers walking up the center of his abs until she reached his neck.

The quickening rise and fall of his chest gave her all the information she needed, but the expanding ridge in his jeans didn't hurt. Ruby curled her fingers around his neck, lifting his chin up while she licked his neck, tasting every inch. She swirled her tongue around his earlobe, imagining it was his cock, and lightly pulled her teeth back down the column of his neck. He shuddered against her, his nipples hardening beneath his shirt. Ruby lifted a knee and pressed it gently but firmly against his growing dick, eliciting a moan from him that sent a wave crashing between her thighs.

Wrapping her fingers in his hair, she pulled his face down to hers.

"I need you to take me, Colton."

"Baby girl, when I'm done with you, I'm going to own you."

He growled before diving his mouth into hers, and desire swept through her to her core. His tongue was insistent, demanding, as he turned them around so she was against the fridge. He placed one hand on her chest and the other around her throat before taking a step back.

"Follow me."

The heat in his voice was enough to make Ruby drop to her knees and crawl after him as he led the way to her bedroom. Colton closed the door and knelt in front of her so they were eye level.

"You may need me to take you, Ruby, but I need you to know I am as much yours as you are mine. Do you understand?"

Ruby was in awe of the sheer power before her and could only nod. He radiated a force that could make her do anything he asked, and the way he looked at her with so much love only reinforced that. She would do anything he asked, purely because that love was there. And he knew that. He knew he didn't need to rely on power or strength, demands or insistence.

Colton pulled her up and slowly undressed her, removing her shirt and pants. Ruby's body shivered as the air met her bare skin, and he moved behind her. His cock rested in the cleft of her ass, his chest pressed against her back. He pushed her hair to one shoulder, leaving lazy kisses along her shoulders and collarbone. His fingers found their way beneath her bra strap, the band of her cheeky bottoms. Hi lips were hot with every kiss, his fingers cold with every movement as he peeled her panties off and pushed her straps off her shoulders.

"Leave your panties around your ankles," he murmured into her neck. Ruby's breath shook, her body trembling at the way he deftly unclipped her bra, letting it fall to the floor, his thick cock nestled between her but cheeks. Her breasts ached for his touch and, as if reading her mind, he grabbed them both and kneaded, grinding against her bottom. They filled his large hands, her nipples peaked as he pinched and pressed, and Ruby's head fell back on his shoulder.

If she died, she knew what heaven would be.

She relished in the way his mouth marked her, in the way his hands commanded her body, pushing her over the edge of the bed. She heard the slide of a zipper, a crinkling, the rip of a wrapper, her body tightening in anticipation.

## 49

"Take off your pants, Colton. I want to feel your legs against mine while you pound me."

Ruby's voice was muffled against the bed, but Colton followed her directions quickly. His jeans, underwear, and socks came off together and hit the floor, followed by the soft thump of his shirt. His heart was pounding at the view before him, perfect peach of an ass rising high into the air, begging for him to take her.

Colton sheathed his cock and ran his hands down her back, gripping her waist until she whimpered. He traveled to her hips, loving the way her lush body fit in his hands, the way when he squeezed her ass she pushed her hips back. Begging for more.

He slapped his hard cock against her cheeks, the thickness surprising even him. She was the only one who'd ever turned him on like this, the only one who ever made his body respond in such a primal way. He slipped the head of his length between her slick folds, enjoying her heat. He brought a palm down hard on one cheek, burning into his brain the way her back arched, hips pressing against him, her cries muffled. Massaging her ass, he pressed his tip into her core, slowing pulling out and pushing a little more in, out and more in, building a rhythm while she stretched around him. Colton held onto one hip, digging his nails into her skin while the other found a fistful of glorious red curls, making her arch even more. Her tight little waist highlighted the spread of her hips, his thick thighs beating against her lean ones with every thrust.

Her body quivered around him, her heat escalating and drawing him closer and closer. He knew how to read her body, knew every path he could take for every second leading up to the edge. Colton switched his hands, releasing the pull on her head and diving for her clit while he continued to rock her sweet cunt, his other hand marking her back.

By the end of tonight, he was going to own her body.

But in the morning, he would stop at nothing to own her heart.

Her muscles tightened around him, her panting becoming more frantic as she gasped for air, her body trembling beneath his ramming. He leaned over her, covering her body with his, and swept some of her honey with his fingers. He rubbed the hot cum on her clit, his fingers gliding across her sensitive bundle and causing her to tremble harder. She pressed further back onto him, her muscles tightening around him as she found her precipice and jumped, bringing him with her. The wave took over and Colton cried out her name, holding her hips tight against his while they pulsed as one.

This was what he missed. Not just the sex, but that kind of intimacy with another. With her. The kind where they knew everything about the other, and even through disagreements and long days, they could still move as one. Become one.

Colton sighed into her skin, holding her shaking body against him, sprinkling kisses across her scratched back as he pulled out and cleaned them both up.

Ruby fell in a heap on the bed, watching him as he moved about.

He pulled on his underwear and was about to hop into bed to cuddle her when she sat up and started dressing.

"No, we can't, Colton. We need to order food, I'm sure my mom's starving."

"But after we order?"

Ruby giggled. "Sure thing, teddy bear. But first: food."

"Fine, fine." He found his jeans at the foot of the bed and put them on, his shirt tossed across the room. Pulling out his wallet, he handed Ruby his credit card. "Go ahead and place the order, whatever you want. And some garlic knots. I'll be back with water."

Colton kissed the top of her head and shut the door behind him, careful of where he was stepping so as to not creak the floor more than necessary. Until he could prove to Ruby's mom he would take care of her, he felt like an intruder.

He pulled out his phone and saw a California number and one new voicemail. His heart raced. Maybe they changed their mind? He listened to it while filling to large glasses with water, his racing heart almost immediately dropping into the pit of his stomach.

Annette said they moved up their work timeline and needed a decision by tomorrow.

Colton pocketed his phone.

*In, out. In, out.*

Leaning his hands against the counter, bowing over the water glasses, his mind raced. This wasn't supposed to happen this way. None of it. He wasn't supposed to lose Ruby, and then his football career. He wasn't supposed to still love Ruby over the last ten years, or lose her again. Not so soon.

He was supposed to have more time.

He didn't know how he would tell her, but he did know he had to do it tonight.

But first, he was going to cuddle the fuck out of the love of his life. He was going to try and hold her in a way so she would know exactly how he felt, what she meant to him, even if he might end up breaking her heart.

## 50

Ruby took her and Colton's emptied plates and put them in the sink. When she turned around, Colton was leaning against the island, chewing the inside of his mouth and staring into space.

"You okay?" She leaned against the other side of the island, her stomach forming knots.

That was his *'I'm thinking something serious and need to say it'* face.

Although the old Colton would've carried it with him for days, Ruby was learning the new Colton was much more forthcoming.

"I —" He dropped his head, staring at the counter instead of her. "I need to tell you something. And I know I should've told you sooner. I thought I had more time to figure it out."

*Coward.*

Ruby tried to stifle the electricity zipping through her, the slight shake in her hands, the quickening of her breath. Her mind immediately flashed to Cara. But he mentioned time being a factor...

Her face blanched. "Colton, look at me."

He did, slowly.

"Is it what I think it is?" Her voice was shaking.

He cocked his head, worry spreading across his features. "Given how you look, I really don't think so? What do you think it is?" He started to walk toward her but she held up a hand.

"D—Does it have to do with... Cara?" Ruby could hardly get the name out, her throat tightening around each letter.

But the look of relief and confusion on his face was comforting, and he resumed trying to get to her, but Ruby took a step back. She needed to hear what he had to say.

"Cara? Absolutely not. Ruby, I've never been interested in Cara. I've never had a fling with her. I actually told her off at Cheers the other night. Why would you think it had to do with Cara?"

Ruby sat in his words for a moment, taking them in before shrugging. "I know you guys have been... close over the years and you mentioned time..."

Colton looked horrified and tried to reach for her again. She let him hold her arms, but she wasn't ready for a hug. And she couldn't meet his eyes. His announcement may not have to do with Cara, but it was still something big. Something that the pit in her stomach said was life-changing.

"Oh, Ruby. No, I know she hangs on me and flirts with me all the time but —"

"Years, Colton. Since we were fourteen. But go on."

"— but trust me, nothing happened. I've never been interested. Okay?" His finger tilted her head up, and she saw the truth.

Ruby nodded. "Okay. But you're still not in the clear. What's going on?"

Colton sighed and let her go. He paced the kitchen, running a hand through his hair. She crossed her arms over her chest, wishing she had a blanket fort before the battle started.

"I have a job offer in San Francisco under my idol, French chef Pierre Hermé."

Ruby shook her head, processing what he said. If he had an offer, that meant he applied and interviewed. But he never said anything about that. "I—I'm confused. How did... Why didn't you tell me?"

"Tell you? I'm telling you now."

This fucker was genuinely confused.

Frustration and anger seeped through her body. "No shit, Colton. But why didn't you tell me about the application? Or the interview? Because clearly you had to interview for it, and if it's your idol he must be pretty big. Which also — now, forgive me if I'm wrong but after listening to you talk about this shit for years — probably includes a kitchen interview."

She couldn't stop herself from gradually entering the Yelling Phase of arguing, but as soon as she said 'kitchen interview', it dawned on her. Her mouth dropped.

"That's where you were this week, wasn't it? When you disappeared for two days?"

He looked ashamed.

"Answer me."

"Yeah. It was." His admission was whispered. "I didn't say anything because I didn't think I'd get it, and I didn't want it to be a thing before it needed to be. But I did get it, and they originally gave me a week to sort it out but they left me a voicemail saying they needed to know by tomorrow."

Unbelievable. Ruby scoffed, chuckled, wanted to throw something and scream how much she hated him. She took a deep breath and tried to keep things calm. But as soon as she opened her mouth, that all went out the window.

"Great, so just pretend we're friends but then also fuck me, and then drop this huge bombshell? You've known about this for days, Colton. And you're telling me now? Because they changed their timeline? Were you ever going to tell me, or where you just going to ghost since you clearly had no problem doing it for the interview?"

"Ruby, I love you but we were seeing where things were going. This is exactly why I didn't want to tell you about the interview—" he waved his hands between them. "— This. We don't owe each other anything, and I thought I was making the right decision."

"'We don't owe each other anything?' Colton, we're only having this—" she mocked his hand wave, not having the bandwidth to address his paltry excuse of an 'I love you' and incredulous that he had the audacity to say what he said. "— because you hid things from me. You were dishonest, and you were dishonest about something that impacts me."

His jaw clenched, arms crossed over his chest making him seem bigger. An ego boost, and Ruby shook her head.

"We were supposed to see where things could go, that's all. We knew this might happen."

"That doesn't address the dishonesty, Colton. Why would you be dishonest?" Goddamn, her eyes tearing. "With me, of all people. Why would you do that?"

He softened, hurt lining his face before he looked at the ground and turned away. "I didn't think I'd get it, Ruby. Why would they want me, an ex-professional athlete with a fucked up knee and back, who's known for his anger issues? I applied because... why not? I wasn't doing anything else but working a job I loathe in a town I needed to escape. I didn't mean to hurt you. I just... didn't think I'd be good enough. But I was, for them. But I'm not for my dad and I know I'm not for you. I'm sorry I didn't tell you, Ruby."

"You have to go, Colt. You have to take the job." Fuck the tears. Fuck that she felt lied to and used, even if she knew the truth behind his words. But that didn't mean she deserved the level of disrespect he showed her, and if there was one thing Ruby had learned by dating fuck-boys in the city, it was how to let them go.

"I also think it best if you leave."

"Ruby — "

"Let me rephrase, Colton. You need to leave. Now. You were dishonest with me, and that is very disrespectful. So get out of my house. Please." She tacked on the 'please' because it was Colton who stood before her. Her first love, her only love. After all these years, he finally had a chance to follow his dream. He went about it the wrong way and made her feel like shit. But she wasn't going to stand between it and him. So she walked to the front door and grabbed his coat, standing with it hanging out of her hand until he slowly walked from the kitchen to join her. Ruby held it out but didn't look at him, and he didn't reach for it.

"Ruby, please."

"Please what, Colton?" She turned to him, tired of the bullshit. "What do you want? For me to not be mad at you? Are you kidding? You fucked this up. You want your dream job? Great — go get it, it's literally waiting for you. I know you say we don't owe each other anything, but given our history, I thought you would've at least been honest with me. Thanks for helping me with the bus and coming to IKEA with me, I wish you luck in your new venture." She shoved the coat into his chest.

"You wish me luck in my new venture? Ruby, seriously? What the fuck is that?"

"Colton." Ruby stepped closer to him, wanting to breath him in one last time. "We had one chance to see if what we had back then could work now. I thought ten years might be enough time. But clearly, this doesn't work. And given our history, I think it best if we don't stay in touch."

She left out the part of how much it hurt, being near him and not having him. How much it hurt that what they had maybe could've worked, if he hadn't lied. How much she still loved him, even after all these years. Maybe he would always be The One That Got Away, and she would find a way to make peace with that.

"One chance? I didn't know I was working with such a finite timeframe. Ruby, life is long and it's weird and I don't want to put any caps on who I love or for how long. But fine. If you want me gone, I'm gone. But know that I do love you. I did love you, all these years." Colton snatched the coat from her and opened the door, stepping onto the porch before looking back. "I wish you luck in your new venture, Ruby. Sounds like your marketing business is going to change Oak Valley for the better. I know you changed me."

And then he was gone. The slam of his car door and the gunning engine of his car barreling down the driveway was the last Ruby heard from him, and her heart ached with something she'd never felt before.

The finality of it all was overwhelming, and while in her heart she knew Colton would never do anything to purposefully hurt her, she knew she couldn't continue with a precedent of dishonesty.

But she also knew that if she couldn't get over Colton Taylor the first time, there was no way in hell she'd get over him this time.

## 51

*In, out.*

*In, out.*

These goddamn fucking potholes.

Colton was feeling so many things, but mostly anger. He'd call a gravel company tomorrow, Ruby and her mom couldn't continue driving this fucking shitty ass driveway. He knew he should've told her about San Francisco far sooner than he had, he'd felt that in his bones, but if he had, she would never have given them a chance.

And that's all he wanted.

Colton pulled over into the lot of the abandoned church a few roads down and screamed. He had never been good enough until he'd been great, and then he had lost it. And that mentality is exactly what landed him here, with the one thing he ever truly wanted.

His dad was right: he was never good enough. His coach was right: if he wasn't careful, he'd scorch all of his greatest opportunities. His mom was right: if he tried too hard, he'd fail — and that would test if he could stand back up. Katie was right: if he stayed so far inside himself, he'd lose Ruby.

He'd done it all, every single thing they'd warned him about.

When he finally stopped screaming into the void and his hand hurt from hitting the steering wheel, Colton's anger had turned into anguish. Grief. He blew his one chance with her, by trying not to blow it. And it was his own damn fault.

So he'd go to San Francisco. Getting as far away as possible from the one woman he ever loved was the only way he could move forward.

He sent a text to Dragan asking if he could come over, letting him know he'd had a night and could use a drink. Or a bottle.

The incoming text sent Colton back into overdrive. Who gave a fuck if it was nighttime and he was on back-country roads? He needed to feel the car swerving, dipping, as he drove into town. He needed to feel in control of something.

He plowed into Dragan's short driveway, slamming the brakes and barely stopped before hitting the rear of Dragan's used car. Leaving his coat in the car, Colton stomped his way up the stoop to the front door and rang the buzzer, which was immediately returned. It was just past dinnertime, and the sounds of laughing neighbors and the occasional barking dog followed him past the elevator and up the stairs.

Dragan lived on the top floor, his two-bedroom apartment occupying the right side while a second two-bedroom occupied the left. Everyone was right; it was past time for Colton to move out. To move on.

The door opened before he could knock, and he entered, shoving off his shoes and barely hearing Dragan over the heat rushing through his head.

"I could hear you a mile away man, you walk like an elephant," Dragan said, walking through the expansive living area to the small kitchen on the far wall. He opened a cupboard, pulling down two tumblers, a bottle of tequila, and a bottle of whiskey.

"I prefer the term ox, but whatever."

Dragan grunted in response, over-pouring both glasses and handing the one with tequila to Colton. His large friend clinked their glasses before moseying to the couch. Colton followed, grabbing both bottles as he went.

Once he was sitting, he didn't want to move.

He settled into Dragan's couch, a second-hand beat-up thing that wasn't as uncomfortable as Colton always expected it to be. One of the great things about his friend was his silence. There was never any expectation of conversation, and rarely was there any judgement on what was said. So Colton pounded his drink while Dragan sipped his, both men staring into space while Colton settled down. Just because he could be angry didn't mean he needed to be.

Dragan cleared his throat and re-poured both their drinks, and just as much. Another great thing about his best friend: he knew when it was time to get fucked up.

"I fucked things up with her."

Dragan continued staring into space but nodded.

"I got the job in San Francisco and told her. But since I hid everything from her, she thought it was a bit dishonest."

Dragan looked at him and raised an eyebrow. "A bit? This is Ruby we're talking about, right? Nothing's ever a bit with her." He chuckled.

"Fair point." Colton sipped his drink. "Do you think it was dishonest?"

"I definitely don't think it was honest. I think any woman would feel a little used, but especially given your history with Ruby, I see why she'd be hurt."

"Dude, she was pissed."

"Pissed? I see why she'd want to cut your dick off and feed it to you. But Colt, I've found people either act out of fear or out of love — she's probably scared. Weren't you?"

Colton scoffed. "Scared? Of being trapped in this town forever? Hell yeah."

"No, dipshit. Of losing her again."

"I mean," Colton said, taking another drink. "Of course. But we were just seeing how things played out, we weren't... together, you know?"

Dragan shook his head. "But weren't you? Haven't you always been?"

Colton stared at the worn coffee table, turning the glass in his hand. Given the way he still felt about her, had felt about her, after all these years said something. And based on her reaction tonight, Colton would bet money she was harboring similar feelings.

He downed his drink, the spice easier to take since he was halfway drunk, and banged the glass down on the table.

"It doesn't matter. I'm leaving for San Francisco, and she's staying here. We tried, but it didn't work out."

"If you say so."

"What the fuck's that supposed to mean?"

Dragan shrugged his wide shoulders and gently set his glass down. "If you really want to give up, that's on you. Personally, I think it's a mistake."

"That's rich, coming from you."

"Mine and June's... relationship... is different than yours and Ruby's."

"Yeah, you've never had the balls to try. I have — twice. You know what, thanks for the drinks, Dragan. I'm gonna call it, I'll catch you later."

He pushed past his friend, knowing he hit a nerve at the way Dragan clenched his jaw and didn't say anything after Colton forcefully opened the door and slammed it behind him. It was too late with Ruby — ten years wasn't enough to change things. Obviously, since he'd fucked it up both times. So he'd do something he hadn't done before, and he'd run. Far away. A new town, a new state, a new career. He didn't need this fucking town or the memories it held. He didn't need his bright-eyed red-head with a gap-toothed smile and a skin full of stars

No, not his.

Hadn't been his for over ten years, even if the last month made him feel otherwise.

It was too late.

Colton sat in his car, knowing he was just past the point of driving safely home, and called his sister, the only person who would pick him up without judgement.

## 52

Jesus Christ, Colton was a piece of work. Dragan knew he himself wasn't a walk in the park, but at least he could keep his anger in check.

He preferred a slight undertone of existential crisis, anyway.

But Colton knew how to dig, how to find the weak point and slice it like a jugular. Dragan had valid reasons for not risking things with June — their friendship was built on twenty-three years of late night talks, family fights, funerals, study sessions, and book sharing. Even mentioning his feelings for her could tear all that away, and Dragan would never be ready to lose it.

He grumbled, cleaning up the drinks mess, knowing Colton would regret his decision. It may take a week, or a few months, even a couple years. But just like how he was able to fill the void Ruby left with football and fame, even ten years later he came back.

Dragan knew he would again, but this time Ruby might not want it.

Peering out the street-facing windows, he saw Katie pick Colton up in the light of the street lamp. At least he had sense enough to not drive in the state he was in. Dragan had been worried about him driving even before he got there but mix that with alcohol and there was no telling what the damage would be. Katie peered up through the car window and gave a small smile before peeling off.

Well, he'd started the night off well so he might as well end it on the same note.

June responded quickly, saying she'd be over in ten. It helped she literally lived down the street and her grandparents were usually in bed right after dinner. Dragan finished tidying up, trying to ignore the welling in stomach, the anticipation of her coming here. He'd always been nervous around her, but over the last couple years it had intensified.

A knock at the door grounded him, if only for a moment, before he opened it to the beautiful blonde. June bounced into the room, kicking off her low heels and throwing her coat on the dingy armchair beside the couch and giving him a quick hug. He watched her, tight black jeans hugging her delicious curves, the silky black halter showing off her defined arms and back as she reached into his cupboard for the drink glasses he just put away. Her shirt lifted as she reached, displaying a sliver of smooth skin. Dragan averted his gaze, hoping his cheeks weren't as red as he felt.

"D—Do you need help with that?" He needed to pull himself together.

"Nah, I got it," she said, turning to him with a smile, her mission successful. June set the glasses on the counters and pulled down the whiskey, pouring a healthy amount into both tumblers. Handing one to him, her eyes pierced his, the greens dancing blue in the low light. She clinked her glass gently against his.

"To better Saturday night plans than going to Cheers."

That explained her outfit.

"To better plans, and better company." He gave a small smile back and took a sip, trying not to get lost in her eyes or the way her smiled warmed him from the inside out. His plans were sweaty, and he set the glass on the coffee table and sat on the far end of the couch, hoping she'd take the other end.

Eventually, he'd have to find a way to not have this reaction around her. Or maybe Archer would be right and he'd get so sick of it, he'd have to come clean to her.

But June didn't take the other end, instead curling up in the center. Not up against him, but close enough that when she relaxed into her position, her knee would definitely touch his.

"Colton just left." He swallowed and adjusted his pants, contemplating grabbing a throw from his bedroom. It was winter, and she was in a thin top. But she acted like she lived here sometimes and would probably grab one of his sweaters before he got the chance.

"Oh, really?" She pursed her lips, eyes wide and staring at him over the rim of her glass.

"Yeah, him and Ruby had a fall-out."

"Of course they did, I don't understand why they don't just fess up to being madly in love with each other," she said, chuckling. There was a nervous energy to it, and she adjusted how she sat.

Her knee rested against his.

"Basically what I said, but I guess he's taking a chef job in San Francisco."

Goosebumps were starting to erupt across her golden skin.

"Oh. Oh wow. She… She wouldn't go with him?" June cocked her head, and Dragan glanced at her chest, immediately returning her gaze when he noticed her nipples hard against the fabric.

Of course she wasn't wearing a bra.

"I'm gonna steal a sweatshirt, I'll be right back." June hopped up, setting her glass on the table as she pranced down the hall.

He didn't watch her leave, instead desperately trying to school his cock from jumping to attention and the images of June without a bra on. Or with one on. Frankly, it didn't matter to him, and that was part of the problem.

He heard her feet patter down the hall, and when she entered the room she had on his Will's Auto hoodie and a pair of wool socks in hand. The sweatshirt swallowed her, hitting her knees, and she pulled her curled hair into a ponytail. She'd left her red lipstick and cat eye liner on, giving him a seductive look as she put on the socks and took her spot.

A little closer this time.

"So Ruby wouldn't go to San Francisco with him?"

Dragan shrugged and stared at the blank TV in front of them. "He didn't say, only that she was staying in Oak Valley. I think her mom's pretty sick."

"Aw man, that's so sad," June said, anguish in her voice. That was one of his favorite things about her — she genuinely felt what others did and didn't hide it very well.

"I was thinking... Ruby's staying in Oak Valley, and Colt had mentioned she does marketing. Maybe she could help with the store?" He looked at June, who was staring off and nursing her drink.

"Yeah, maybe." She shrugged and looked at him, settling even closer, her arm was pressed against his, enveloping him in her vanilla scent. Dragan wanted to drink her in but could hardly breathe, needing her and not daring to risk a move.

"Wanna watch a movie?" she asked, casting a bright smile his way. As much as she empathized with everyone else's feelings, June was generally good at hiding her own. Dragan had learned her cues, when to push and when to go with her flow.

"Sure, what were you thinking?"

"There's a new horror movie out I'm dying to see, if you don't mind me hiding behind you." She laughed, pulling up his Netflix queue.

"Of course not." He gulped. "I'm going to get a blanket, need anything else while I'm up?"

"Nope, a blanket is perfect though." She looked up at him — he could swear the word adoringly would apply — and smiled.

Yeah, he definitely needed that blanket.

## 53

Olive sat across from Ruby at the back table in For Goodness Cakes. Ruby wanted to go over her publicity plan with her friend and called ahead to make sure Cheri Taylor wasn't working, or that Colton had no other reason to drop by.

He'd made it clear this was where they ended, and she drew the line.

Besides, he was leaving Oak Valley. It gave her a somewhat clean slate to finish building her life here, at least for the foreseeable future.

"Ruby?" Olive cleared her throat. "You good?"

"Yeah, why?"

Her friend chuckled. "I know you, and given your questions earlier, clearly something happened with Colt. So if you need someone to talk to, I'm here."

"Thanks but I'm good. Anyway," Ruby placed her laptop between them so they both could see the screen, where she had a slideshow presentation set up. "Here's what I was thinking, and obviously I can't promise results but I can promise I know what I'm doing and I have a lot of contacts. You create some sort of Valentine's Day dessert so we have pictures, and over the next few weeks I'll reach out to my contacts and try to hook you up with a feature in a wedding magazine. I'll work the traditional angle — press releases for events you work, features for magazines and websites," Ruby said, moving through the slideshow.

"But I have some things you could do to help bring people in. An easy one would be to find a space in here to put a photo wall — so when people do come in, they want to take a picture. You could even set up mini-layouts, where patrons can prop their awesome baked goods and take photos for them to share. If they tag you, obviously share. I checked out your socials, and they're good, though a bit inconsistent. It's also very static — all photos, and very few signs of people. I recommend having more life, plants or even a hand in the frame. Content can get up to 70% more engagement if you show a person. You could also consider having a baking show or giving baking tips. And for holidays, really come up with something special, if you're able."

Olive took over scrolling through the screen as a call came into Ruby's phone.

"One minute," she told her friend, answering the unknown number across the shop.

"Hello?"

"Hi, Ruby?"

"May I ask who's calling?"

"Oh, yeah! So sorry, this is June Beaumont," her voice chipper.

"Oh! Hi, how's it going?" Ruby remembered June was close with Dragan and therefore Colton, but had no idea why the sunny blonde would be calling.

"It's going. I saw Dragan the other night and he told me you worked in marketing, is that right?"

"Yeah, when I lived in New York City and up here I've picked up a couple local jobs. Is there something I can help with?"

Ruby caught the past-tense of her life in the City, but the pang of missing it wasn't as strong as it'd been.

June was quiet for a minute. "I hope so. I don't know what you charge, but as you probably know, my family runs The Little Prince Bookstore. I'm taking it over from my grandparents soon and want to revitalize it."

"I love The Little Prince. I'd love to give a free consultation, what's your schedule look like?"

Ruby vaguely remembered June's family owning the store, and her parents tragically dying when they were kids. She genuinely would love to help and while she didn't always want to give free consultations, she really wanted the bookstore to stick around. Plus, helping a fellow female business owner was what Maven Media had been founded on, and a principle engrained in Ruby from her time there. They swapped schedules and settled on a date, post-Valentine's Day Festival, and Ruby hung up.

Sitting down at the table, Olive was almost in tears.

"Oh no, is it bad?" Fear gripped Ruby — it couldn't be *that* bad, could it?

"Ruby... Are you kidding, this is amazing. Not only did I not think of those things that I can do, but there's no way I'd be able to have the reach you do. This could literally change our lives."

Ruby breathed a sigh of relief and laughed. "You scared me, Olive. And please, don't oversell. Let's just see how this goes, but it will help increase your visibility. Especially since I think both of us should work on distribution."

"What do you mean?"

"If you could sell your baked goods online — especially while simultaneously working weddings and having articles published about you — you'll have limited supply, high demand, and low overhead. You can charge what you want and have enough to expand."

"Oh my god."

Ruby smiled. "I know, right?"

"You're a genius, free hot chocolate from me for life!" Olive jumped up and started pouring their drinks.

"Right, because I don't already have that perk for being your friend?"

Olive laughed, and Ruby added her meeting with June to her calendar. She started researching and writing down initial ideas for the bookstore.

She could do this. She could work up here, in Oak Valley, while taking care of her mom and living on her own. Her bus was already laid out — she was taking care of plumbing and having solar installed that weekend. She could turn lemons into lemonade, and she could do it alone.

She certainly didn't need Colton Taylor to help.

## 54

Colton stepped out of the airport and into the crisp San Francisco air. A light breeze was rolling off the Bay and the sun was just starting to set.

Yeah, this beat Oak Valley any day.

He'd left two days after his fight with Ruby, saying goodbye to his friends and family before quickly dipping out. He didn't need to risk running into Ruby on the street or at the grocery store.

It helped his new job started tomorrow, evidence for everyone that he actually did have to leave town sooner rather than later. His dad wouldn't look him in the eye, and his mom had cried but with a smile on her face. He'd privately given Katie the paperwork for her new plot of land. Which she was pissed about and refused to do anything with it, citing how when she asked for help she didn't mean spend over two million dollars and put investment capital into it. But that was hers to do with what she willed — there was a relief in not being in control of her well-being, not when she had everything at her disposal.

No, this was good. This was right where he needed to be, and as his car drove him to his new, high-rise apartment, he was overcome with excitement. This was truly a new start. He didn't have team obligations, he didn't have to worry about making the hour and a half trip from his place in Englewood Cliffs to Oak Valley to see his family, he didn't have to worry about randomly running into Ruby on New York City streets.

The car stopped outside of Avalon Valley Apartments, the modern facade looking more like a hotel than an apartment building. Colton had managed to fit everything that mattered into one large suitcase and a carry-on, and he wheeled them into the lobby. The front desk security checked his ID and handed him two sets of keys, and he made his way to his old luxury lifestyle.

His two-bedroom apartment on the twentieth floor was an open-floor plan filled with large windows, brightly colored walls, and a washer and dryer in-unit. The kitchen was updated, white cabinets and stainless steel appliances. It was bright and welcoming and, with enough time, Colton could make it his home. He unpacked his suitcases, enjoying the navy blue on the master bedroom wall, and shoved the cases to the back of the walk-in closet before standing in the middle of the living room and looking around.

He wasn't ready for the quiet.

It'd been well over a year since he'd had that level of quiet where he lived. For two months before his injury, he'd been traveling with the team and staying in hotels, where it was almost always rowdy. Then his family's home, his mom humming in the kitchen or Katie-Cat yelling down the hallway, his dad stomping up the stairs.

He pushed missing the noises of comfort, familiarity, from his mind, asking Alexa to play music while he poked around the apartment. Might as well start to get familiar, even if the time change was starting to get to him. He checked his phone. 8 p.m.

here was... 11 p.m., plus travel. Colton sighed. Normally he'd go to Dragan's or...

Ruby.

*No. Don't think about her.*

Colton shook his head. Maybe it'd be worth taking a shower and getting to bed early. Pierre had said work started at 5 a.m. and ended at 6 p.m., with the weekend schedule being slightly different, with team rotations. But the first week was prep, to make sure every hire could fulfill their position. His knee twinged at the thought.

Yeah, there was a lot he needed to try and ignore.

Or forget.

He hopped in the shower, using his micro-fiber travel towel until he got around to buying new linens. He stared at the bed — at least the apartment came furnished, well worth the extra expense — but he was also missing bedding.

Fuck.

He wandered around, finding a throw blanket in the living room ottoman and taking that back to the bedroom. Turning off the music and adjusting the thermometer, he tried to sleep. Colton wasn't sure what time he passed out, but he knew he missed Oak Valley right before he did.

The alarm blared, waking him with a jolt. Sitting up, he looked around at the unfamiliar room, a thin blanket tossed to the sky. But being greeted with the silence that came after the alarm brought it all back. He'd made the move to San Francisco, and it was his first day at his new job.

And he was alone.

The thought followed him into his wake-up shower, when he opened the fridge and was disappointed, when he tried to figure out how to lock the door from the outside because the key was weird. He walked down the carpeted halls and was hit with the feeling that he was in a hotel, not an apartment, and wondered if he'd ever get to know his neighbors. Maybe he should host a house-warming.

Colton decided the twenty-minute walk to work could be good, breathing in the slightly chilly sea air rolling in from the Bay. There was a slight fog hanging in the air, the street lights illuminating it before the sunrise could. It was a pleasant walk, the buildings slowly going from modern to graffiti'd and mural-ed as he made his way back to the Sucre in the Mission District.

The door was locked and Julien opened it with a smile. Adam ran in behind Colton, and as soon as the door shut, Eliza pushed it open. They gave each other smiles and greetings, the nervous excitement of a first day sitting between them. Julien led them to the back, where Pierre and Annette were waiting.

"Good morning, everyone!"

"Good morning, Chef!"

"I will supply you with two chef uniforms to take home, but in the meantime you will find chef jackets in that cupboard —" he pointed to the far wall, "— please be sure to choose a cubby in that locker and make it yours. Annette and I will show you the morning prep, and then we will get started on croissants, brioche, chausson aux pommes, pain aux raisins, and abricots à l'anglaise."

The sous chefs picked their cubby and their jackets before scattering to the stainless steel work table. Colton felt a little out of place, accidentally bumping into a stack of mixing bowls and bumping his hip on a marble table he assumed was used for rolling out dough. Eliza and Adam seemed to be hitting it off, none of the friendship he'd had with Adam during the kitchen test coming through.

Pierre immediately went into instruction, moving quick and flipping between English and French. Annette and Julien brought out ingredients for the croissants, and they got to work while they and Pierre looked on. For the next breakfast dish, they swapped out the ingredients, and so on. Colton found his hands not rolling as tightly as they should, over- or under-sprinkling raisins, occasionally bumping into someone while they moved about. It got very hot, very fast. Sweat trickled down Colton's spine, his chest, he had to keep wiping his forehead with his sleeve to keep it from dripping.

And even after an hour lunch break at the sixth hour, his knee was killing him with a vengeance by hour eight.

By hour twelve, Colton was leaning against the table for support.

When they were finally released at 6 p.m., Colton was trying to use kitchen tables, shelves, carts, anything to get to his cubby and out the door. Eliza and Adam had left together, laughing, best buds. Annette and Julien had joined Pierre in a back office. Colton was left in the dark kitchen. Alone.

Again in the silence.

It was spacious and gray, metal and tile and cold despite the ovens being all day.

It was nothing like For Goodness Cakes.

As Colton hobbled out of the shop, his back starting to twinge from all the movement and standing and ways he tried to alleviate pressure from his knee, he tried not to think about if he made a huge mistake.

## 55

Ruby passed the length of red PEX tubing to Olive's older brother, Rhys, who was helping plumb her bus, Olive out picking up lunch for everyone. The other Dougherty boys, Finn and Kade, were setting up the water tanks with Mr. Dougherty, the grey tank being housed beneath the frame and the freshwater being plumbed inside Ruby's soon-to-be utility closet. The solar company she'd hired were affixing the panels to the roof as she sat on her plywood floor, listening to all the people helping with her project.

By the end of this weekend, her bus would have running water and electricity.

When she thought that, her heart swelled. It'd taken a lot of hours, a lot of manpower, but they did it. She'd pulled it off, and while she was confident she could've done it alone, it would've taken four times as long and there was something about knowing her home was built by people who cared that made her feel even more accomplished.

Even if most of the heavy lifting had been done by Colton, the last person she ever would have wanted touching her home, and exactly for this reason. Every time she saw the plywood floor or the exposed ceiling metal, she thought of him. Every time the back emergency door was open and a man leaned through with his arms on the floor ledge, she thought of him. When she eventually placed her IKEA order, she knew every time she saw the couch he sat on sitting in her living area, she'd think of him.

And that kind of fucking sucked.

"Pass me that fitting, would you?" Rhys nodded to a bag of gold circles, and Ruby handed one to him. Now that she'd decided to stay in Oak Valley — especially knowing Colton was gone and would hopefully stay gone — a sense of calm had settled over her. Like she could move on with her life, could start letting go who she'd been in New York City. And dating would probably be a good start. When they'd gotten to an appropriate adult age, Penelope had started saying, 'The best way to get over a guy was to get under another one.' Ruby never disagreed, but she rarely put it into practice. She preferred to be alone.

But getting over Colton again would take every trick in the book.

Rhys asked for another fitting, his blue eyes piercing hers, ruddy cheeks extra flushed with the cold and labor. He was pretty cute — she understood why all the girls in high school swooned — but messing with Olive's brothers was probably out of the question. Ruby didn't need the drama. But that didn't mean he didn't have friends…

Olive's car came down the driveway, and Ruby yelled out to the workers.

"Damn, you make quick work," Olive said, getting out of the car and passing out the boxes of ten pizzas and six dozen wings to the guys, who traipsed into the basement where Beryl insisted they set up several folding tables for lunch.

Olive turned to Ruby as they brought up the rear. "Are you going to live in your mom's driveway when it's done?"

"I'm not sure, actually. Probably depends on how she's feeling, or if I can buy land close by."

"That makes sense, although I'm sure your mom would love it if you lived literally next door."

"I mean, I would, too," Ruby said, smiling at the idea. "Maybe I can talk to Mr. and Mrs. Cunningham, see if they would be willing to part with some of the old Ryder Farm."

Olive pursed her lips and nodded. "Not a bad idea, Ruby. Not a bad idea."

The guys were already seated, a chair left empty for Ruby. But she made sure to plate a slice of cheese and deliver it to her mom's room, where Beryl was sitting up in bed with a smile. The color was starting to come back to her cheeks, despite looking like death for the past week or so.

"I could hear you guys hammering away or somethin', how's it coming?"

Ruby smiled. "Amazing. Sounds like they'll all be back tomorrow, so we may have to make room in the fridge for a fuckton of pizza tonight, but by end of day tomorrow I can technically register the bus as a motor home."

"I'm so proud of you, honey," Beryl said, looking Ruby in the eyes and grabbing her hand.

Ruby shook her head and chuckled. "It wasn't just me, Mom."

"That's part of the point. And not just for the bus."

"Not just the bus?"

Her mom laughed, causing her to have a small coughing fit. Ruby passed her the water on her nightstand, and she drank before continuing. "Oh, no. Honey, you left your life in New York City and moved into your childhood home. You re-dated your high school sweetheart and — while I don't really know what happened — he's not here today but you're still standing. You and I both know nothing would've kept him from helping today, especially with those fine Dougherty boys hanging around, which means it must've ended. But you're... okay. Even if you're sad, or hurt, you're okay. And I see what a beautiful, mature, ambitious woman you've become, something I didn't really have the chance to experience when you lived away. So yes, I'm proud of you, Ruby Delacey."

Ruby let the tears fall. She couldn't remember the last time someone had told her they were proud of her, and it was extra special coming from her mom. It'd been the two of them for as long as she could remember, and they weren't just mother-daughter. They were friends.

But her mom was right — she had done all those things. She pushed and stretched herself, she learned and grew and she'd never felt stronger or more capable than she did in that moment. She really could do anything she wanted, and she finally proved to herself she didn't need to do everything alone. She'd found the balance, and she'd found herself.

She leaned over and hugged her mom, careful not to squeeze too tight but still leaning into the type of hug only a mom could give.

"Go back to your party, I'm sure one of Olive's brothers would like to take you out.

Ruby laughed. "I'm not touching Olive's brothers, it's too messy."

"If you say so, but life's too short not to make out with a hottie," Beryl said shrugging. "Youth is wasted on the young."

Ruby shook her head, trying to ignore the pang that came with thinking of making out with a hottie other than Colton. But she'd gotten through it before, she could do it again. "I hope you enjoy the pizza, just text me if there's anything else I can get you."

She closed the door behind her and joined the raucous group in the basement, taking another look at the group. The solar guys were a touch too old for Ruby, two of them married. The brothers...

They weren't Colton.

It was as simple as that, and Ruby wondered how long it'd be before she could look at a guy and not think of that asshole.

## 56

The last week was nothing short of hell, and Colton found himself waking every morning wanting to die and coming back to the apartment feeling like he already had.

And it had nothing to do with Katie's constant reminders about the Valentine's Day Festival, now just days away, or how he hired a gravel company to smooth over Ruby's driveway and had heard nothing back. Not that he had expected to, not really. He thought it might have helped in smoothing things over, but he could only read her non-response as it hadn't done anything.

Although he could picture her getting pissed off, and that made him chuckle.

Colton hopped in the shower. Or, better yet, nearly dragged himself in and after a solid forty-five minutes, back out and onto his bed. He was in a state of his knee always hurting, his back twinging when he moved too fast. They were baking so many items at such a high speed, Colton forgot what it was like to love it.

But this was supposed to be his dream job, his new start.

His phone lit upon his nightstand, Katie's name on the screen. He answered it and mumbled a hello.

"Well, hello to you too, Mr. Sunshine," she laughed. "I take it the Hermes bag man is putting you to work?"

Colton didn't have the energy to laugh at her stupid joke, instead just sighing.

Katie dropped the playfulness from her voice. "Dude, what's going on?"

"Dude, I'm exhausted."

He heard her breathing on the other side, and what sounded like she was chewing her nail.

"Colton, you know it's okay if you're dream job ends up... not being your dream job, right?"

"What do you mean?"

"Well, I mean, life is long, right? So who said you have to pick one thing and stick to it? You're allowed to try new things and have them not work out. You're allowed to... fail."

He stared at the phone from his bed, head smashed into the pillow he ordered after his first day at work.

"Katie, I've been failing all my life."

She took so long to respond, he almost repeated himself. But making the admission once was hard enough, so he bit his tongue right as her sigh came through.

"But you haven't, Colton. Just because a job is beating you to death doesn't mean you failed — don't argue, I can hear it in your voice, you're miserable and you've been gone a week. It's okay to set the boundary that it's not working for you. You have other options."

"Is that what you did?" The words slipped out before he could stop them, immediately wishing he could take them back. His goddamn mouth.

"Actually, yeah. I gave Dad my two weeks yesterday. I'm not sure when or how I'll start what's next, but I have money saved. And money buys freedom, and I could use some of that right now."

Colton sat up, groaning as his back throbbed. "Wow, Katie-Cat. You did it. I—I know I don't say this often enough, but I'm proud of you. How'd the old man take it?"

Katie snorted. "He just about shit a brick. But I don't care, man. You and I both know I was going nowhere staying there. And — thanks to you — I can do what I want. So I'm looking for a cheap apartment and will figure out what's next. And Colt?"

"Yeah?"

"Thanks. That means a lot."

"Of course."

"Hey, Colt?"

He chuckled. "Yeah?"

"You know you have more than enough money to just... sit pretty for a bit right? You have plenty of money to buy your own shop and be your own boss, right? You have plenty of money — and support — to change your mind and fail and pick yourself back up and fail some more. And keep picking yourself up."

Colton sighed, his brain on overload.

"Okay, big broski. I know you're tired, I just needed to give my two-cents. Have sweet dreams, I love you. And I'm proud of you, too."

She hung up before Colton could respond, but her words rang in his ears.

She wasn't wrong. He knew he had plenty of money. He just also knew plenty of professional athletes — let alone ex-professional athletes — who had special talents for losing all their money very quickly. Colton had vowed he'd never be that guy, and he'd gone to great lengths to keep a steady income so he wouldn't have to touch his millions.

Until he spent some on Katie, and that had felt really fucking good. Especially knowing she took it and got herself out.

His phone buzzed with a text.

A link from Katie with flights from San Francisco to New York.

He might as well humor her.

Scrolling through, he could leave tomorrow morning. Hell, in a few hours.

Colton set the phone down. He'd been at his dream job for a week and felt like his body was going to disintegrate. He'd lost his love of baking. He had no friends — and it was clear Adam hadn't known who Colton was before the kitchen test but had found out, and that fucking hipster said things that alluded to athletes being useless in the kitchen constantly — and was far from his family. As painful as it was, Colton missed Oak Valley.

And he hated himself for it, but knew he'd hate himself more for not going back.

## 57

Macy finished checking her itemized list for the Valentine's Day Festival, passing it off to Ruby. Some of the local businesses were making their own floats, so Macy and Ruby asked the police department to up their street presence and provide metal barriers so the crowd could watch safely. At the end of the route, they'd set up a stage for local bands and local businesses and artisans could rent tables for their wares. In the lot were the four Country Kissing Booths. Each booth represented a Valentine's Day tradition, with a man and woman in each who asked trivia on the subject. If the guesser guessed the right card, they could choose a chocolate candy or which person they wanted a kiss on the cheek from.

Macy had been right: this would be the biggest festival Oak Valley had ever seen. Ruby had managed to get several press releases published in larger newspapers, and Macy had been receiving emails all week from excited would-be patrons.

Ruby had also been receiving emails, from more businesses who wanted her services. She'd put some of them off until after the Festival but at the rate she was going, she'd have to decide if she wanted to continue her work at Maven Media. Even part-time, she was struggling to balance those clients with Macy, Olive, and June. While she'd lose out on that sweet paycheck, she also didn't have as many living expenses, and they were far cheaper than what they'd been in New York City.

It was just her mom's medical bills she was worried about.

"Okay, Ruby. I'll catch you later. Thanks again for your help and let me know when you've got confirmation from the vendors." Macy waved a gloved hand and left the old room in the Town Hall where they'd taken over and set up shop.

Ruby shuffled the papers and put them in her bag, pulling out her project list for Olive and her ideas list for June before heading out onto Center Street. The large tree to the left still had all the Christmas light on it, but Macy had gotten the crew to wrap red and gold tinsel around it as well. At night, the white lights illuminated bounced off the colors and cast everything within twenty feet in the most beautiful soft raspberry.

She tightened her scarf, turning right onto Main Street, actually excited for the Festival. The center main strip was covered in decorations, from the sidewalk trees and bushes to the window paintings on the shops done by artists in the middle and high schools. Ruby waved to Marco Romano, The Crispy Crust pizzeria owner who had emailed her for help, and passed Cheers and Beers next door. Ruby was blissed out at how everything was working out, she almost fell to the ground when she bumped into someone.

They caught each other, rucking out sorry's and excuse me's before realizing who the other was.

"Ruby! Oh my god, I'm so sorry."

"Katie! No, no, *I'm* sorry. I totally wasn't looking where I was going."

She laughed, and Ruby's heart sank at how reminiscent of Colton's it was. "H—how are you? How's... the family?

*Slick, Ruby. Real slick.*

Katie gave her a knowing look. "You know, you can just ask. And he's good, he actually came back yesterday. Things are good, I actually left the shop and am contemplating opening my own." She shrugged, passing off everything she said.

Ruby was still reeling from what she started with. "He's back? Like, for good?"

"Oh yeah, way for good. He may actually have to go back to physical therapy. And, you know, he actually admitted to missing it here," Katie said with a shake of her head and a laugh. "But how are you doing? Are you settling in okay to moving back here?"

"Physical therapy?" Ruby could barely keep track of what Katie was saying. "Wait, he actually said he missed it here?" She needed to clean out her ears or Katie was lying out her ass or something. There's no way in hell Colton got out just to come back, not of his own decision.

Katie just paused her lips and nodded. "Yeah, the long hours at the pastry shop fucked up his knee a bit. But he actually managed to steal the apartment across from Dragan, I think he's signing the lease right now at Robertson's. I was going to meet him for pizza, he's been shitting on San Fran's garlic knots for the last week."

"Ruby."

Her breath caught, and she hesitated to turn around. And when she did, she was both glad and hated herself. She hated how good he looked beneath the bright blue sky. She hated how his tailored coat still showed off his bulging biceps and tapered waist. She hated how he looked at her like he missed her.

No. He couldn't lie, and then leave, and get her driveway re-graveled — because she knew it was fucking him, probably because it drove him crazy he had to baby his car when he came over — and he sure as fuck couldn't come back and say her name like he owned her.

It didn't work like that.

She didn't work like.

Ruby stood her ground, standing taller and keeping her face straight. "Colton."

He fucking smirked, and those dimples nearly undid her.

Ruby turned to Katie before he could see the blush in her cheeks. "It was so nice to see you, Katie. I'll catch you around."

She pushed straight through them, stopping herself from breathing deeply as she brushed against Colton. But that didn't stop her from catching a whiff of his earthy scent, and instead of the hint of grease she could usually catch, there was just him. His sweat, his musk. The scent that

covered him after he helped her with the bus. The scent that covered her after they made love.

Ruby refused to look back as she walked away.

If she did, she knew she'd find a way to forgive him.

## 58

He watched her walk away, begging her to turn around. To give him a sign it wasn't too late. She didn't, but he refused to accept that.

"Yo, Romeo. Earth to Romeo."

He turned toward his sister, rolling his eyes and walking back towards Robertson Realty.

"You know she's still in love with you, right?"

Colton shrugged, setting his jaw and hoping Katie got the picture.

He didn't need her as much as she didn't need him.

"And you're still in love with her too, so..."

He stopped short and turned to her. "So... What? What, Katie?"

"Jesus, you're a moron," Katie said. It was her turn to roll her eyes and she kept walking. "Win her back, before it's actually too late."

"I wouldn't know where to start, and I'm pretty sure it *is* too late."

"Colton, you're not the sharpest with women. Trust me, it's not. Do you want her? I need you to say it."

They stopped outside of the realty office door, and Colton faced his sister. Her big brown eyes, doe-like, like their mom's, stared up at him. Pleading.

He signed. "Of course I want her. She's the love of my life. I basically came back from California to get her back." He said it with a smile and opened the door, Katie laughing hysterically at the half truth. Yes, his dream job sucked ass and his body was basically dying because of it. Yes, he missed Oak Valley. But he would've missed any town he left behind, if Ruby were there.

"So what are we doing here, Hoss?" Katie picked up a brochure with fancy houses on it and flipped through it.

"Liam works here, he helped me sign the lease on that apartment in town. And I bought a commercial kitchen space in Fox Hollow, so I'm only fifteen minutes away from you and mom. But I need your help on one last thing."

Katie stared at him, wide-eyed and mouth open. "Holy shit, Colt. You really went for it. What else do you want?"

"I want Ruby. I have a couple tricks up my sleeve, but I want your input. The biggest one... I want to buy Ruby some land for her bus."

Katie whistled and looked around the office. "Honestly, I think that's a great idea. But only if it's the perfect plot of land."

"Obviously."

"I think we should talk to Olive. Mr. Dougherty was at the shop yesterday and while he was waiting for his tire alignment, he mentioned to Mr. Cassick he was out at Ruby's working on a bus with his kids. Olive will have more info."

Colton led the way, a new spring in his step while he mulled what else he could do to win her back. Because he knew now, without a doubt, he could never go back to a life without her. He tried that, and after being with her again showed him how empty he'd been. He barged into the bakery, Olive jumping two feet behind the counter.

"Jesus Christ, Colton."

"I have questions."

"Jeez, say it again, I can't wait to help you." She shook her head, short hair swinging as she pounded some keys on the tablet register. "What do you want?"

"Colton's in love and he needs your help!" Katie piped up, grabbing a cookie from the New Flavor plate.

"Shut up, I'm not." But his face heated. Olive had one eyebrow raised and half a smile. "Okay. Fine. I'm in love with Ruby. I need her. I want to win her back. I don't care what it takes, but you're her best friend. And I know we've always been friendly, Olive."

"Would you help this poor sucker out?" Katie asked, grabbing another cookie. Cranberry Maple, read the card. Colton filed it away for his shop.

*His shop.*

He was finally making all his dreams come true — he didn't need anyone.

Except Olive. He needed Olive for his last dream.

She was chewing her lower lip and tapping her fingers on the counter. "You don't care what it is?"

"Nope."

"I have some heavy-hitters. Like, really heavy."

"Olive —" he started to lower onto his knees. "I will literally beg you."

"Hold out a little longer, Olive, I need to see him do this," Katie cackled.

Olive shook her head, smiling. "Stand up, you fool. Okay. Here's what I know. Do with it what you will."

Colton listened intently as she told him about Ruby maybe talking to the Mr. and Mrs. Cunningham about selling some of their farmland since it was next to her mom's. She told him about the medical bills, how Ruby mentioned leaving Maven

Media once she had paid more of them down and had more clients. And she told him how excited Ruby was for the Valentine's Day Festival, even if she was sad about not having a Valentine — because this year, she thought she'd have her favorite one.

Katie looked at him when Olive was done, a wide grin on her face.

"I think we know what to do. Thanks, Olive."

"Don't you dare hurt her again, Colton. I'm only helping you this one time because I think you guys belong together, now. It's your time."

"I know it. Don't worry, Olive. She's my girl."

He left, Katie close on his heels, knowing exactly how to make Ruby Delacey his Valentine forever.

## 59

Ruby placed her massive IKEA order and carefully shut her laptop, breathing a huge sigh of relief at finishing one of the final pieces to her bus. All that was left was to install the kitchen cabinets and appliances, build the furniture, and move in. She was excited to do it herself, even if there was a piece of her that itched to call Colton, ask him to help.

He'd come back.

After only a week away, he'd come back.

And if the way he looked at her or said her name was any indication of how he felt, she knew a piece of him came back for her. But he needed to work a bit harder to show her, and she had yet to hear or see anything from him.

She carefully packed her mom's knitting into her bag, watching as the nurse unhooked her from the IV. Ruby helped her stand, handing Beryl her cane as they left the facility and walked to the car. Ruby had a lot to do, with the Festival in two days and a steady stream of businesses wanting to hire her. She was sure in large part because of the changes Olive had made to For Goodness Cakes, with the photo wall taking off faster than they thought and the social media videos steadily gaining steam. Being the small town that it was, Oak Valley businesses almost all followed one another on every platform they were on. Word spread fast, something Ruby used to find annoying.

Ruby started helping her mom into the car. She might be able to leave Maven Media by the end of the year, if not sooner, depending on the medical bills. She remembered her mom's manifesting books, how she'd managed to pull the bus together, and remembered that exact numbers were important.

"Hang on, Mom. I'll be right back." Ruby turned the car on and shut the door, running back to the receptionist.

"Excuse me, would you please tell me the balance on my mom's bills? Last name, D-E-L-A-C-E-Y, first name B-E-R-Y-L. Date of birth, December 28, 1969." She waited as the stoic woman scanned the computer screen.

"There is no balance, ma'am."

What?

"No balance?"

The woman's eyes scanned again, and she shook her head. "No balance. It looks like... An anonymous donor paid off the balance yesterday, and left an account number to run anytime a charge comes in." The woman looked at Ruby, betraying no emotion.

Ruby stared back, unsure of who it could be. Her mom was relatively beloved in the town — she worked at the library, organized events for kids, attended as many of the town festivals and showcases that she could. She always had a smile, always asked how people were and genuinely wanted the answer.

She knew the bills weren't as astronomical as some people — about $20,000 a month, and they were in month three, and that was including what had stacked up over the years for check-ups and tests — but for people like them, that was a lot of money to pay off. But if the town got together...

Or if one person with far too much money sitting in an account was trying to win her back.

Ruby sucked in a breath. "Are you sure it was one anonymous donor?"

"I don't know about one. There's just a note of an anonymous donation, paid in full yesterday, and an account number for future charges. I'm sorry, ma'am, that's all the information I have. I hope you have a wonderful rest of your day, this seems to be a tremendous good deed."

"Th—Thanks, you... you too." Ruby backed away slowly, walking in a stupor back to the car. When she climbed in, she could only stare at the steering wheel.

"What is it, honey?" Worry etched her mom's face, new wrinkles besides old friends grown deeper and ones from exhaustion.

"Mom..." Ruby turned to Beryl, still not sure how to tell her.

"Honey, you're scaring me."

"Someone paid off the bills."

"What?" Her brow furrowed.

"Someone... Someone paid off the bills. A—And they left an account number. So charges will go through that."

"I don't know what you're saying, Ruby."

Ruby stared at her beautiful mom, realization hitting her. She started laughing, crying, every emotion coming out from places she never knew existed. "Mom, an anonymous donor is taking care of all your medical bills. We... we don't have to worry about them anymore."

Ruby's head fell into her hands, and she sobbed with the relief of it all. For years, she'd worked multiple jobs to help her mom. And she would've done whatever needed to be done in order to continue doing so. But someone had answered her dreams.

And she was pretty sure who that someone was.

She could build the life she wanted, living in Oak Valley because she wanted to, not because she felt there was no choice. She could spend time with her mom instead of working multiple jobs. She could quit her job at Maven Media, focusing instead on the everyday people and businesses she grew up loving.

For the first time in her life, Ruby felt truly free.

## 60

Colton had implemented Mission Get Ruby Back, but now he was doing it mainly because he just enjoyed the feeling it brought him to treat the people in his life. And with Ruby, while he started with the driveway, he knew she needed more. She deserved more.

He set up an account with more than enough money, calling the clinic where Beryl's oncologist and treatments were, and arranged for everything to be taken care of. He didn't know how often Ruby checked the balance, but that was part of the fun. He never knew when she would find out, only that when she did, it would lighten the weight on her shoulders.

Up next: talk to the Cunningham's about their land, the old Ryder Farm.

He asked Dragan to drive, since his car was inconspicuous, Liam in the back seat as his real estate agent and Katie just along for the field trip. He found the Cunningham's number in the phone book at the Town Hall and called ahead, careful not to give all his cards away. They agreed to talk but had a hard edge in their voices.

They'd talk, but they wouldn't listen.

Dragan pulled into their driveway, and Colton could just peek Ruby's bus next door. It was now painted a soft butter yellow, the roof and windows trimmed in white. It was sweet, cozy. It made him smile to think of her living in a home she helped build, one that she could make all hers. She earned it, and she deserved it.

"You ready?" Katie patted his shoulder and got out, the guys following her. They walked up the grand white porch to the old farmhouse front door and knocked.

An old man opened the door. "'Ello?"

"Hi, Mr. Cunningham? Glenn Cunningham? It's me, Mr. Taylor. I called about wanting to speak with you and your wife?"

The man stared at him, shock of white hair standing in a ring around his head. "Oh, right!" He jolted back, and then opened the door more. "Please come. I see you brought company. Muriel's in the back sunroom, you can follow me."

Colton introduced the crew, and they followed his shuffle down a long hallway to the back. It was a beautiful house, if not needing a little TLC, but Colton appreciated the original hardwood floor and the high ceilings. Mr. Cunningham stopped before another door, slowly opening it into a back porch, entirely white and with glass walls. It almost didn't seem to fit with the rest of the house, even though Colton knew it was probably one of the more original and well-maintained aspects.

Mr. Cunningham sat in a white wicker armchair with a floral cushion beside Muriel, introducing them as they tried squeezing in on the matching loveseat across the way, with Dragon deciding to stand.

"Let's cut to the chase, what do you kids want?" Muriel asked, leaning back in her chair.

Colton cleared his throat. "I'm hoping to negotiate the sale of a parcel of your land. It doesn't have to be big, but it does have to abut the Delacey property. Name your price." He didn't expect they'd know who he was, but no amount of money was going to keep him from getting Ruby what she wanted.

The Cunningham's stared at him, glanced at the others, and then moved their gazes back to him.

"Could we have the room, please?" Glenn asked.

"Of course." They filed out, Dragan ducking his head at the threshold and Katie poking her head into several rooms with doors slightly ajar. Colton and Liam leaned against a wood-paneled wall, trying to figure out what their number would be, and for how many acres.

"You can come in," Muriel called through the closed door.

They filed back in and took their places.

"Ten acres, $749,000. It's mostly wooded, has river access in the back, and runs the length of the Delacey's lot. Final offer."

"As long as it all tracks, done. Liam here can represent both of us, if you agree, and get the paperwork started."

Muriel stuck out a hand, shaking Colton's and Liam's. "Wonderful. You bring us the papers when they're ready, we can have an attorney present to review. Hopefully we can sign on the spot."

Glenn stood, limping his way to lead them out. As they walked back to the car, Liam shook Colton's hand and chuckled. "Thanks, man. That was one of the easiest deals I've ever been a part of."

"My pleasure, thank *you*."

"Okay lovebirds, we get it. You guys both rock each other's socks off. Can we go get pizza? I'm starving," Katie said, sliding into the backseat.

They joked around on the ride back to town, but Colton wasn't concentrating. Tomorrow was the Festival, and his heart was ready to beat out of his chest. He had one more gift to pick up, and it felt the most important.

## 61

Ruby was running around the lot, checking in with the vendors and Kissing Booths. Everyone was running on fumes, despite the festival being a little halfway through. She looked up at the sky, thankful the weather had held during the day, even if the clouds moving in were starting to block the brilliant orange-pink sunset.

The next band was starting to set-up, and Macy was attempting to help them sound check. The parade had been a huge success, even though only six business had contributed a float. Given the interest from the businesses that hadn't participated, and the six already being more than they'd initially figured, they would have to make the route longer next year.

Because of course Macy had already started planning for next year's Festival while the current one was still going. And of course she needed her 'right-hand-wo-man' to help, as Macy called Ruby.

Ruby had been so busy running around, she hadn't had a chance to see if she recognized anyone. She thought at one point she'd seen Dragan — he was so fucking tall, he stood out like a sore thumb — but when she looked again, he was gone. Better that way. Where he was, Colton was likely to follow. And she didn't need his distraction, even if her body said otherwise.

Even if she wanted to ask about the medical bills.

"Ruby, did you do that pulse-check I asked you to do? How's everybody feelin'?" Macy popped up behind Ruby's right shoulder, sending her jumping.

"Yes, yes I did. Half the vendors will be running out of stock in a matter of minutes, but that may be best — we can reconfigure the space to be more of a sit and relax, buy food at any of the local restaurants and eat while you enjoy the show."

"Amazin', Oh, darlin', what would I do without you? You're a dream." Macy gave her a quick hug before darting back into the crowd, disappearing as quickly as she appeared. Macy had turned out not half-bad, becoming almost like a second mom or maybe a grandma, and Ruby felt a twinge at judging her so harshly when she first moved back.

"I don't know what I'd do without you, darlin'."

Ruby froze at the deep voice, husky and low in her ear. The rest of the world fell away as she tried to steady her breathing, trying to focus on his. She could sense the wide expanse of chest behind her back, without being pressed against it. But knowing it was there, her body needed it. Called to it. Craved it.

"Well —" her voice cracked, and she took a shaky breath. "You seemed to do just fine the last week or so."

"Turn around." Soft, but commanding, Ruby had no choice but to obey. She kept her eyes trained on his chest, basking in the power radiating from him. This was not the Colton that had left Oak Valley. That Colton had power, but it was untamed. It was wild, acting on impulse.

But this? This power was controlled. This power stalked, hunted, found its prey and played before devouring.

And Ruby was desperate to be devoured.

She slowly raised her eyes to meet his, her knees wobbly at

the way he looked at her. Hungry, but like he'd feed her first if she said the word.

"The last week or so, I had some things to sort out. But the ten years before that? That nearly killed me."

Ruby sucked in a breath, waiting for him to continue. He bent his face low to hers.

"I have a very important question, Ruby. It doesn't need an answer. Not now, not even anytime soon. Not ever, if that's what your heart desires. But I need you to know that everything I ever felt for you, from the time we were fourteen until the day I die, was true."

Ruby's whole body shook, from lust or fear, she couldn't tell. She didn't care. He was so close she could kiss him, and she started to lean forward. Just a taste...

Slowly, Colton started lowering himself to one knee.

## 62

Colton felt his knee shake the entire time he was lowering onto it, but he needed to do this before his knee decided to give out. It saw him to the hard pavement, sharp asphalt gravel biting into his leg. The people milling about had stopped and gathered around as soon as he started lowering, but he wasn't seeing them.

He didn't give two shits about anyone except the goddess before him.

He gazed up at his angel, her brilliant head of fire backlit by the last remnants of a golden sunset. The clouds stood at Colton's back, and flurries drifted around them and caught in Ruby's hair. Her hazel eyes went from shock to lust to love, her hands trembling as she watched him. He pulled his hand out of his pockets, the smooth leather of the small robin's egg blue box in one hand a reality check for what he wanted, needed, to do.

Holding it up, he popped the lid. Ruby gasped, the crowd of onlookers following suit. He imagined the single large Tiffany diamond was shining brilliantly in the gold light, but he was too transfixed by the woman before him. He took a deep breath, trying not to fall back on his slightly-rehearsed speech.

"Ruby Delacey, I saw you when we were thirteen years old, in Mrs. Kocsis' science class. I fell in love with you on the spot, but it wasn't until the next year when we finally started dating. I thought I knew what love was — who at fourteen doesn't? — but every day you showed me how very wrong I was, and how much deeper we could go. You challenged me and accepted me, loved me and helped me grow. I never for the life of me understood what you saw in me, and when we were eighteen, it broke me when I realized that what you'd seen in me was more premonition than reality. But here we are, ten years later. And Ruby Delacey, I have known all that time that I was in love with you, would always be in love with you. You are the love of my life. I don't need you to give me an answer — I just want you to know that I would give my life to give you the life you deserve, every day, and that it would be an honor to marry you."

Her hand had gone to her mouth around the halfway mark of his speech, tears slipping down her cheeks blooming pink.

"Ask me."

It was hardly a whisper, but he didn't need her to repeat it. He saw it in her eyes, the way the corners of her mouth were turned up.

"Ruby Delacey, would you allow me the honor of becoming your husband? Will you marry me?"

She nodded, ferociously, and dropped to her knees before him. Her soft hands cupped his face, pulling him into a kiss that consumed him, burned him to the bone until he was ash against her. She had always been a part of him, but now he knew he had always been a part of her. They found each other, again, and Colton knew that they would continue to do so in every moment, every lifetime.

She was his heart and his soul.

# EPILOGUE

Dragan whooped and hollered as Colton got engaged, kissing his future wife while they kneeled in the parking lot, surrounded by the entire town at the Valentine's Day Festival. He brushed up against June, his body heating without hesitation. He glanced down at the curvy blonde, his best friend, and wondered:

What would it feel like to kiss her full lips?

To feel her body pressed against his, not in friendship but in love?

To hold her wide hips in his hands, showing her he could protect her from the world?

To wake up to her every morning, knowing, without a doubt, she was the love of his life, and she knew it, too?

Tears were streaming down her cheeks. He knew they were of happiness, but that didn't stop the need to wipe them away from rising through him, threatening to break free in a kiss that would surely, horrendously end their friendship.

But... What if it didn't?

*Thanks so much for reading Break Me Like a Promise!*

*Read Kiss Me Like You Mean It:*

*Dragan Carter has been in love with his best friend June since childhood. But he's from the wrong side of the tracks, and beautiful, smart women like June Beaumont don't love men like him.*

*When June comes to him to help save her family's bookstore, he's faced with the truth: she has the same feelings.*

*As things come down to the wire, they need to decide if following their hearts is worth risking their friendship.*

**Click here to read Kiss Me Like You Mean It, the second standalone in the Oak Valley series!**

# LINKS

*Want to receive news first and get exclusive content? Sign up for my newsletter!*

*Did you enjoy this book? Leave a review and let others know!*

**Find me online:**

Facebook
Instagram
Website

Printed in Great Britain
by Amazon